FAMILY REUNION

FAMILY REUNION

SHADOW VANGUARD™ BOOK SIX

TOM DUBLIN   MICHAEL ANDERLE   CRAIG MARTELLE

DISRUPTIVE IMAGINATION

Copyright © 2021 LMBPN Publishing
Cover by Andrew Dobell
Cover copyright © LMBPN Publishing
A Michael Anderle Production

LMBPN Publishing
PMB 196, 2540 South Maryland Pkwy
Las Vegas, NV 89109

Version 1.00 October 2021
eBook ISBN: 978-1-68500-507-8
Print ISBN: 978-1-68500-508-5

THE FAMILY REUNION TEAM

JIT Readers
From each of us, our deepest gratitude!

Rachel Beckford
Micky Cocker
Veronica Stephan-Miller
John Ashmore
Peter Manis
Misty Roa
Jim Caplan
Diane L. Smith
Dave Hicks
Dorothy Lloyd
Veronica Stephan-Miller
Tim Bischoff

*If we missed anyone, **please** let us know!*

Editor
Lynne Stiegler

No Space, Space Station, The Marble Key, Night Club

Naka-Lee didn't need to be in water to survive, but she preferred it that way. Her *gills* preferred it that way, and it proved to be the perfect place to watch the club without anyone noticing her in the windows beneath the raised pool. Aliens from a variety of places came in and out at all hours, or as she liked to call them, "undesirables." They would drink in the booths, make secretive deals with one another, and then leave without anyone being the wiser. The Marble Key was one of the finer establishments in the Ordanion Hub, and it provided cover for the nefarious type of criminals throughout the galaxy and especially the rich ones.

She was waiting for someone, although she wasn't expecting him any time soon. Not for another hour, at least. Naka-Lee liked to relax first and keep an eye on things, monitoring for any changes and adjusting herself as needed. Using her webbed hands, she swam elegantly to the top of the pool and pulled herself out and into the dry.

An attendant offered her a towel, but she refused. Instead, she willed herself to change.

Naka-Lee was a Mutanaraian, a rare and rarely seen species in this part of the known galaxy for the simple reason that hardly anyone trusted them. A Mutanaraian could change their appearance at will; nothing big, but enough to blend in with others.

Their true forms had more in common with goldfish than anything else: gold scales, large bugged-out eyes, and webbed fins with an orange glow. They were naturally fantastic swimmers, and it was a form Naka-Lee enjoyed as often as she could manage. It could be exhausting being fake.

As she moved past the pool and into the club, her appearance transmogrified from the traditional Mutanaraian to human. A mane of gorgeous blonde hair cascaded from her naturally bald scalp, her skin was warm and tanned, and her body assumed an hourglass shape.

She was sophisticated and beautiful, but most important, she was officious in her new appearance. She didn't want anyone thinking they could get the better of her. Naka-Lee shook the last drops of water from her body and grabbed a glass of champagne as a server passed with a tray.

As she sipped, she watched the entrance from the balcony on the second floor. There he was; an Alstublaft had entered the building. His attire looked worn but clean, but she didn't care for the red X that had been plastered across his face. What's more, he was early, and by a good margin, too. She didn't know whether she liked that.

"I have a guest down there." She stopped one of the

attendants and pointed at the door. "Would you please have him come to the Crown Suite?"

"At once, miss." The attendant bowed.

The station operated many different things: a casino, a nightclub, a number of high-class restaurants, and of course, a hotel. It was the latter that had brought Naka-Lee here, and she had permanently reserved the Crown Suite, the most expensive and classiest suite, for herself. One of the best parts was the private elevator for her exclusive use. She pushed the button, and a few seconds later, she was inside her stellar hotel room, or as she preferred to think of it, her home away from home.

The contact she had summoned was an Alstublaft, and despite dealing with him a few times, the only thing she really knew about that particular race was that they were similar in appearance to human children. That was why she had become a beauty. She'd found that people were easier to deal with when they were dumbstruck. She hoped this form worked. She didn't want to change herself into a human child, not that she could if she wanted to. She could only resemble people who were just about the same height as her, so she'd be an exceptionally tall child.

Naka-Lee turned to a creature that had appeared at her side, a pet of sorts. The werewolf was as large as they came, and she had picked him for his unusual blond and black fur, but he wasn't like any other werewolf you could find. He had a heavy collar around his neck that kept him in line, shocking him whenever he had a thought that was disobedient. Naka-Lee gave the werewolf an affectionate stroke, the same way one would stroke a whining dog. He was growling at the other elevator, the peasant elevator. Her contact was on his way up.

"You behave now, Biscuit," she cooed, rubbing beneath his chin. "No making trouble, okay? Mama doesn't want to get mad today."

The creature whined and turned toward a pile of blankets on the floor, his tail tucked between his legs. He dropped his heavy body on his bed, but he didn't stop glaring at the elevator door. Soon the doors opened, and the Alstublaft stepped inside. Biscuit was the first thing he noticed, and Naka-Lee was the second.

"You're early, *Benjamin*." Naka-lee took a sip of her champagne. "I wasn't expecting you for another hour."

"Traffic was clear." Benjamin stepped into the room, keeping an eye on the werewolf in the corner. "I was going to hang around, get a few drinks, but they told me you wanted me upstairs straight away."

"Please, take a seat." Naka-Lee gestured at the white leather couch that seemed like it went from this room straight through to the next. Despite the furniture's luxury, Benjamin was anything but comfortable. He knew, like a thousand others knew, that Naka-Lee was the most dangerous person someone could do business with. A weapons dealer of the highest caliber. She strolled casually across the room and languorously stretched out next to him. She rhythmically stroked his knee with a single finger. "Tell me, Benjamin, what goodies you have for me today?"

"Information," the creature replied. "Good information."

"Oh, boo." Naka-Lee stood up. "I thought you had a

new toy. It better be good. I don't think you want Biscuit getting upset."

Benjamin pulled out a disk from his jacket. "Plans for the Federation terraformer. If you can reverse-engineer it, you can use it to destroy whole worlds in a matter of hours."

Naka-Lee reached for it, but he pulled it back. "Two million credits?"

"I won't accept an amount that high," Benjamin replied. "Truth is, the whole thing can't be operated without the help of someone that knows how to use it. Unfortunately, there's only one person in the galaxy who knows it well enough, its inventor. Chances are, you won't get it working without her."

Biscuit growled, baring his teeth.

"Fifty thousand credits," Naka-Lee said, snatching the disk. "I was hoping for better, Benjamin. I really was."

"I do have something else," Benjamin said. "I've heard you recently went into, uh, werewolf training... keeping...domination?"

Naka-Lee beamed proudly. "These experimental collars have worked wonders. With them, the werewolves are subservient to their masters, and it keeps them in a primal state, as they should be. They make perfect body-guards or assassins, or even just laborers. Although trans-porting the collars throughout the Federation carries significant risk because too many of those in charge are sympathetic. They are animals at heart and need to be treated as such."

"What if I told you that there was a werewolf out there that had an immunity to the effects of DNA-dampening drugs?" Benjamin said. "Would that be something you'd be interested in?"

"You've piqued my interest," she replied. "Please tell me more."

"Oh, there is more," Benjamin replied. "I know of a werewolf out there who is not only immune to the effect of DNA-dampening drugs but can alter specific parts of her body at will and is perhaps the strongest werewolf on the Federation's records."

"You're pulling my leg, Benjamin." Naka-Lee finished the last of her champagne. She resumed stroking his knee.

"Then believe this." Benjamin pulled another disk out of his pocket and handed it over. She examined it and started reading its contents.

She looked at it, then at Benjamin.

"Two hundred thousand," Naka-Lee said, placing the disk down. "I'll even transfer it direct before you leave the building."

"That won't be necessary. I trust you." Benjamin got up to leave. "Deal."

"Wait. Who am I looking for exactly?" Naka-Lee asked. "Where can I find this individual?"

"Her name is Adina Choudhury," Benjamin replied. "She shouldn't be too hard to find with the right contacts, although I should warn you that she might be a challenge to pick up. She's a member of the Shadows."

"Shadows?" Naka-Lee smiled the way a snake must when it saw a fat and juicy mouse. "Perfect."

2

No Space, ICS *Fortitude*, Bridge

"I'm afraid he was found dead this morning."

There was a tightness in Adina's chest, and she clutched at it before the uncontrollable sobbing took her. For a moment, she thought she might change into her werewolf. Jack and Tc'aarlat were preparing for that possibility by flexing their fingers and preparing to wrestle the wolf into submission before she could do any damage.

Yousuf Choudhury had died. Her uncle, her last connection to a family she'd once had, was dead, and she hadn't been there to comfort him. Nothing else mattered, and the struggles she'd dealt with in the past few months didn't matter either. Not the hackers. Not Renasta. Nothing.

Adina didn't transform, but her face did. A muzzle stretched out, pointed teeth popping through to replace her regular ones. She dropped to her knees and let out a howl of grief loud enough to shake the souls of her friends.

She was alone, but she wasn't. Not as long as she was with the Shadows.

Jack ignored her wolf face and pulled her close. "I'm sorry, Adina," he said, gently stroking her hair with his left hand. "I really am. I know what he meant to you."

Tc'aarlat found himself at a loss for words. He stroked his Raal hawk Myst. "Fuck." He had nothing else. "Just, fuck."

Jack gave him the side-eye before deciding it was best if Tc'aarlat didn't try too hard to deliver sympathetic words.

"Whatever you need us to do, we'll do it," Jack promised.

Adina got to her feet and hurried off the bridge. Jack and Tc'aarlat watched her go.

"She'll be fine," Jack said. "It just takes a little bit of time."

"Great, two funerals in that many weeks." Tc'aarlat crossed his arms. "The joy."

A frowning Nathan Lowell had delivered the bad news personally since the Shadows worked for him. Afterward, he hadn't signed off. He watched from the comfort of his temporary office on Federation Base Station 11.

Jack faced the main screen, surprised to see that Nathan was still there.

"Is that everything, Nathan?" Jack asked curiously. "Or is there something else?"

"There is, Captain Marber," the man replied with undue formality. "Given how far out your ship is, I want your team to make the trip to Station 11."

"Right now?" Jack glanced at Tc'aarlat and gave him a

look. "We were on our way to follow up on a new lead regarding Don Gan'barlo. Has there been trouble?"

"You could say that," Nathan said. "While your crew is docked there, I thought you could help me on a personal matter. A crisis on a friend's station."

"What kind of crisis?" Jack asked.

"The worst kind, but I don't want to discuss it over an open channel, just in case."

"Understood," Jack said. "We'll report to your office first thing after we arrive on station."

Jack kept his hands behind his back as he stalked across the bridge, ending next to Tc'aarlat. He crossed his arms over the Yollin's terminal.

"Did that seem odd to you?" he asked. "I wonder if everything is okay?"

"Maybe it's serious?" Tc'aarlat suggested. "He said it was a crisis. I want to go after the Don. I know you feel like we must do the personal favor for Nathan. We need more information from him. The morest he can give us."

"Morest?"

"Yes. The most there is of more. He knows more, and he hasn't told us. Don Gan'barlo cannot hide forever. The Federation must have an idea where he is. They know more than they let on." Tc'aarlat's mandibles clicked in his agitation.

"Cool your clickers, big fella." Jack clapped him on the shoulder. "But we do need to ask. A personal favor should get us everything we deserve to know."

"Maybe that's it. Nathan doesn't think we deserve to know. If we do know, then we take out the Don. What if he's doing favors for the Federation, and they're protecting him?"

"Throttle back a little, my friend. You're starting to sound like a nutjob. I promise you, we'll ask. I think they're holding out on us, but not because they're protecting the Don. I think they're doing it to keep us on the hook, doing job after job."

"If I can suggest something, Captain Marber?" The ship's ever-present matronly AI Solo spoke through the din. "After assessing Nathan's vocal patterns, body language, and facial expression, I am ninety-nine percent sure that I can't tell if he's lying or not."

"You are as helpful as a nun in a brothel." Tc'aarlat turned his attention to their AI assistant. "You can analyze someone's body language? Why did we not know this?"

"I've only been able to do it since my upgrade," Solo argued. "And the results, as we see from my analysis of Nathan Lowell, are less than spectacular."

Tc'aarlat scowled and Jack shook his head. "Solo, set course for Base Station 11. Quickest route, please."

"Yes, Captain Marber." A few moments later, Solo delivered the bad news. "I've calculated the quickest route, and it will take twelve days."

"Twelve days?" Jack said. "Are we that far out?"

"Every mission has taken us farther from the base," Solo informed him. "I could try to find another route if you're—"

"No, Solo, that'll be fine."

"Hey, Jack," Tc'aarlat said. "Maybe you can finally get your nanos fixed, whatever the problem is with them.

Can't have you waddling around with a broken arm again. That was totally fucking stupid."

"Yeah, that's a good idea," Jack replied. "I'll ask Nathan if he'll hook me up."

No Space, ICS *Fortitude*, Adina's Room

Adina retired to her room after she had left the bridge and locked the door behind her. She climbed onto her bed, reached beneath it for a small wooden box, and pulled out a picture of her and her uncle. She was the little girl with the bewildered expression, and he was the guy rocking her on his knee. It was a memory that had comforted her even in her darkest moments, and she clutched it to her chest, wishing that it was her uncle instead.

"I can't believe he's gone." Her tears dropped onto the photo, making little pings as they did so. Adina had known this day was coming; it had been coming for a long time. Uncle Yousuf had been long in the tooth and was admitted to a care home when he could no longer look after himself. In there, he developed a particularly nasty strain of dementia. That was how Adina had left him when she joined the Shadows and left on the *Fortitude*.

There were two things she could always count on in her darkest moments. The first was the comfort of her memories, which was why she collected souvenirs of the wonderful moments in her life. The few she had stayed within her box. She thumbed through them. It wasn't the quantity that mattered but the quality. Adina hugged the picture of her uncle to her chest and rocked. The second was Solo, who seemed to pick exactly the right time to appear on the small cracked screen on the other side of the room.

"I just wanted to let you know that I'm here for you," Solo said, her face motherly. "I hope you feel better."

"I'm fine," Adina choked out, wiping her tears with her sleeve and trying to sniff the sadness away. "It's just a shock. I've been expecting that call for so long. When I left him, he was...I mean, he wasn't in a good place. I never thought he had that long left, but I left him."

"That's what it means to be human," Solo told her. "Death is inevitable, but sometimes it doesn't have to be sad. Your uncle doesn't have to suffer anymore."

"I thought if I could...if I could cure his dementia, then maybe..." Adina was breathing in gasps. "Sorry. He was like a father to me, and I feel like I let him down. Like I could've done more."

"You did everything you could for him. I'm sure he knew that, just like you do."

Federation Base Station 11, Dock 17, Freight Bay D

Moving to the open hangar door, Jack stretched for relief from the long journey. Twelve days stuck on a ship with Tc'aarlat was even less appealing than it sounded.

He took a deep breath of recycled station air, but it wasn't *Fortitude*'s air. "Solo, steal some of the station's air for a full refresh of the systems. Too much Raal hawk, too much Tc'aarlat, and then there's the sweat."

"Your sweat. I'll take care of it. Maybe get a maintenance team to replace my filtration system. I have feathers clogging it up." Solo didn't sound happy.

Jack smiled as he watched the activity in the station's hangar bay. Individuals from a dozen different races were going about their business, helping each other carry and move things. Others had their heads together as they spoke quietly. For Jack, this was like coming home. Getting back to the place where he felt most welcome, where he didn't have to worry about fitting in.

"Can we get something to eat or what?" Tc'aarlat moaned, breaking Jack's moment of reflection. "I'm starved. I don't know if you've noticed, but there's no real food on my ship."

"How can you be starved? It smells like toxic waste down here. That doesn't dampen your appetite?"

Tc'aarlat looked at Jack as if a third eyeball had appeared in the middle of his forehead.

"And we *have* real food. You've gone on a health-food kick. It smells like my ass."

"That might affect my appetite, but it doesn't. I have business to take care of, and it's inside a Yollin diner."

"Adina. What about you? Coming with us for some Yollin food? Tc'aarlat says he's paying."

"I muchly did *not* say that."

"You meant to, my friend. I know what a kind soul you are."

Tc'aarlat backed up a step. "You want something."

Adina leaned out. "Has Tc'aarlat ever bought dinner anywhere we've been?"

Jack shook his head as the Yollin vigorously nodded. "Always buying."

Adina joined Jack in shaking her head.

"Let's not beat the bush to death here," Tc'aarlat offered. "Dinner. On Jack. Thank you for accommodating my Yollin tastes."

"It's beat *around* the bush," Jack corrected. "Why would anyone beat a bush to death? Never mind. Dinner it is. Yollin restaurant." Jack leaned back through the hatch into the ship. "Solo, order whatever repairs you need and send the bill to Nathan Lowell's office."

Tc'aarlat looked annoyed. "English is a hard language to grasp."

"You have the translator chip. Just use that." Jack spread his arms wide. "Bring it in, big guy."

"What the fuck? Nooooo... I don't want any of your weird human mating rituals." Tc'aarlat pointed at his open mouth. "Hungry."

"Guys?" Adina threw her backpack across one shoulder and rubbed at the dull pain throbbing in her forehead. "I can't join you for dinner."

Jack groaned. "I'm sorry. Take the time you need to make your arrangements. Just let us know if you need anything. Anything at all."

"What time will you be back?" Tc'aarlat turned to Adina. "We'll come for you if you're not here. Leave no one behind, like you didn't leave me on Renasta. For that, I am grateful."

Jack wondered why Tc'aarlat had softened. He had refused to talk about quitting the Shadows but had returned once Jack had agreed to continue hunting the Don.

"I don't know when I'll be back. I've never arranged a

funeral before," Adina admitted. "Could be a few hours, though…at least. You guys will be done with Nathan long before I'm done at the care home. Guaranteed."

Jack didn't know what to say. He gripped Adina's arm with one hand and tipped her chin up with the other. Her eyes were red and cried out. He pulled her in for a hug and held her until it started to get uncomfortable.

"I'll see you guys later," Adina said, turning to walk away before calling over her shoulder, "Keep me updated on what's happening with Nathan."

Jack gave her the thumbs-up.

Tc'aarlat waited until she was out of earshot. "Can we eat now?"

"On me, Tc'aarlat, but do we have to get Yollin food?"

Federation Base Station 11, Nathan Lowell's Temporary Office

Nathan welcomed them like old friends in the outer ring of the massive station. He led Jack and Tc'aarlat to his office and offered them seats near his desk.

"You guys look like a bag of donuts stuffed inside a wet bag, without the donuts," Nathan said as he sat down and leaned back with his fingers laced on top of his head.

"Damn. What happened to Nathan? He usually doesn't give me a high hard one so early in the reaming." Jack scrubbed his chin with a dirty hand.

Tc'aarlat cocked his head. "Why would someone let a bag of donuts get wet?"

Nathan stared at the Yollin, who stared back. Jack watched them as if he were following a tennis match.

Finally, he broke the staring contest. "I could use a spin in a Pod-doc, Nathan. I broke my arm when I got tossed around the *Fortitude,* and it took a solid three weeks to heal. There's something wrong with my nanos."

"No wonder you look like shit," Nathan replied, raising one eyebrow.

"I don't look like shit." Tc'aarlat shook his head. Myst squawked, and he stroked her absentmindedly.

"You always look like shit!" Jack exclaimed. Tc'aarlat gave him two fingers for his trouble, and Jack gave him one back.

"Gentleman," Nathan interrupted. "It's good to see you again. I'm sorry we couldn't meet up for a meal like last time. I'm a bit behind on my paperwork. The Bad Company is a high-risk business endeavor that is taking a lot of my time, but it seems to be paying off. Regardless, I'm a bit buried."

"Shame. I'm still tasting that steak we had on Talth," Jack replied.

"The roasted rodent was particularly tasty." Tc'aarlat rubbed his stomach. "Just like Mother used to make. Well, not make exactly, but catch, and not my mother, either. Let me rephrase. Just like a woman I knew that worked in the kitchens of my boarding school used to catch, dispatch, skin, and roast in the furnace."

Jack shook his head.

"I can get you in the Pod-doc as soon as we're done here." Nathan tapped on his screen. "Done. When you leave, head to the medical unit."

"I like how you work," Jack said.

"What happened again?"

"Grenade," Jack said quickly. "I got hit by a grenade."

Tc'aarlat snickered. "He fell over his console."

"Yeah, that was *after* the grenade!" Jack exclaimed. He looked at Nathan, who was gazing at him. "It was a grenade, Nathan."

Tc'aarlat silently gave Nathan a few words when he was sure Jack couldn't see his mouth. Nathan couldn't be sure what Tc'aarlat had said, but he was pretty sure he could make out the words, "He fell over."

"You say you've been swamped. Is everything okay? I'd like to offer help, but we can't take any new missions until we've dealt with Don Gan'barlo."

"I wish everything was okay," Nathan replied. "Unfortunately, things around here have never been further from the word *fine*. Have you ever been to City Station Hopefill, otherwise known as the Frontier Zone? It's about an eight-hour journey from here."

"A few times, but I never stayed for long," Jack noted. "Some of my training for the Force de Guerre was there."

"I have an acquaintance, Timothy Grand. He is having issues," Nathan said. "A drug problem has swept across the city, and gang wars have turned the place into a warzone. I've been wracking my brain to think of a way to help him."

"Can't you just knock heads together?" Tc'aarlat asked, punching a curled fist into the palm of his hand to demonstrate. "What knockers you could be."

Nathan closed his eyes and tilted his head back as if praying for patience. "It's a problem I was hoping you'd help me with," he replied. "They have a werewolf problem."

"Only weres I know of work with the Federation."

"That's the problem. Someone acquired one of our Pod-docs and modified a bunch of willing volunteers before we noticed it was happening. These people aren't fully aware of what they have. From what we've seen, they have little connection with the Etheric beyond the ability to change form. They can't see into it like our more evolved weres can."

Tc'aarlat rolled his head sideways to look at Jack. "Don Gan'barlo," he said, enunciating clearly.

Nathan ignored him. "There's been an increase in werewolf activity around that city, and the WRU has been going wild because of it. The governors of the city have transferred emergency power to them, and they're power-mad now."

"The WRU?"

"Sorry, of course you wouldn't know," Nathan said. "Because there's been such a dramatic increase in werewolf activity in the past six months in that city, the officials there decided an appropriate reaction would be to make a response team that's specially trained to deal with werewolves. They're called the Wechselbalg Response Unit."

"Dog catchers?" Tc'aarlat suggested.

"Crack-snackers?" Jack countered.

Nathan waited until Jack and Tc'aarlat were finished. "It's a damn nightmare."

"I'm guessing the werewolf problem and the drug problem are connected, then?" Jack didn't need to ask the question. He knew the answer, but he wanted to be sure.

Nathan nodded. "Gangs in the city have been using werewolves to attack one another. Seems like every day, we're getting new reports of a bloodbath somewhere on the station. It's a clusterfuck for sure, and one that has kept Timothy and me wrapped up in paperwork."

"Where do we come in?" Tc'aarlat asked. "I assume that's why we're here and you're telling us this? We come in somewhere…also to get paid, but I don't give a flying squirrel fuck about anything other than Don Gan'barlo. I already quit the Shadows once, and I'll do it again right fucking now if we don't get to resolve this mission."

"I want your team to go investigate. Get to the bottom of it all and collaborate with law enforcement there. The En-D," Nathan replied. "We're pretty sure we've found a source to tell us where the drugs are coming from, a person who goes by the name of Bloody Darling. If we can stop the flow of drugs at its source, it could give us a real edge in dealing with these gang wars."

"Cute name," Jack said. "I'm guessing you want us to find this Bloody Darling and bring them to justice?"

"That's right," Nathan said. "If it's not too much trouble. And this one is for you, Tc'aarlat. We think the Don is behind it."

Tc'aarlat sat up straight. "You could have started with that." He poked Jack's shoulder. "Shouldn't he have started with that? Justice for the Don? Yes. I am game for that."

"What's the drug they've been dealing?" Jack asked.

"It's called Eternity," Nathan replied. "It gives an instant high that can last for hours, but it is addictive from the first use. It makes a majority of its users blind with regular ingestion. You can spot them by how misty their eyes look."

"We'll be on the lookout, then. Have you got a lead on this Bloody fellow?"

"Not so much," Nathan admitted. "At least not on our end. I want you to travel to the city as soon as you can and collaborate with the WRU. See if they've got a place you can start, seeing as solving this problem will solve theirs."

"Are they going to like outsiders coming in?" Jack asked. "Don't strike me as the kind of guys who would like to hear someone else's opinion."

"No, but despite that, you are doing official work for Tony's division, the En-D," Nathan said, then sighed deeply. "The number around my acquaintance who can be trusted has been dwindling. Pretty soon, he'll find himself on the wrong end of it all."

"What do you mean?" Jack asked.

"This WRU has been headhunting his top agents," Nathan said. "Leaving everyone else to pick up the slack. There's also word that they're keeping watch over his department for any signs of mistrust. The WRU is convinced that the werewolves are coming through official lines, and unfortunately, that starts with him as the head of the En-D."

"I can see how this would look," Jack said. "Hiring outsiders."

"Do we get badges?" Tc'aarlat asked. "If so, I want to go rogue now and have my badge taken from me. Save some time."

"I doubt you'll have any trouble getting information, especially your team," Nathan said. "One of the higher-ups in the WRU is someone you've worked with before. You remember Draven Maynard?"

"NO!" Tc'aarlat exclaimed and shot out of his seat. "No. No way. Nuh-uh. I'm not working with that guy again."

"Tc'aarlat didn't get along with Draven," Jack explained. "Even though he was nothing but pleasant the last time we saw him."

"If you can call being a snobby smooth-talker *pleasant*," Tc'aarlat snapped. "God, I hated that guy's stupid face."

"In any case, that's your contact, and frankly, the only one I'd trust," Nathan said. "You haven't got a choice."

"Damn it." Tc'aarlat sat roughly back down. "Why must we always do the things I hate? *Why*? And how much are we going to be paid?"

"Last question," Jack said, ignoring Tc'aarlat's outburst. "Is there anyone in the WRU we should watch out for? Someone we should avoid?"

"Mikhail May," Nathan came back with instantly. "Some people call him No-Arm Mike for obvious reasons. He's the current head of the WRU and is a stubborn bastard. I guarantee he won't like your group getting involved."

"Wait?" Tc'aarlat said. "He has no arms, and we should be careful around him? What could he possibly do?"

"Get a bunch of werewolf hunters to hunt you down."

"Yeah, well, besides that." Tc'aarlat looked at the floor.

"*Mikhail May*," Jack repeated, committing the name to memory. "We'll be on the lookout for him. Thanks, Nathan."

Federation, Base Station 11, Residential Zone 9, Rosemere Care Home

Adina swallowed hard to tamp down the nerves that had built up inside her. It had taken her about an hour to travel from the freight bay, and although the trip would have only taken a few minutes on public transport, she had opted to walk to clear her mind.

This was Adina's first time back here, not counting nightmares, since she had joined the Shadows. Uncle Yousuf hadn't known who she was at the time, with dementia destroying his mind. If he had forgotten her, it wasn't because he wanted to. The uncle she knew was the one she remembered. In the next life, they'd meet again.

"Adina?" A large and kindly woman approached. Worry lines creased her forehead. She tried to smile but couldn't manage it. Adina nodded and waved.

Wendy Lintern had been her uncle's nurse during his time in the home, and Adina had gotten to know her personally. They had always gotten on well. She was a lovely woman with a face like a freshly plucked tomato. Seeing her was almost too much. Adina's eyes glistened.

"Hi, Wendy." Adina moved to the front desk. "I think you know why I'm here."

"We were told you were coming," Wendy replied with a nod. "Just not when. It's good to see you, Adina, but never under these circumstances. I'm so sorry about Yousuf."

"Thanks." Adina looked around sheepishly, afraid to ask the next question. "Can I see him?"

"Are you sure?" asked Wendy. "It could be upsetting."

"I wouldn't forgive myself if I missed the opportunity to see him one last time," Adina replied. "Where is he?"

"Downstairs, dear," replied Wendy. "Yousuf was preserved for the funeral. You got here just in time. En-D just gave him back to us yesterday."

"En-D?" Adina asked. "Why did the En-D have him?"

Wendy moved around the desk and beckoned for Adina to follow her. "I'll take you to him and explain along the way."

Adina had walked these halls a hundred times. Visiting her uncle had not been an occasional thing; it had been a solid part of her weekly routine, and she'd made sure to catch him up on the details of her life as often as she could when she had lived on the station. As they walked and talked, a thousand memories flooded into her thoughts. Things she had already been thinking about, but they appeared much clearer in her mind's eye now. The day he had been admitted. The first time she had visited. The first time he forgot her name.

Wendy was taking her somewhere new. Adina had seen the elevator on every visit but had never used it, mostly because her uncle was on the ground floor. They got in, and Wendy pressed the button for the morgue.

"The En-D took him for a few days over some abnormality," she was saying. "They originally thought his death was suspicious."

"Suspicious? How?"

"Your uncle had had a check-up the day before. Pretty routine; we get a doctor in every three months to check on all our residents," Wendy replied. "It was unusual because he'd been given a clean bill of health despite his condition. Then the next day, he suffered a heart attack and died. I guess these things happen."

"So, the En-D didn't find anything?" Adina's mind raced with theories of why they had been interested in her uncle.

"Not that I know of. If they had, they wouldn't have given the body back so quickly."

Adina had heard of the En-D, otherwise known as the Enforcement Division, but not had many interactions with them. They were the ones that kept the peace in the Frontier Zone, the place where human settlements outside the official Federation stations made their beds. Their primary goal was making sure laws were enforced and keeping the peace where they could. Other than that, she'd never dealt with the En-D, but like any law enforcement, they were a mixture of detectives and officers.

A brisk chill was noticeable when Adina stepped out of the elevator, and her breath was visible. Following Wendy, they arrived in a locker room with large metal drawers. She searched the tags on the doors and found the appropriate one.

"Are you ready?" Wendy gripped the handle.

Adina took a deep breath and nodded in reply, then Wendy pulled it open. Adina found herself face to face with her uncle again. They had done a wonderful job of preserving his body. He looked like he was peacefully sleeping, but the reality hit her like a brick to the head. It was her uncle like she had never seen him; there was no pain or suffering. Tears rolled down her face, as she had expected they would.

"Do you want to say a few words?"

Adina looked down at him as he rested the way a proud daughter would look at her father. "No," she said. "I think he already knows everything I'd want to say to him."

Wendy closed the drawer, and oddly, Adina felt that a chapter of her life had come to a sudden and complete end. Now she had to arrange a funeral, find anyone and everyone who had been important in his life, and make sure her uncle had the best possible send-off. She had faced off against every kind of foe, dealt with deception and backstabbing, violent mobsters, and alien races, but as she watched the drawer close, she thought this would be the most difficult thing she would ever do.

3

Frontier Zone, City Station Hopefill, Commercial Zone 5, The Picky Pouncer

City Station Hopefill was unlike most other stations floating in the void of space. It was more like a city, with a thousand buildings housed beneath a large dome through which one could see to the stars beyond. It had streets, alleys, roads, and infrastructure like a planet-based city. It even had days and nights, using artificial lighting to support its cycles.

Built as a private enterprise to show what was possible, Hopefill was in the Frontier Zone, outside Federation control but within its sphere of influence. It was the best of both worlds for those who wanted access to Federation members without being subject to its laws.

Being an independent entity with its own laws and rules made it a chaotic place.

The Picky Pouncer was not the most upscale of pubs. It was quiet at this time of day, with only a few locals parked on barstools, nursing their drinks. Draven could count on one hand how many times he had been here. It was a miserable place with watered-downed booze, but it was quiet, unlike many places in Hopefill. That was why he came here with his important clients—to have the peace to conduct sensitive negotiations in the privacy of a public space.

Draven had been excited to get the call from Nathan arranging a meeting with the Shadows, whom he hadn't seen for the better part of a year. He had left the group in an unfortunate state during their last adventure together after getting blown up in a small cruiser while defending the *Fortitude* from a missile attack. Still, Draven had gotten better in time, thanks to his quick healing and werewolf nanos, and he was stronger and more handsome than ever.

Smiling, he watched Jack and Tc'aarlat stride into the pub, heads swiveling as they searched for his familiar face. Draven waved as they cast their eyes in his direction, then stood up to greet them. Jack came up to the table eagerly and shook Draven's hand. Tc'aarlat was less enthusiastic.

"You suck." The Yollin didn't waste words.

"Ignore him. If it isn't Missile Man!" Jack took the seat directly opposite. "You've certainly recovered."

"It was a rough couple months, I have to admit." Draven drew a hand through his blond locks to drag the radical strands out of his eyes. "Here I am, though, stronger, faster, and dare I say, a little more careful?"

"Well, it's great to hear that you've been keeping busy," Jack said. "How are things with the W—"

"No, no," Draven said. "No business yet. I want to know more about what's been going on with the Shadows."

"He fell over a terminal," Tc'aarlat offered. "We saved a world with two races of people. You know, the usual."

"I did not." Jack scoffed. "I was hit by a grenade."

"Then he fell over a terminal."

"Oh, Tc'aarlat, ever the charmer." Draven turned to the Yollin and flashed those impeccable white teeth. "How have you been?"

"Fine, real fine. Saving the universe, no big deal," Tc'aarlat replied, thinking that Draven was the only person he knew who could be hit by a missile and come out better for the experience. The guy had a tan, for the gods' sake. "Big-picture stuff. You wouldn't understand, but I'm sure you'll get there one day."

"Where's Adina?" Draven looked around for her, and the others couldn't mistake the disappointment on his face. "Is she going to be along soon?"

"She won't be joining us today," Jack replied. "She's at Base 11 for a funeral, a close relative. Speaking of which..."

"Nathan's getting you to investigate the drug problem on behalf of the En-D," Draven started, leaning back casually in his chair. "I don't envy you. It's getting to be one hell of a problem for the city. Been keeping me busy, that's for sure."

"We were told that if we could find someone called the Bloody Darling, we might have a chance of stemming the flow," Jack said. "Do you know anything about them?"

"I've heard the name. It came up a couple of times in my work, but I only know the legend," Draven said. "Bloody Darling is selling drugs to the gangs in the city, and the gangs are going to war over their territories. My job isn't about that. With the WRU, it's about werewolf activity.

29

The gangs have been employing werewolves as soldiers to expand their territory."

"Solve the drug problem, though, and you'll solve the werewolf problem," interjected Tc'aarlat. "But Nathan only mentioned rumors of werewolves. We are supposed to check their truthliness."

"If only it was that easy, my young Yollin," Draven replied with a sweet sigh. "With or without those drugs, the gangs will want to expand their territories. A higher priority for us is to figure out where these werewolves are coming from and stop it there. They are real, but they are not a concern for the Federation."

"We were hoping for a bit more than that," Jack admitted. "We have no idea where to start finding this Bloody guy. As to the werewolves, they are very much a concern for the Federation."

Draven flicked his hand as if chasing a fly away. "I can keep my ear to the ground for you. Let you know if I hear anything. I'm sure the En-D has its own resources when it comes to finding drug dealers."

"Maybe," Jack said. "Maybe." He decided to shelve the conversation about the werewolves. Draven wasn't coming clean, which suggested there was a lot more to it. They would find out in due course, and Jack would let Nathan know. Then the En-D and WRU would both be in a world of hurt.

"How about the next time, you investigate werewolf stuff?" Tc'aarlat asked. "This isn't two problems but one. You rub my carapace, and I'll itch your back."

"Scratch your back."

"My back isn't itchy," Tc'aarlat replied.

Draven raised one finger before deciding he wouldn't win. "If you think you can handle it," he said nonchalantly instead, and Tc'aarlat narrowed his eyes. "I'm supposed to receive a tip soon on the whereabouts of a den in the city. We're going to try to take down as many as we can. You're welcome to tag along as long as you don't get killed. I'm not big on the paperwork side of this business. Your dumb ass dying would mean a lot of paperwork."

"Would your superiors be okay with that?" Jack asked. "We're not WRU."

"It's my team going in, so it's my call," Draven replied. "Besides, I've seen you guys fight. I know you can handle yourselves when it comes to danger."

"Yeah," Tc'aarlat said. "I can." He looked pointedly at Jack, who smirked.

"Will Mikhail May be there?" Jack asked. "I've heard he's in control of the WRU."

"He is, and for a reason," Draven said. "He's getting the results the governors want to hear. The more werewolves go into the ice blocks, the more at ease they make people feel. What he won't tell you is that most of those outbursts are from regulars in the city. People discovering their werewolf sides for the first time, not gang affiliates."

"And you have no problems with that?" Tc'aarlat snapped. "I thought this was about fighting gang warfare?"

"I see it as a holistic problem," Draven said. "It's the broken windows. Take care of the little things, and the big things will go away. We end the werewolf creation process, and the rest of it will dry up."

"Broken chairs. No place to sit down, and they'll give

up. Maybe we should eliminate all the donuts, too," Tc'aarlat said. "You know. The little things."

"Have you been huffing reactor coolant?" Draven leaned close to examine Tc'aarlat's eyes. The Yollin snapped his mandibles, barely missing the beautiful man's face.

"Maybe you'll end up in one of those ice block things yourself, whatever they are." Tc'aarlat tapped the table for emphasis.

"It's where they take dangerous werewolves," Jack explained. "And I've got to agree with Tc'aarlat here. This smells funky, Draven."

"It's the results the governors want right now. They're trying to give the people in the city some reassurance that we're working to make sure they're safe." Draven shrugged off the thought. "And I'll say this as well. We don't take in werewolves that haven't done anything. If they kill their neighbor or harm an innocent bystander, though, it's game over. Under the new rules, they don't get a second chance."

Tc'aarlat gave Jack a look, and Jack gave him the same look right back. Neither of them liked this.

Federation, Base Station 11, Residential Zone 9, Rosemere Care Home

Planning her uncle's funeral turned out to be easier than Adina had originally thought because the home took care of the arrangements. If Adina didn't want to do anything, she didn't have to, but that made her feel guilty on top of the emotional burden already wearing her down.

Ultimately, all Adina ended up doing was signing a

series of forms and transferring a commensurate stack of credits for Rosemere to file the forms, something she did willingly. They would invite the guests, organize the dates, find a place for him to be cremated, and so on. There was a problem, though, and that concerned Yousuf's personal effects.

Adina wanted the funeral to be held in the Frontier Zone, with her uncle's ashes deposited in space beyond Hopefill. That was where her grandmother, Uncle Yousuf's mother, had been scattered on the infinite voyage to become stardust once more.

It felt right to her that she could put her uncle in the same place. It was an endeavor that required a lot of paperwork, but the home promised to prepare the ashes and make the travel arrangements.

With her part of the paperwork taken care of, Adina strolled through the care home's halls to clear her mind before she could take one of the many transporters to Hopefill City, a journey of about eight hours, to meet Jack and Tc'aarlat.

The care home was popular, and the death of her uncle had created an opening for another fortunate elder to take his place. Adina had twelve hours to organize her uncle's things and take them away before the rest would be burned or donated to a local charity.

Now came the hard part she hadn't realized would be the hardest. The paperwork and final arrangements had been easy, but this? Adina had to go through everything that had been her uncle's in life and decide what she would take with her and what would get destroyed. At least she didn't have to do it alone.

"How about this?" Wendy held up a box of old shoes, and Adina shook her head. Into the trash it went.

Adina cleaned out her uncle's drawers. His clothes meant nothing to her, but one thing caught her eye beneath a pair of threadbare trousers. She moved them out of the way to retrieve a small cardboard box. It piqued her curiosity since it was a box she recognized. Adina opened it and gasped. A pair of earrings. *The* earrings.

"Everything okay?" Wendy asked after Adina's audible gasp.

"It's... He kept them." Adina blocked out everything around her as she removed them from the box and held them up. She spoke as if talking to herself. "On my thirteenth birthday, Uncle Yousuf gave me some earrings, and then... Well, after it all, he kept them."

"They're very pretty," Wendy said. "Maybe you could wear them to his funeral?"

"Clip-ons." She laughed, then her face turned solemn. "My parents didn't think I was ready for earrings. He bought me clip-ons." She clutched the earrings to her breast. "I am going to miss him."

"We all are," Wendy said, handing her some tissues from the pocket of her scrubs. "We all are."

Frontier Zone, City Station Hopefill, Dock 23, Freight Bay F, ICS *Fortitude*, Bridge

"I want to thank you again, Captain Marber, for coming to my aid." The man on the screen had very little in common with his acquaintance. Timothy was rotund, with cherub cheeks and a mouth full of spit. He looked like he hadn't slept in weeks. "Nathan speaks highly of you."

"I just hope we can help," Jack said through a smile. "Hopefully, we'll get to the bottom of it."

"Here's hoping. As the name says, Hopefill."

The screen went black, and Jack was left staring at nothing. For an hour before the call, he had gone through recent news reports covering events in Hopefill City. The werewolf problem was bigger than they were led to believe. The attacks were far-reaching and frequent, with as many as one or two a week.

They were the main topic of many reports, and the headlines were mostly unforgiving. One was *Another attack in Residential Zones.* The leading headline, which gave no room for misinterpretation, was *Werewolves: Menace or Menace?* More: *Five ways to tell if your neighbor is a werewolf. Will the WRU actually succeed?* And finally: *Big Doug's auto repair is slashing prices!*

Jack had clicked one too far. That last headline was an advertisement for a repair shop located near the hot border between warring gangs. He chuckled. Opportunists were everywhere. Whoever thought the ad was in bad taste wasn't living life to its fullest.

"This city *is* in crisis," Jack said aloud. "But it doesn't feel to me like the werewolves are to blame. They're tools, just like a blaster."

The bridge door opened. Jack swung around to see Adina, tired and red-eyed, walk in with a box under her arm. She took a seat at her workstation after passing Jack.

"How was it?" Jack asked. "Okay?"

"Tiring," Adina replied. "I had to organize my uncle's

stuff, all of it, before they throw the rest of it away tomorrow."

"Sounds hard."

"How's your arm, Jack?" Adina pointed to the captain's formerly busted limb.

"Nathan arranged a Pod-doc for me in the city, and we shouldn't have a repeat of that three weeks to heal a broken bone nonsense. That was the absolute butt-nimbies." Jack smiled and flexed for Adina.

Adina glanced at the main screen and saw the many reports Jack had been looking at. Curious, she glanced at him. "What's all this about? Is this for Nathan?"

"Yeah," Jack replied with a nod. "Hopefill City has a real werewolf problem right now. It's something I think we should have a conversation about."

"Oh?"

"Have you been doing your breathing exercises like Zorxia taught you?" Jack asked. "The ones that help you control—"

"I have," Adina interrupted.

"I don't think you can afford to lose control here, Adina. It's important that you don't change," Jack urged. "Werewolves aren't being regarded in a kind light, and the old ways of doing things have been replaced by the WRU. They seem to only care about getting werewolves off the street and not about the person that's part of them. They shoot first and ask questions later. I don't want to see you hurt."

"That's awful." Adina glanced at the screen.

"It is," Jack said. "This means it's important you remain

in control. I don't know what'll happen if your unforgiving side comes out. We might lose you."

"I'll keep it in check," Adina promised. "I'll do the exercises."

Jack nodded. "When's the funeral?"

"They said it would take a week at the most," Adina replied. "Then I'll be on this with you."

"No, you should take a break. You don't have to come back on board right after. Give yourself some time to grieve."

"Honestly, I think it might be a good way to keep my mind off things." Adina grabbed her box and started the short trip back to the door. "I only came in here to see if you guys were back. I think I'll just head to bed."

"If you need anything, Adina, just let me know," Jack said as she reached the door. "Always here to talk."

"Thanks, Jack."

He gave her a smile that quickly became a frown when he was sure she was gone, the door secured behind her. The whole werewolf mess exacerbated the situation with her since she was still learning to control the beast. Jack was worried about her, extremely worried.

Looking at the headlines and reports he had on the screen, his stomach did a summersault. All it would take was one slip, and Adina would be thrown in the ice blocks. The WRU didn't forgive, and they didn't need much reason to capture a werewolf.

Jack had promised to keep a close eye on her. He started reviewing the headlines again, looking for any sign of Don Gan'barlo. He could smell the mobster's stench on this.

4

Frontier Zone, City Station Hopefill, Dock 9, Freight Bay A

Theo nervously looked over his shoulder. The station was dark at this time of day, and most of the population had crawled into bed. Not him. The man, who was dressed in torn rags, scratched the scabs surrounding his eyes beneath his sunglasses and picked up his pace to transit the long-abandoned dock. It was nothing but worn-out ships and smashed crates, but he couldn't discount the danger there. This was Silver Diamonds territory, the domain of a notorious and successful gang operating within Hopefill City. They were who he had come to see.

Moving farther into the darker parts of the docks, Theo stopped. A silhouette stepped out of the shadows. He knew without looking there would be others behind him, blocking his exit, no doubt heavily armed and uncaring about whether he lived or died.

But they weren't the greatest danger. As Theo squinted into the darkness, the nightmare came into focus. A large beast on all fours, covered in fur, with fangs that could tear a man to shreds. A werewolf.

"Yo, man, whatcha doin' down here?" The voice was low, slow, and concise. The figure it belonged to stepped out of the shadows. Theo saw him for what he was: a big guy, a muscle builder, covered head to toe in tattoos and body piercings. He wasn't the sort to let Theo go in peace. He tapped his switchblade, and the spring sent the blade snapping into place. "You get lost or somethin'?"

"Riddle, it's me. Theo."

"Aw, shit, man. I was hopin' to get some cuttin' done today. You here to buy or what, Theo?"

"Yeah, I'm here to buy," Theo said, showing him the color of his credit stick. It had been heavily modified and repurposed, but that was not uncommon in Hopefill City. It allowed a user to make transactions with encrypted currency so their history couldn't be monitored by the banks. "I'm looking for some more Eternity. You got any?"

"Got plenty." Riddle pulled a tube out of the inside pocket of his jacket. "Three hundred credits for a full pack. Fifty for a single dose."

"I'll take a single." Theo made to step forward but froze when he heard the low growl of the werewolf at Riddle's side. He had seen the werewolf before and had always gotten the distinct impression that it didn't much care for him, but this was what he had to deal with if he wanted the drugs.

"Bonkers don't like you, man. Don't get too close," Riddle said, stepping forward and taking a credit reader from his pocket. "Place your credits on here, then get the fuck outta here, man."

Theo did as he was told, putting his credit stick on the device and transferring the necessary amount.

Riddle put the reader away and stared at Theo, making him wait before pulling out a smaller tube and playing with it. He acted like he was dropping it, only to catch it and hold it out of Theo's reach.

Theo waited as patiently as he could, refusing to play Riddle's game of chase the tube. It wasn't good business to renege on a deal, and the man knew that. He finally gave him the tube.

Theo scurried into the night, away from the gang members and their werewolf pet. As he moved, his eyes itched, and he couldn't resist scratching them. He grabbed the tube the moment he was sure the gang wasn't following him.

Eternity was a powerful drug, highly addictive, and produced a meteoric high. It instantly made everything in a person's life better, and the high lasted for days or weeks depending on the dose. Theo removed his shades, revealing pupils misted over by prolonged use of the drug, and pulled down his eyelid. He opened the tube with its glittery contents and dripped the liquid into the space between his lid and eyeball.

The effect was instant. Theo felt like he could take on the world.

He left the docks and went back into Hopefill City with confidence in his stride. There was nothing that could stop him and nothing he couldn't do.

Unfortunately for him, the dose would only last for a few days at most, and after it was gone, he'd go back to being a bedraggled stranger begging for change and living in the darkest alleys.

Frontier Zone, City Station Hopefill, Crematorium

The group gathered in the crematorium. Adina sat in the front row with the rest of the Shadows. Looking around, she found that she knew fewer people than she would've liked but was pleased with the number who had come to honor her uncle. They were the family, friends, and acquaintances he had built up over the years. There were perhaps thirty of them, and they sat quietly, listening to the service.

Uncle Yousuf lay in a sleek black coffin at the end of rows of chairs, on a sliding ramp that would lower him into the ovens for cremation. The service was like any she had heard before: a man at the front in robes dictating to the crowd the achievements of Yousuf, a person he had never met. Through it all, Adina couldn't help but think about the last time she had been in this room, staring at the coffin of her mother. The emotional burdens of the room hung heavy in the air. Tears welled in her eyes as she lost her will to fight them.

"Now it is time for the people who knew Yousuf Choudhury to come and say a few words." The robed man up front spread his arms, but Adina knew no one would step up. She had wanted to say a few words herself, but she couldn't bring herself to commit them to paper for him to read aloud, and heaven forbid she stand in front of the crowd, trying not to cry. A few moments passed with no one volunteering, and Adina's already heavy heart sank.

Finally, a stranger at the back stood up. "I'll say a few words."

All eyes turned to the man. He wore the obligatory black suit and sported an overgrown beard heavy with gray. His face looked haggard and defeated.

Adina watched him, mouth agape, as he took the stand and retrieved a piece of paper from his pocket from which he made to read. Adina couldn't stop staring; he was the last person she had expected to see. He was her father, Usman Choudhury.

"I, uh, I just wanted to say a few things about Yousuf." Usman coughed nervously. "I didn't know him too well, especially these past two decades, but I couldn't find a person I'm more grateful to have in my life...or not have, as the case was. There was a great deal of pride to Yousuf, and he always knew what was important. I want to take this last opportunity to thank him for everything he did for me, and for taking on the responsibility of raising my daughter. Adina. I know he was more of a father to her than I could ever be, but I'm grateful that there was someone to catch her when she fell."

Before he was ushered from the podium, Usman took one quick glance at Adina, knowing that she was there. She was looking back at him dumbfounded, words completely lost to her. The last time she had seen him was at the wake when she was thirteen, when he had told her that he couldn't stand the sight of her and there wasn't a place for her in his home anymore. Her father, who could never forgive her. This was too much for Adina and she intended to run off when the ceremony came to an end.

People lined up to walk past Yousuf's coffin, to place a

rose and whisper a goodbye. Jack and Tc'aarlat were at the front of the line so they could go through quickly, having not known the man.

Adina stopped for a good long while. This was the last time she'd ever be next to him, and it was to say goodbye forever. Adina placed the rose on top and gently stroked the coffin, then whispered, "I shall miss you, Uncle."

She turned her back one last time, head hanging in despair.

"Was that really your father?" Jack asked the moment they had left the service and were outside again. "I thought your father was dead?"

"My father is dead," Adina said. "To me."

"Yeah, I get that," Tc'aarlat said. "No point dying over cried milk though, right?"

Jack gave him a look.

"Adina." There he was, her father, calling her. Adina wanted to go to him and run away from him at the same time. She hadn't seen him in twenty years, and he had chosen this moment, this damned day, to come and see her again. As he approached, Jack stood between him and Adina, thrusting out his hand to stop the man in his tracks.

"Hold up there, big guy," he said. "I don't think she wants to see you."

"What do you want?" Adina hissed. "You threw me out when Mom died. You said you were done with me."

"And I was, then. Your mother's loss was hard on me, and I never considered how hard it would be on you, too," Usman replied. "I'm...I'm sorry. I've been thinking stuff over, and I...I made a mistake, Adina."

"I don't want to hear it!" she snapped. "You made it

clear that you don't care about me. If Uncle Yousuf hadn't brought me up to be so respectful, I'd have a couple of words for you. But I don't. I just want you to leave me alone."

"That's fair," Usman said before reaching into his pocket. Jack was going to break his arm off until Usman removed a business card and handed it over. "My contact details are on there. I know I don't deserve it, but if you're ever willing to give me a chance, I'd like to talk."

"You've said your piece," Jack said, gesturing toward the exit. "If she wants anything to do with you, she'll give you a call."

Usman walked like a very old and sad man toward the gate at the end of a long path. Before he reached the end, a woman joined him. She interlaced her fingers with his and gave him a supportive peck on the cheek. They continued out the gate without looking back.

"Son of a bitch." Tears ran down Adina's face, but she made no effort to wipe them away. Her uncle's funeral, her mother's funeral, her father. Her mind raced, trying to regain the control she'd ceded to her heart. She finally closed her eyes, but couldn't stop crying. Her muscles tightened. "SON OF A BITCH!"

Jack, seeing what was about to happen, grabbed Adina's arm and started pulling her toward a wall behind which they could hide. He gestured for Tc'aarlat to follow.

They marched her to where guests could no longer see, and once there, they tried to calm her down. Fur was growing from her exposed skin. Her eyes had sunk and turned a dangerous yellow.

"Adina. *Adina!*" Jack snapped his fingers near her face. "You've got to breathe, okay? Just take some deep breaths."

"Jack, we're about to have a problem." Tc'aarlat watched over the wall. "There's a lot of people around here."

"Adina, look at me." Jack grabbed her forming muzzle and brought her eyes to meet his. "It's okay. I know this is a hard day for you, and I know what you're going through. You've got to calm down. You don't have to do anything you don't want to. Calm down for your uncle. You don't want to hurt the people that cared enough to come, do you?"

Adina shook her head at that last part and started breathing slowly, gathering control of herself. Breathing in, holding it, then breathing out over and over until the transformation receded, until she reverted back to her human self. The tears stopped as her mind regained control. She looked at Jack, her eyes glazed with pain. "Why did he come, Jack? Why was he here?"

"I don't know." Jack continued to hold her.

"Hey, do you guys know if the wake is going to have any grubs?" Tc'aarlat said. "I'm really craving a grub snout."

Adina snorted and rubbed the back of her hand over her eyes.

"You're asking this now? We're in the middle of something." Jack glared at his friend.

"She's fine." Tc'aarlat waved the comment off. "I'm starving, though, which isn't fine. This place makes people sad. Maybe we can go somewhere that makes people happy. Like a restaurant."

"For fu..." Jack shook his head in disbelief. "Fine, we're going."

Jack left to find out where their transport was. Tc'aarlat leaned against the wall with his arms crossed. Adina looked at him gratefully, and he tried to wink at her, but it was just a flutter of his eye.

"Thanks," she said. "It's been a long day."

"You've not been doing those exercises," Tc'aarlat remarked. "I know. Isaaca told me."

"How did Isaaca tell you?" Adina asked.

"She didn't, but you did," Tc'aarlat replied. "Why aren't you doing them? I thought you wanted to be in control?"

"They don't work," Adina said. "I need the medication again. There has to be a good substitute for them. Every time I calm myself and close my eyes to concentrate, I think about every horrible thought I've ever had. I come out of it more frustrated than ever."

"Have you tried *not* thinking about those terrible things?" Tc'aarlat asked. "Does me a world of good. Hope for a breast and expect the worst."

"That's...that's not how that saying goes at all. It's hope for the *best*, and prepare for the worst."

"Why wouldn't I hope for a breast? Expecting the worst is the Yollin way."

"Guys!" Jack shouted, beckoning them over to a waiting black vehicle. "You ready to go?"

"I know what you're going through." Tc'aarlat looked at Jack and nodded. The Yollin ushered Adina out from behind the wall. "I lost Wo'fek, then I regained her only to lose her again, but she survived. My soul was tortured. Although she is still around, I understand."

"I thought you never wanted to talk about that. Under pain of excruciating death."

"I don't because I don't need anyone to think that I'm not hard as *Fortitude's* landing skids," Tc'aarlat said. "When I fall asleep and in my dreams. It sounds pretty…what's the word? Well, anyway, you can never have enough fucking people that care about you around you, you know?"

"Are you, of all people, saying I should give my father a chance?" Adina asked. "The guy who abandoned me?"

"I think he's the guy who made you who you are," Tc'aarlat said. "Life's too fucking short for leaving things open-ended. Believe me, I know. There's no harm in hearing what he has to say, and there's no reason you can't tell him where to stick it when he's done talking, either."

Adina and Tc'aarlat moved toward the waiting vehicle, a hoverlimo, that waited to take them to the wake. Adina took Tc'aarlat's hand and gripped it tightly. "You're pretty good at this, you know? I like seeing this side of you."

"Don't get used to it," Tc'aarlat replied, opening the car door for her. Adina climbed in.

Frontier Zone, City Station Hopefill, Residential Zone 8, Anderfall Pub

The party was catered as part of the funeral services the care home provided. The wake allowed Adina to meet the many elders who had become friends with her uncle over the years, ones who had been brought to the station by transport. Despite having to travel to the City Station, they were happy to get out.

She knew what a good man her uncle had been, and his friends reinforced that. They would have made the trip had it *not* been comfortable. Unfortunately, she found herself

reflecting on the appearance of her father and the myste-
rious woman she had seen him with. He wanted to make
amends after all this time, and at the funeral of the man
who'd raised her.

It was plaguing her and keeping her out of discussions
about her uncle, which depressed her further.

"I am sorry for your loss, Adina." She forgot about her
father issues when her eyes landed on the once and still
great Draven Maynard with his silken hair. He was dressed
appropriately in a tight black suit, and he was holding a
bouquet of blue daisies, which he handed to her.

"I hope you don't mind me just turning up like this. Jack
and Tc'aarlat mentioned you were attending a funeral, and
I haven't seen you in ages, and I was in the neighbor... This
is weird, isn't it? I shouldn't have done this."

"No, it's okay." Adina stood to hug him. "It's good to see
you, Draven. How have you been?"

"Less explosive," he replied. "Any day I don't get hit with
a missile is a good one in my books. Oh, I love your
earrings, by the way. They are beautiful."

"Thanks," Adina said, self-consciously reaching for
them. "You're with the WRU now from what Jack was
telling me?"

"Yeah, I am," Draven said. "Have been since I recovered
from my injuries. You know, I could use someone I trust to
help me fight the werewolves if you ever—"

"How did you know I was a were?" Adina asked
abruptly, missing the point of his statement.

"I didn't until you just said it. You haven't come up in
the WRU's database," Draven replied.

Adina groaned. "Well, crap. Don't tell anyone else."

"It's no big deal," Draven replied. "I do work for a big werewolf hunting group, after all."

"That's what concerns me."

"What do you say? You would give us an edge no one else has. Multiple weres working together."

"It's not for me," Adina said politely. "I've never been a fan of turning wolf. Changing is a nightmare. It happens when I don't want it to. I took pills to stop it, but they don't work anymore. Can I ask you something?"

"Sure. What's up?" Draven shrugged as if her revelation were nothing, but his eyes never left her.

"How do you, uh, how do you control that other side of you?" Adina asked. "I've been having trouble remaining in control lately."

"I don't. I change. I do my thing. I change back." Draven laughed, but he shut up when he remembered he was in the middle of a wake. "I don't know what to tell you, to be honest. I thought all werewolves were in control of their change. I guess you're the exception."

"How do you control it, then?"

"I can't help you there," Draven replied, but he could see this issue was upsetting her. "It's all about understanding your other side, not controlling it. You being a werewolf is as much a part of you as Adina is a part of you. When you fully understand that, the rest should be easy."

"Really?"

"It's how I do it," Draven said. "When was the last time you let yourself just be a wolf, Adina? Let your other side walk wild without you needing something from it?"

"I don't think I've ever done that." Adina took in all of his words.

"It's like anger, or at least, I think it is," Draven explained. "It builds up and up until one day it just gets released and does some real damage. You need to find an outlet for your anger to stop that from happening. Same thing here. Let me guess; you get angry and then change, so your wolf is the release of your emotional energy?"

Adina nodded. "How do I release the anger to embrace a calm wolf? How do *you* do that?"

"Fortunately, I have a good job," Draven replied, then just behind her, he spotted Jack and Tc'aarlat, two people he wanted to talk to right now. "Don't be afraid of it. That's the best thing you can do. It was really good to see you again, Adina."

"You too."

Draven gave her another giant hug before moving past her toward the odd couple. Jack and Tc'aarlat. They had been eagerly eyeing the buffet that had been arranged and were now carefully picking out the bits they wanted and putting them on paper plates.

Adina watched him go, thinking about what he had said to her. It made a lot of sense, and she silently promised herself she'd find an outlet for her other side, so she could change into a calm wolf who was more a friend than an enemy. That revelation alone eased her troubled mind.

Before she knew it, she was embroiled in conversations with people who had known her uncle in life.

Tc'aarlat saw Draven first and rolled his eyes. He desperately tried to get Jack to move away before the guy could catch them, but Jack wasn't having any of it. Draven got between them and grabbed a paper plate, stacking it high with mini-sausage rolls. "I love these. There's always such a good spread at wakes."

"You come here to eat? That's morbid," Tc'aarlat declared.

Draven looked at him with a finger to his lips. "Before your dumb ass asks, I wasn't invited. I thought it'd be nice to see Adina and offer my condolences."

"Wait!" Tc'aarlat snapped. "You missed the boring part and just came here for the good part when there's food and alcohol? I didn't know we could do that!"

Jack scowled. "We can't. Well, decent people don't do it that way. We were there for Adina, and now we're here for the food."

"I love watching you two talk." Draven shoved one of the sausage rolls into his pie hole and attempted to talk with a full mouth. "I bet you guys get compared to an old married couple a lot."

"Yeah, what's the deal with that?" Tc'aarlat asked. "I've never gotten that. Do human marriages have a lot of hunting gangsters across the galaxy or something?"

"I get the feeling you're here for more than just the food," Jack interrupted. "Have you got something for us? And what do you know about gangsters? We think the Don is behind this. Are you on his payroll?"

Draven nodded and swallowed. "My team's being deployed tomorrow to the northern side of Hopefill City. We've heard word that some old storage units are being used as a holding base for unreported and illegal were-wolves working for the Silver Diamonds gang. They've been pretty aggressive with their werewolf tactics, so we're expecting a lot of resistance. Wanna join?"

"I don't know. I'm busy organizing my guns tomorrow," Tc'aarlat replied idly. "Then I've got ironing and my hair, not to mention watching re-runs of *I Love Pukey*."

"We'll be there," Jack said. "Just give us the time and place."

5

Frontier Zone, City Station Hopefill, WRU Head-quarters

Rola Foste checked her watch for the fiftieth time and counted the seconds, but mostly she was paying attention to her reflection. The claw marks she had received a month ago—the ones that ran down the left side of her face—had finally healed, but they were still visible. They had gotten the bastard who did it to her, but she'd have to live with the scars.

"Where is he?" To her left, Tinio Attes cooled his heels. He had a face envious of his ass but a body built for battle.

No one answered because no one knew. To his left stood the last member of the crew, a buff man-mountain they fondly called Reward. They had seen him knock a hole through a wall before considering turning into a werewolf.

The three of them had been waiting for close to an hour next to a black hovervan. Their mission was clear, but there was no sign of their squad captain Draven Maynard.

"He's late by one hour, two minutes, and twenty-seven seconds," Rola said. "Last time, it was fourteen minutes and five seconds. He's getting later each time."

"Maybe he ran into bad traffic, like usual." Reward shook his head. "Or he could learn to leave earlier to get here on time. Makes me want to question his motivation."

"Draven's picking up the tag-alongs," Tinio added. "That's why he's so damn late. I don't see why we have to entertain them."

"They'll probably just get in the way," Rola countered. "Draven can't just expect us to adopt two new guys an hour before we go into a mission. It's unprofessional."

"He won't expect them to fight, surely?" Tinio was less than amused.

"I don't know what he expects," Rola replied. "He ain't here. All I know is that we haven't had a good bust in weeks, and No-Arm is riding our asses hard about it. We need to get some results, and that needs to happen tonight."

"We'll get results." Reward hammered a big fist into his hand. "Don't panic about these tag-alongs. If they get in our way, we eliminate them."

"I'm really getting to dislike that pretty boy." Tinio lifted his head as if he heard something.

"Draven is a good fighter, but he's a shit leader," Rola admitted.

They froze as three figures strolled through the cascading shadows of the buildings around them. They recognized Draven immediately with an annoyed grunt, but the other two were a mystery. A Yollin and a human.

Draven marched up to his team and apologized profusely for how late they had arrived.

"This is Jack and Tc'aarlat. They're working for the En-D, and as you know, they're going to tag along tonight and see how we do things," Draven said, then he turned his attention to the Shadows. "This is my team. We're responsible for wolf retrieval and investigation. This is Tinio, Rola, and the big guy is Reward."

"I hope you guys have some chops," Tc'aarlat said, opening the hovervan and getting inside. "I don't want to have to be watching your butts all night."

"Sorry about him." Jack hopped in next. "He gets like that before he has to do real work."

"The Yollin is going to be watching a butt, all right. His own, when I shove his head up there," Rola whispered to the others before they too climbed into the hovervan. It wasn't very impressive since the vehicle was designed to blend in with a crowd, and it was the minimum needed to get them there in one piece.

"Where are your weapons?" Tc'aarlat asked, and the three of them grinned at him.

"We don't need weapons," Rola said. "We *are* the weapons."

"I use a gun, so..." Tc'aarlat shrugged, pulling out his modified Jean Dukes Special. "I don't have to be directly in front of anyone to kill them."

"I'm kind of surprised you remembered to bring it this time," Jack said. "You've been forgetting it in your room lately."

Tc'aarlat glared at him, followed by a moment of

silence. "Thanks for that, wiper of the hairy ass. What do these guys know about Don Gan'barlo?"

"Ask them, not me. And it's 'asswipe.'"

"Yes. You are an asswipe. We agree." Tc'aarlat faced the others. "Tell me where the Don is. I know he's behind this."

Draven looked at the others. They broke eye contact and looked at the floor of the van. "We don't know anything about a dude named Don," Draven answered for his team.

Jack and Tc'aarlat turned to each other after watching Draven and his crew. Neither believed Draven's reply. What did their body language say? They were afraid? Constipated?

"All right, enough fun." Draven rubbed his hands together, eager to get started. "Let's get everyone caught up and ready. We've received one-alpha intel that the Silver Diamonds are hiding unregistered werewolves in a series of storage units in the commercial zone. Now, I don't think I have to tell anyone here that the Silver Diamonds have been particularly aggressive with their werewolf tactics thus far, and according to our intel, we're expecting to meet a lot of resistance."

"Wait, unregistered?" Jack asked. "I didn't realize that werewolves had to register here?"

"That's the WRU for you," Draven said. "Things have changed a bit since you were last here, Jack. In an effort to keep the city safe from rogue werewolves, we needed to know who is one and who isn't. Being an unregistered were is an instantly jailable offense."

"What's the plan, boss?" Reward asked.

Tc'aarlat looked like he was going to say something but

settled for clicking his mandibles and leaning back to watch the others. He dug at his crotch to scratch an itch and found the others staring at him. "What?"

Draven filled the silence. "It's not going to be easy. This particular facility has upwards of a hundred different storage units, and I'm sure they have contingencies in place. As soon as we get there, Rola and I are going to transform and try to sniff them out and make them run while Tinio and Reward block off the possible exits. Jack and Tc'aarlat, you are going to stay in the hovervan and keep an eye on us."

"Fuck off!" Tc'aarlat exclaimed. "We'll be that much farther away if we have to come in and save you."

Jack shrugged.

"You're not familiar with the team. I'm afraid you might get in the way," Draven replied. "Once we've cleared them out, you can come in and take a look."

"How are you going to stop them if there's more than a few?" Jack asked, genuinely curious. "Beat them unconscious?"

"We use these." Draven turned around and brought a large metal box into his lap, opening it to show a gun. An injector gun. There was a needle on one end and a tube of yellow liquid sloshing on the top. It was large, too, bigger than any human could be expected to handle. It had been made to be used by a transformed werewolf. "Are you guys familiar with the nano-slash-DNA-dampening drugs? They aren't common, usually found in pill form. This is just like that except in a liquid form with a quick applicator for a nearly instantaneous effect."

"I thought you guys didn't use weapons?" Tc'aarlat tried to smile, but it came across as a leer.

"I get it," Jack said. "Once they've transformed back, they're pretty easy to capture."

Draven nodded. "Exactly."

"We're getting close, boss," Tinio said. "Couple of minutes at most."

Draven nodded. "Okay, guys. That's our plan of attack. Look out for each other, and let's get as many of these guys off the street as we can."

Frontier Zone, City Station Hopefill, Commercial Zone 1, Storage Units

Getting into the storage unit was easy because the unit didn't care if they broke anything. Draven and Rola leaned into a pry bar and broke the lock off like a knife cutting through butter, then shoulder-rammed through the wooden doors to get inside. That was when they changed into werewolves.

Meanwhile, Tinio and Reward assumed their were forms and circled the building to find exits and watch for anyone trying to escape.

As soon as they were inside, Draven and Rola sniffed the air and locked onto an aroma that could only be described as wet dog.

Draven, who had noticed the smell, nodded at a corridor and they both ran toward it. Jack and Tc'aarlat had been restricted to sitting inside the hovervan and listening to their grunts and growls through the radio as they raced through the complex.

"We should be in there doing something interesting." Tc'aarlat crossed his arms. "This is crap."

"We haven't been hired to hunt werewolves," Jack replied. "We're here for the drug lord, Bloody Darling who I think will lead us to Don Gan'barlo."

"Something tells me he won't be here," Tc'aarlat said. "It will be an end of ultimate deadness. It will be the mummified remains of a lead. Why are *we* here, Jack?"

"The werewolf problem and the drug problem are connected; that is clear to me," Jack said. "I think if we can figure out how, we'll have a shot at finding this guy."

"How do you know it's a guy?" Tc'aarlat asked. "Are you holding something back from me?"

"I just meant in a general sense. All suspects are guys until they're not, even if they're girls."

Tc'aarlat nodded but continued to watch Jack for signs that he knew more than he was letting on. "You are liking this Draven like he is some school crush. You are bromancing."

"What crawled up your ass and made you feel jiggly inside?"

"Aha!" Tc'aarlat declared. "You *are* hiding something. You didn't answer my question."

"You didn't ask a question, dickweed."

Tc'aarlat accepted his comeuppance with dignity and grace. "You suck."

Jack tapped his fingers on the dashboard while he stared through the window at what he could see of the complex. He focused on a light spot where there shouldn't have been one.

"Stay here," Jack said and jumped out the front door.

"Fuck that!" Tc'aarlat slid the side door open and ran after his partner.

Jack approached a dumpster to the side of the complex. Jack pointed at a light gray powder that had collected on the ground and the streak running up the side of the refuse bin.

"What is that?" Tc'aarlat asked after looking more closely and seeing nothing that meant anything to him.

"Epperin." Jack reached into the dumpster and pulled out a sack hanging across the front of it that read Epperin in bold letters. They knew what Epperin was. It was a chalky gray powder that was used in mining operations to turn big rocks into little rocks.

Because it was a powerful explosive.

"Holy butt-snuggler!" Tc'aarlat shouted. "They're in a building that's about to be blown into three weeks from now!"

Jack didn't hesitate. He ran to the hovervan and grabbed the radio to warn the team inside. "Get out of there!" he shouted, but they were in werewolf form. He tucked his fingers in his mouth and whistled as loud and as long as he could.

Before he ran out of air, the shock wave of the explosion tossed him and Tc'aarlat into the van right before the dumpster slammed into it. The night turned into ringing ears and falling debris. They couldn't see through the choking dust cloud.

When it cleared, one side of the building was gone. It leaned and tottered before a second explosion turned the top floors into a raging fireball. Jack and Tc'aarlat crawled under the van and waited for the last of the fallout. The automated fire control systems were useless since the damage was so extensive. Sparks signaled live wires in their death throes. Random bricks fell. Metal screeched as it tore free and crashed into the refuse.

Jack found his feet wobbling as he tried to stand upright. "Tc'aarlat, are you okay?"

"What?" Tc'aarlat shouted, rubbing his ears. "I've become really good at hearing a loud ringing in my ears, but nothing else." He shook his head.

Jack worked his way to the far side of the hovervan and tried the radio once again. "Draven! Draven, are you there? Report!"

After a few haunting seconds of silence, Draven's voice came through crystal-clear. "This is Draven, I'm fine, but Rola has been injured. She needs medical assistance *now*. Call an ambulance."

The radio came to life again. "This is Tinio and Reward reporting in. No injuries beyond going ten rounds with the reigning kickboxing champ."

Jack turned to look at Tc'aarlat, and he could tell that the Yollin was going through the same thoughts as he was. "This wasn't just a trap to cover an escape. This was planned."

"Someone knew they were coming," Tc'aarlat agreed. "Doesn't look like they were planning on leaving any survivors, either."

Jack radioed En-D. "This is Jack Marber. I need medical assistance at the storage units in Commercial Zone One. We have one badly injured person. Please hurry."

"Jack, look!" Tc'aarlat pointed at a silhouette looking down from a nearby wall. It was hard to mistake the toothy grin of a werewolf. The Yollin pulled out his gun and gave chase. The were ran.

"Wait!" Jack called after him. "It could be a trap."

Tc'aarlat was engrossed in chasing the bad guy, and with a bad case of ringing in the ears, he never heard the warnings. Jack pulled his gun and ran after his friend.

The werewolf was fast, leaping over walls without losing its momentum and dashing across the landscape of old buildings and worn-out vehicles. Despite being on a station, this part of the city looked eerily similar to a planet-based rundown section of town. The werewolf took paths and routes a mountain goat would have found challenging.

What the werewolf didn't count on was Tc'aarlat's determination. The Yollin had kept pace with the beast from the deck to the rooftops above, finding a shortcut when necessary, diving over obstacles when one was presented. The wolf ran like a greyhound but faster, maintaining its speed through turns and leaping vast distances between buildings.

Tc'aarlat did the same, angry and letting that fury drive his body to fantastic speeds. To get the criminal, Tc'aarlat needed to keep it in sight. As long as it was, he had a chance of catching it.

Tc'aarlat's problem lay in ending the chase, and he knew it. Despite how well he was keeping up, it was hard to ignore the fact that the werewolf had more stamina and would be able to go much farther than him without tiring. Time worked against him.

In the next alley, he grabbed a thick freshwater pipe. He clambered down the pipe with ease, thanks to a building façade that offered decent footing. "So far, so squid."

Tc'aarlat jumped that last five meters to the ground. There he squinted into the distance and spotted the beast. It had extended its lead on him. "There you are, Mr. Butt Breath."

The Yollin steeled himself for a new sprint. He accelerated toward the werewolf but stuck to the shadows. He pushed himself harder than he had ever done before. His body screamed in torment, but he ignored the pain. He was gaining on the were. It slowed as it looked in the wrong direction for him. Then it stopped and licked a paw.

Tc'aarlat leapt majestically through the air, bounded off a nearby wall, and slammed into the werewolf. Both of them went sprawling. Tc'aarlat pulled his Jean Dukes Special and lunged forward.

"Gotcha." Tc'aarlat straddled the giant wolf, pinning him to the ground before twisting his face around. One crazy eye locked onto Tc'aarlat while the beast tried to open its jaws, but the Yollin's free hand had it clamped shut. Tc'aarlat jammed the business end of his gun into the werewolf's cheek.

"You know what this will do, don't you? Your head will become nothing more than a mess of yogurt. That's right, good boy, settle the fuck down. I have some questions."

Tc'aarlat took a few deep breaths and took in the werewolf. He noticed something suspicious.

"What the fuck?"

Tc'aarlat grabbed the collar that had been obscured beneath its fur. As a guy that had seen his fair share of werewolves, he had never seen one wearing this kind of accessory before. The werewolf was looking up at him with pleading eyes, and he could tell it was about to transform back. First its eyes became human again, then the fur began to recede. That was as far as it got, though, as the collar revealed its purpose: giving the poor creature a massive surge of blue lightning around its neck and bringing it back to werewolf form.

The thing pleaded with its eyes. Tc'aarlat didn't have to be a mind reader to know what it would have said if it could have spoken. "Help me."

The creature spun into a rage, flailing and bucking, and threw the Yollin off. Tc'aarlat hit and rolled to put distance between himself and the creature. It snapped at his face, and he slashed back with his mandibles. The beast crouched. The Yollin dove to the side, ducked, and jumped sideways a second time before coming up ready to fire on a low setting to stun the werewolf, but it was gone.

Tc'aarlat had nothing left in his fuel tank. It had taken everything he had to catch it the first time. There wouldn't be a second time, at least not today. All he could do was look around and wonder which way it had gone.

"Tc'aarlat." He turned to see Jack approaching and sighed in relief. "What happened?"

"Something strange, Jack," Tc'aarlat said. "These guys aren't losing control. I think they're *being controlled*."

6

Frontier Zone, City Station Hopefill, Dock 23, Freight Bay F, ICS *Fortitude*, Bridge

Adina sat in Jack's chair monitoring the feeds Solo said he had been looking at lately while turning her father's card over and over between her fingers. She never looked at it properly. Her pet Raal hawk perched on the bar over Tc'aarlat's position, where Isaaca's mother Myst usually stayed, much to Jack's chagrin.

Adina sighed. Her father's request for reconciliation had been on her mind all day. She found herself no closer to making a decision about what to do.

Tc'aarlat's words bounced around her head. *Life was too short to fill it with people who don't care about you.* Now that her uncle was gone, she wondered who would be there for her.

"No, he made his side clear. He had all the time in the world to contact me," Adina said, sitting up and grabbing a lighter she had swiped from the kitchen. "Fuck him."

Caw. Caw.

Adina gestured at Isaaca. The hawk flew to her, landed on her shoulder, and started pecking the card.

Adina flicked the lighter, bringing it to life. She dangled the card over it before plunging it into the flame. The corner caught and flared. Once it started burning, it went quickly. She let it fall from her fingers to the deck, then kicked at it with her toe to help it burn to ash.

She had hoped that act would feel like the right thing to do, would give her confidence in her decision to stay away, but all it had done was make her more unsure. She knew she wouldn't have closure until she talked with her father. She had to know if it was a ploy by her father to alleviate his guilt or if he was doing right by her.

"Hopefill City has been rocked tonight by reports of an explosion in a suspected werewolf habitat, leaving people to wonder if the werewolf threat has just reached a new level of terror. I'm Lucy Luce reporting for Channel Two Thousand."

Adina leaned toward the quiet voice speaking from a pop-up window showing a breaking report. Solo had been keeping her eyes and ears open, watching for werewolf activity in the station. The reporter stood in front of a building that had recently been torn apart. Debris and smoke drifted through the air. In the background, emergency medical technicians loaded a wounded individual into an ambulance.

"Solo, can you turn that up, please?" Adina asked.

"Of course."

The reporter continued, holding her microphone close to her face and going through the supposed events that had led o the building's destruction. Then she and the cameraman turned their attention to the gentleman next to her. An older man with fading gray hair, he looked like he had been stitched together from reclaimed body parts like a Frankenstein monster, and it was hard to notice that he didn't have any arms. "I'm standing here with the department head of the recently established Werewolf Response Unit, created to tackle this growing threat. Mikhail May. Mikhail, is the werewolf problem that is currently plaguing the city getting worse?"

"Well, first of all, Lucy, it's the *Wechselbalg* Response Unit. No, I don't think the problem is getting worse. We've had setbacks like tonight, but we're pleased to announce that there were no fatalities and certainly no danger to the general public. We take extra precautions on every mission we undertake, and if you look at our reports, you'll see a sharp decline in the numbers of dangerous werewolves walking our streets."

The reporter barely waited for him to finish before blurting her follow-up. "It's hard to deny, though, that there *have* been attacks. There are weekly reports of new assaults by crazed werewolves. How is the general public supposed to react?"

"With a calm demeanor." Mikhail May flashed his multicolored teeth, a mixture of pearly white and sickly yellow. "I think we have all heard the adage 'things must get worse before they get better,' yes? That is the case here. We're doing our very best to reduce casualties and keep our streets safe."

Adina listened closely and heard a remark off-camera. "I thought it was, 'When things get worse, we make them better,' you butt-crack-snacking jaghole?"

"Thank you for joining us, Mr. May, and addressing some of our concerns."

"Of course."

"You heard Tc'aarlat too, right?" Adina asked. Solo's motherly face appeared on the screen and nodded solemnly. "I guess I know what they've been up to tonight. Tc'aarlat!" She smiled at his impudence. "I wonder where they are now?"

"If I had to guess, I'd say they were being questioned about the explosion. Is everything okay Adina, you seem a little…"

Adina considered her answer carefully, petting the crimson feathers along Isaaca's body and enjoying how soft they were beneath her fingertips. "I'm fine, Solo. Just trying to get on with life."

"Have you done your breathing exercises today?" Solo asked.

Adina didn't answer.

Frontier Zone, City Station Hopefill, WRU Headquarters, Interview Room

They were stuffed into a cramped and sterile room with a single table, four uncomfortable steel chairs, and a camera with a continuously blinking red light. Jack and Tc'aarlat had been taken to the WRU headquarters. They thought it was to keep them under cover, but after being forced into an interrogation room to wait for nearly two hours while they remained handcuffed to the table and each other, the truth became apparent.

"So, we're under arrest, right? Fuck Draven right in his eyehole," Tc'aarlat said. "This is us being arrested."

"That's for damn sure." Jack's lip twitched into a feral snarl of its own accord.

"That means Draven is a dickhead. I called it. You should have bet me on that. I would have won."

"Something tells me this wasn't Draven's idea. And I have to agree with you. Draven is a fuckstick."

The pair sat up straight when they saw a silhouette in the translucence of the door's window. It opened and in stepped Mikhail May, the armless leader of the WRU. The stern-looking elder came in and took a seat. A few seconds later, Draven walked in and closed the door.

"Well, I finally get to meet Nathan's golden boys," Mikhail said. "You're the guys who solve his problems."

"Certainly does sound like us," Tc'aarlat said. "You've met us. Now take off these cuffs."

Jack leaned forward, which inadvertently brought Tc'aarlat forward as well with a rattle of chains. "I'm sorry, Mr. May. Are we under arrest?"

"Of course not, guys. We just need to—"

Mikhail gave Draven a look that shut him up instantly. "The short answer is no. The long answer is yes. I want you two to answer a few of my questions before I allow you to go back to Nathan Lowell with everything you know."

"You apprehended us and chained us to a table because we work for Nathan Lowell? What kind of utter bullshit is that? How small must your willy be to be so threatened by me and this guy?" Jack gestured with his head since he tried not to make any sudden moves with his hands. "What questions, you fucking suckhole piece of dogshit?"

Mikhail ignored Jack's tirade. He was apparently used to prisoners being less than cordial. "Simple stuff, like why Nathan brought you in, and why he isn't depending on the official agents of the En-D?"

"Sounds like a question you should ask him, you ass-munching, triple-chinned, dickweed." Tc'aarlat nodded at Jack, earning a small chuckle in response.

"The reason he brought us in is that he wanted a fresh set of eyes on the problem of Bloody Darling, in addition to locating Don Gan'barlo."

"You're after Bloody Darling?" Mikhail snorted in derision. "He's a myth propagated by the gangsters that run this city. A fear tactic. And who is Don Bun Grabbo?"

"That sounds like something Bloody Darling would say," Tc'aarlat countered. "Or someone trying to cover for them. Are you giving us an ice-cold shoulder?"

"What?" Mikhail leaned back and scowled. "Is either of you capable of giving a straight answer?"

"He means, are you stonewalling us?" Jack explained.

"Once in a green moon, we say what we mean. If you want to know what Nathan is doing, ask him. If he tells you, then you deserve to know. If he doesn't, you can fuck off."

"Cute," Mikhail replied. "Anyway, Bloody Darling is what the gang members say when we haul them in. All of their drugs come from the same source, this Bloody Darling. It's an excuse, a scapegoat. There are several suppliers coming through the city. The higher up we go through the hierarchy of the gangs, the more we hear that name. It's a diversion."

"Interesting theory." Jack crossed his arms, forcing

72

Tc'aarlat to whack his head on his shoulder and grunt in pain. Jack mostly ignored it. "No evidence that it's not true, though. The En-D seems convinced."

"Believe what you want. I don't give a fuck," Mikhail said with a shrug. "That ain't my problem, it's yours. My problem is you two ugly fuckers getting involved in WRU business."

"Whoa!" Tc'aarlat snapped. "You can call Jack that, sure, but I'm a *Gott Verdammt* specimen of perfection!"

"We ain't interested in werewolves," Jack said.

"Should've thought about that before you went chasing after one. If one person was harmed in that pursuit, one person, you'd have put this entire department in jeopardy. We rely on public trust to perform our duties."

"What, so we weren't supposed to chase a criminal who happened to be a werewolf?" Tc'aarlat said. "We were doing your job for you, so that very much begs the question. What in the fuck were *you* doing?"

"And how did that go?" asked Mikhail. "Did you catch it? What information did you get from it?"

"It was wearing a shock collar," Tc'aarlat said. "Here's my theory; you're gonna love this. I think they're being controlled, and what's—"

"We know about the shock collars," Mikhail said, rudely interrupting. "Every werewolf we pick up from a gang has a damned collar. They're used to make sure they don't do anything stupid like revert back to human form when our agents knock on the front door."

"That guy did not look like he was in control," Tc'aarlat replied, eyeing their interrogator suspiciously. "His eyes were saying, 'Help me.' I know it. Makes me wonder, what the fuck are you doing out here since you don't seem interested in getting to the root of the problem, you disagreeable fuck."

"What?" Mikhail replied. "He wanted to jack you up. Give himself a moment to slip past you, which he did if you'll remember. These are regular werewolves, changed humans in charge of their faculties. They walk on all fours and are in complete control of their change."

Tc'aarlat kept his mouth shut.

"*Whoa,*" Jack muttered under his breath. First time he had ever seen Tc'aarlat stay quiet when a perfectly good retort was called for. Maybe he'd had enough stupid for one day. He'd reached his limit.

Mikhail stood then, and Draven followed his lead. Mikhail said a few final words before he left. "I can't say it's been a pleasure. Most importantly, keep your noses out of WRU business. Consider this your one and only warning, gentlemen."

Draven's boss strode from the room while he hesitated. "Sorry, guys."

Tc'aarlat stuck two fingers up at him and blew a raspberry. "Go blow your boss silly using your suck hole."

"He's just upset," Jack said, pushing down the Yollin's hand. "We'll be in touch."

"Just be careful. I've gotten you in enough trouble already." Draven looked down before heading out, leaving the door open behind him.

"Unlock us, you fucking asshole!" Jack shouted after him.

. . .

Frontier Zone, City Station Hopefill, Dock 23, Freight Bay F, ICS *Fortitude*, Bridge

Amazingly, it was Isaaca who had woken Adina up when Jack and Tc'aarlat threw themselves through the bridge door. She squawked up a storm, spooked by the pair's sudden appearance. Adina turned around to meet them, forgetting that she had fallen asleep in Jack's chair, before smiling innocently.

"That's my chair," Jack said, moving over to her. "It's supposed to be the one thing on this damned ship that's mine. Sorry, just...pain in the ass."

"Rough night?" Adina stretched her sleep away. It was late, she realized, far too late for them to be getting in from a mission. "I saw you on the news."

Tc'aarlat perked up. "We were on the news?"

"Well, your voice was," Adina replied, pointing at the Yollin.

"Sometimes that's all you need to get a pop star career going." Tc'aarlat preened like Myst did. "We got told off by some high-up prick at the WRU, so we're not in the best of moods."

"Let me guess. They didn't like you sticking your noses into their business."

"We stayed in the van." Jack picked Adina up and stood her to the side of his chair. Isaaca squawked at getting dislodged and fanned Jack's face as she flew to the perch over Tc'aarlat's position. Jack took his seat and quickly began working his back into it. "I don't think we stuck even the tips of our noses in."

"How about things with you?" Tc'aarlat asked. "Love the swear pants, by the way."

"Sweat pants. Yeah, I've just been lounging today," Adina replied. "Forgetting about things. What's new with Bloody Darling?"

"I caught one of the werewolves, and it was wearing a shock collar." Tc'aarlat shook his head. "My running theory is that someone's controlling them like bad dogs."

"That's awful. What did the guy say about—"

"Why is Draven's business card in my trash can?" Jack reached into the small circular bin and pulled out the half-burnt business card. "Adina, were you burning stuff at my terminal?"

"It's not Draven's card, it's—"

"No, it is." Jack swiveled the card around. It was mostly black and ash, but one could still make out the name *Draven* at its center. "Do people sit here often? Is this a habit I need to watch out for?"

"I burnt the wrong card," Adina whispered, suddenly feeling hopeful, although she didn't know why. She started backing toward the door. "Guys, I'm going to bed. I'll see you in the morning."

"Did I sound good, at least?" After she shrugged, Tc'aarlat waved her away. "What are we going to do now? Draven had nothing for us, and we're up the bleak without a shadow since we're persons no *gracias* with the WRU."

"Persona non grata. We'll stay in touch with him. We've just got to keep it on the hush-hush," Jack replied. "I think Adina's got the right idea. I'm going to bed. Maybe I'll wake up fresh-faced in the morning, a new man with vigor and a focused eye. Pay a visit to Timothy and see if he's had any ideas."

"How come every idea you have is all about waiting around for stuff to happen?" Tc'aarlat asked.

"What's your plan, then?"

"Go out on the street, find a drug dealer, and chase the trail. We'll work our way up to the top and beat the crap out of them."

Jack stood up and stretched with a jaw-creaking yawn. "Good luck with that, Tc'aarlat. I'm going to fall asleep watching *Titanic* again."

"Don't forget to cry, you big fat baby," Tc'aarlat teased.

"Always do. No, I won't forget because I remember. All of it," Jack meandered out, waving over his shoulder as he hit the corridor on his way to his quarters.

"You are the wind beneath my wings!" Tc'aarlat called after him with a short chortle.

7

Frontier Zone, City Station Hopefill, Dock 9, Freight Bay A

Tc'aarlat had been scouring the city for hours, trying to find the seediest sections so he could draw out the drug dealers and other career criminals. It was ironic; apparently the city was dealing with daily werewolf attacks, but he hadn't seen an unpleasant person yet. He was greeted by empty streets and a sky full of stars. Grumbling, the Yollin was about to call it a day when he saw something on the other side of the street—a vagabond wearing sunglasses that covered his eyes.

"Longer use can lead to not being able to see," Tc'aarlat muttered to himself, repeating the mantra about the city's new favorite drug. He crossed the empty road and approached the old beggar.

The guy shook the cup in his hand. "Spare some change, mister? Just a few credits."

"You get much tonight?" Tc'aarlat asked, resisting the

urge to rip the sunglasses off and find out what was underneath. "Haven't seen many people coming this way."

"About as much luck as you'd expect." He rattled his cup again. "Might have some more luck now, though."

"Yeah, yeah." Tc'aarlat took out his credit stick and tapped it against the cup, transferring him five credits. The vagabond cheered up, smiling broadly and showing his pearly-white teeth.

"All donations are appreciated."

"Those are some cool glasses. Don't suppose I could buy them off you?"

From the way the guy looked at him, the Yollin could tell he was suspicious, but he wasn't sure what he was thinking. It wasn't hard to notice the glances at Tc'aarlat's gun while wondering how much danger he was in. Still, the guy didn't miss a beat and appeared calm against the potential pitfalls. "They're not for sale. I need them to see."

"You could buy some more," Tc'aarlat suggested. "My species is used to the dark. This place is far too bright. You got a name?"

"They call me Theo. You?"

"Tc'aarlat."

"What's the deal here, Tc'aarlat? You ain't the type to take no for an answer, are you?" Theo asked.

"Unless the question is, 'Have you had enough to eat?'"

"You don't want to fight me, Tc'aarlat," Theo said. "You should walk away now while we still have a bit of dignity left."

"I'm taking this from a guy who sleeps in a princess blanket?" Tc'aarlat gestured at the pink duvet with the cartoony princess logo on it. "Just let me see what's beneath the glasses. End of discussion, end of trouble."

"Why don't you come and get them?" Theo countered in a low and dangerous voice.

"I don't want to do this," Tc'aarlat said. "Violence is my last resort." It wasn't, but it sounded better if he claimed it was.

"Then walk away."

Tc'aarlat shrugged. Quick as a whip, he lashed out a hand to tear the glasses from Theo's face. A forearm blocked it. Theo caught the Yollin's wrist, twisted it to the side, and forced Tc'aarlat away.

Theo settled onto the balls of his feet. His body relaxed, and he stood ready.

"All right, let's try that again." Tc'aarlat feinted left, dodged right, and then came straight up the middle, swinging an uppercut to catch the glasses as his hand passed Theo's face. With a subtle but lightning-fast turn, Theo deflected Tc'aarlat's attack and spun him in a circle.

The Yollin attacked sideways, then low, then with a flying atomic elbow. Each time, his best moves were deflected, and he twisted against his own momentum to end up with his back to the target.

"Give me those glasses before I get mad," Tc'aarlat growled.

"I'd hate to see you mad. You might fall down and hurt yourself." Theo adjusted the glasses casually before settling into a fighting pose. He'd not made any attacks because Tc'aarlat was powerless to hurt him.

"Okay, maybe this time I'll let you keep those glasses, but I don't really want them. I only want to see the eyes behind them. I think you're a user. Your eyes will confirm it. I'll admit it; you're good."

"You're terrible," Theo said strongly and confidently. "Ready to give up?"

"I'm good at hanging in there. I'm stubborn like that."

"*YOU!*" A voice shouted from up the street. They both turned to find three En-D officers running toward them. Theo's eyes went wide and he released Tc'aarlat and made a dash for it, but they were ready for him.

Intrigued, Tc'aarlat followed until they apprehended Theo. Despite his skill in martial arts, Theo was as weak against tasers as the rest of the population. They got him to the ground, put him in handcuffs, and marched him toward a waiting car.

"Why are you arresting him?" Tc'aarlat asked.

"He's been warned about sleeping in this area before. Now he's going to spend twenty-four hours inside," came the reply from one of the officers keeping a tight hold on the stumbling vagabond.

"Will he get a bed?"

"Yes."

"And food?" Tc'aarlat pressed.

"Yes."

"Yeah, I can see why he was hanging around. What do humans say? 'If you feed an animal, it'll keep coming back, then bite the hand that feeds it' or something?"

"Sir, would you please step back?"

"I can step back with the best of them, yes I can. Like my balls were launched from a slingshot. That's how fast I'll step back. Maybe even jump. All the way. Back."

Tc'aarlat moved out of the way, knowing a lost cause

when he saw one, and watched them place the man he knew as Theo behind bars for being in the wrong part of the city. The Yollin was far from done, though, and as soon as the car turned a corner and traveled out of sight, he rushed to the vagabond's stuff, still sitting behind the scraggly blanket.

Rifling through it, he found that it was mostly junk. Old food, bottles of water, and a few personal effects that he thought the guy might want if he could get them. The last place Tc'aarlat checked was beneath the princess blanket. Sitting there was the answer he'd expected.

"I knew it!" he exclaimed, grabbing one of the tubes. Tc'aarlat had worked in the mob for a good portion of his life; he knew drugs when he saw them. He brought one of the tubes up to his nose and sniffed it tentatively, recoiling from the far-too-sweet aroma. "Yeah, that's drugs all right." He coughed through the lingering scent. "Fucking burnouts, toasting their brain cells. Get nothing for it but poor.

Tc'aarlat gathered Theo's things and loped toward the ICS *Fortitude*, the beginnings of a plan forming in his mind.

Frontier Zone, City Station Hopefill, Dock 23, Freight Bay F, ICS *Fortitude*, Adina's Room

Adina stared at the card with her father's contact information on it for nearly ten minutes. He had sounded like he wanted to reconcile, but he had missed the previous twenty chances. History's judgment did not reflect brightly on him.

Her mind raced with possibilities. She was open to

giving her father yet another chance. Mistakenly destroying Draven's card could have been karma telling her that no value would be found in continuing animosity. She decided it was worth hearing his side of things.

Adina knew she had already decided. The debate with herself was over. She had to see her father.

"Solo," Adina said. The ship's AI appeared on the screen in her room and saw the card in Adina's hand. "I've got someone I need to call, but can you make sure it's a private call?"

"Of course, Adina."

Adina held up the card for Solo to see. The numbers transferred to the screen as Solo engaged the comm. Adina listened to the beeps, waiting for someone on the other side to pick up and connect.

"Hello?" A face appeared on the screen.

The woman was gorgeous, even for someone approaching their twilight years. She had the most expressive eyebrows Adina had ever seen, but she had seen the woman before. This was the same person who had joined her father after he had been told to leave the funeral.

"H-hi," Adina said awkwardly. "Uh, is Usman Choudhury there?"

"Oh, my goodness, you're Adina." The woman was trying hard to hide her mix of enthusiasm and surprise. "I'm so sorry, dear, but he's at work. I really hoped you would call. I really did."

"I'm sorry, who are you?" Adina asked.

"I'm Kirandeep." The stranger gave her a small bow of respect. "I'm your father's...well, this might be hard to hear, but I'm his girlfriend, dear."

"*Girlfriend?*" Adina's voice stuck in her throat as she tried to say the word. She had gathered who this woman might be, but it was hard to digest. "You and my father?"

"I'm so sorry." Kirandeep sighed and searched desperately for her next words. Adina could see the gears turning in her head. "I don't want to upset you. I just wanted your father to have a chance to talk to you. It's something that has been haunting him for years, and he has apologies to make."

Adina closed her eyes.

"I can explain everything," Kirandeep said. "I...I don't think it should be done over a vidscreen, though. Can you meet me somewhere, anywhere, in the city?"

"Meet *you?*" Adina looked at her. She was holding a sweet smile hostage. "Again. I can't believe this is happening."

"I love your father," Kirandeep blurted. "I want the chance to explain things to you. Maybe if you hear it from a stranger, it might be a little easier? I don't want us to be enemies."

Adina thought about that. She didn't know whether to yell, cry, or both, but she nodded in any case. "Okay, I'll meet you somewhere."

"Do you know the Gray Sun Café?" Kirandeep asked. "It's in the northern quadrant, Commercial Zone Six."

"Yeah, I can find it. I'll meet you there in about an hour." Adina's finger hovered over the end call button, but she couldn't hit it.

"I hope you come, Adina," Kirandeep pleaded. "I've been wanting to meet you and explain things ever since I heard about you from your father."

Kirandeep disappeared from the vidscreen, saving Adina from ending the call. Her father. It had been so long. Maybe the feelings she had harbored were ill-founded? Or maybe her father *had* changed.

Adina collapsed on her bed, her mind running around the same track. She had gone from considering whether she'd be up for talking to her father to meeting up with his new girlfriend, a woman Adina hadn't known existed. It was time to settle things.

A family reunion where relatives could get together and bitch about each other and their failed lives, followed by "It was nice to catch up." A family reunion. Adina snorted.

"What should I do, Solo?" Adina asked the AI when she appeared on the screen. "Should I go, or should I leave her hanging?"

"What do you want to do? You don't have to do anything you don't want to."

"Part of me wants to just leave it. Get back to normal life and hunt werewolves and drugs dealers with Jack and Tc'aarlat." Adina sighed. "The larger part of me wants to hear what he has to say. What excuse he could possibly have for being absent from my life for twenty years."

"Then you should talk to your father, not this Kirandeep."

"That's just it." Adina sat up to face Solo. "My father kicked me out of my childhood home and abandoned me because...because of what happened with my mother. Yet, here he is with another woman, completely moved on and with only me as a regret. I've got to meet her. I've got to know *why*, Solo."

"I understand that. Be prepared for whatever answer you get, Adina."

"I might not like the answer." Adina shot up and toward the stagnating pile of clothes in the corner, rifling through to find something more suitable than sweatpants for her meeting. "I've still got to do it. I need the one thing I've been missing all these years. I need closure."

Frontier Zone, City Station Hopefill, Timothy Grand's Office

Timothy sat up straight at the knock on his door but slumped a little when he saw who was on the other side. Jack and Tc'aarlat. The pair, who were looking rough from the events of the previous night, came into the room and took the seats before his desk. They sat for a few moments in silence, absorbing each other's presence without a hint of a hello on their lips.

"I saw the news last night," Timothy finally muttered. "I'm guessing you didn't find anything?"

"Oh, no, we found plenty," Jack said, trying once again to rub the sleep from his face while wishing away the headache behind his eyes. "We found out Mikhail May is a bit of a prick."

"*Bit of?*" Tc'aarlat snarked. "Replace 'bit of' with 'colossal' and you'll get my opinion of the guy."

"That's a shame to hear, guys," Timothy said. "I was hoping for some good news."

"Who says we don't have good news?" Tc'aarlat asked. "I, for one, have a plan on how we might get to the top of the drug food chain."

"Can't wait to hear this," Jack exclaimed, turning in his chair to face Tc'aarlat.

"I was walking around the streets last night, trying to find some druggies I could rough up for information," Tc'aarlat started. "I came across this homeless guy. I think he was high on Eternity, but before I could get anything out of him, the En-D showed up and took him away. I thought we could get him and make him tell us who the next higher up is. Follow the chain of command to its source?"

"We've tried that," Timothy replied. "Many times, with many different users of the drug. The problem is, they're usually extremely loyal to the deception. They know if we cut off the source, it means they can't get high anymore."

"That is so ridiculous it makes my carapace itch, like scratchy-itch with real fingernails," Tc'aarlat shot back.

"Why don't you intimidate them with imprisonment?" Jack offered. "If you can't reason with them, threaten them."

"It goes the other way too." Timothy reached into his drawer and pulled out a stack of photos, each showing a person found dead in a variety of creative ways, mostly with limbs missing, torsos torn apart, and slit throats. "Any of the drug dealers get caught talking about who's above them, it doesn't end well, as you can see from the crime scene photos."

"Have you tried being more subtle?" Tc'aarlat asked. "Following the chain without being noticed? That way, nobody gets hurt except for those at the very top."

"We've tried everything," Timothy said. "If you want to try it, though, you have my blessing. You might have more luck since you two aren't associated with us. I think there's a mole in the department, but who knows? I get the feeling that it's more than just the WRU keeping tabs on us."

"Really?" Jack said. "You think you've got a leaky bladder?"

"I don't think it's any secret that I've been finding it hard to trust people around here." Timothy scanned the room as if lurkers might spring from the corners at any second. "That's why you're here."

Tc'aarlat nodded and thrust a thumb in the air. "Let's give it a try, then. I'm going to need that guy your people locked up last night. He'll be the start of our trail."

"I can get that arranged," Timothy replied. "Is there anything else you need?"

"That should do us for now, Timothy," Jack replied, getting to his feet. "We'll be on—"

"There's one more thing," Tc'aarlat interrupted, making no move to get up. "I had an encounter with one of these werewolves last night. It was wearing some kind of shock collar."

"Shock collar?" Timothy asked.

"Although that big no-arm prick denies it, I think someone's controlling these werewolves behind the scenes, like mind control or something," Tc'aarlat said. "Is there any way to find out more about the collars? Maybe where they come from?"

"Not without analyzing one," Timothy replied. "For that, though, you'd need to catch a werewolf and bring it back here, or at the very least, grab its collar."

"Bistok ballsacks! I *knew* you were going to say that." Tc'aarlat gave a casual shrug before standing up to join

Jack. "Guess we'll just have to get one for you. Do you care how much meat is attached to it? A shocked meat-sicle. A meaty shock-sicle. A shocking thing, that collar."

"Please make the ugly noises stop," Jack begged, dragging Tc'aarlat toward the door.

Frontier Zone, City Station Hopefill, En-D Detention Center, Cell A

This wasn't the first time Theo had been inside a cell in the detention center, and he doubted it would be the last. When homeless on the streets of Hopefill City, the options were limited. They made those who couldn't protect themselves easy targets, and more times than not, the purveyors of the pain were the En-D. Still, it wasn't all a bad life. The detention center offered individual cells, free food, a bed that was more comfortable than a pile of cardboard, and most important, the security to sleep in peace. If it weren't for the absence of drugs, he'd never leave.

That was the problem. Theo was rubbing the skin around his eyes raw in his wanting. The growing scabs identified him as a user going without. Desperate. Sick. Every moment in confinement was a lost opportunity for getting money from strangers to support his addiction.

The detention center near the En-D offices was a temporary place for miscreants to contemplate the errors of their ways or for more serious criminals to be held before being moved to a higher security facility. Twenty-four hours and either they were charged and moved or they were turned loose. At eleven hours, they had to feed their prisoners. He wanted a twelve-hour confinement, then he needed to get back on the street if he was to survive.

Theo heard the slider open before he turned his head to see the eyes that looked in on him every now and then. They focused on him for a few moments, making sure he was away from the door before the slider closed and the door lock clicked. Theo sat up and straightened to make himself a little more presentable because one wanted to look their best when getting fed. One never knew if the woman of his dreams would stroll through the door.

Or not.

The door opened into the cell with a tiny squeal. The Yollin he had met the night before stepped in. Tc'aarlat seemed as cocky as ever.

"You dick!" Theo shouted.

There was a second person with the Yollin, a human who laughed at Theo's proclamation.

"He knows you," the man said.

Theo didn't hear the words or see the humor. The man was a ghost. A person who could only be described as a blast from Theo's past, and he jumped at the sight of the stranger and pressed his back against the wall in the hope that it would give way and he could put more distance between him and the stranger who was not. Not in fear but in shock and disbelief. The man with Tc'aarlat was none other than Jack Marber. *The* Jack Marber.

"Theo?" Jack wondered. "That's...no, you can't be here. What are you doing here?"

"Jack," Theo said, trying to calm himself. "Is that really you?"

"Theo, what the fuck? How in the holy ass-banging

ways of the universe are you here and on drugs? Come on, Theo."

"Does someone want to fill me in?" Tc'aarlat said, looking between the pair. "Were you guys in band camp together or something?"

"This is Theo Young," Jack said, gesturing at the vagabond. "He was...well, he was my subordinate when I was working with the Force de Guerre."

"Wait." Tc'aarlat pointed at Theo. "That means he was—"

"That's right." Theo stood. "Jack Marber was my platoon leader."

8

Frontier City Station Hopefill, Commercial Zone 1, Gray Sun Café

Adina hovered her hand over the door's access panel before dropping her hand and peering in through the window. The café was quaint and cozy and looked as if it had been hit by a kitten bomb. The shelves and tables were gross with kitten porcelain, plates, wallpaper, posters, paintings, and cups in a motif of endless cat caricatures. Patrons filled the inside while wait staff bustled around in a kabuki dance of serving and cleaning. Oddly, Adina couldn't see Kirandeep.

The hesitation spoke loudly to her. She didn't know if she could go in and face the new woman her father had gotten attached to, much less speak to her father when the time came. Maybe Kirandeep could prepare her, but only if she was there.

With a sigh of resignation, Adina turned away from the door and made to slink away, but she came face to face with Kirandeep and stumbled back in her shock.

"I'm sorry!" Kirandeep grabbed Adina before she could trip across the threshold and fall inside. "I didn't mean to surprise you like that."

"It's okay." Adina pulled herself together. "I was just going in."

Adina opened the door and gestured for Kirandeep to lead the way, stopping for an instant to gaze up the empty street and wonder how far away she could get before the woman noticed.

She shook off the thought and followed her inside. The stranger led the way to a small reserved booth at the other end of the café, where she took a seat and motioned for Adina to do the same. It was only then that Adina noticed the woman's finger. An engagement ring with a not insubstantial precious gemstone adorned it.

"Would you like anything to drink?" Kirandeep asked, standing up again. "I'm going to get a coffee. I daresay I need one."

Adina nodded, shifting in her seat but unable to get comfortable.

With Kirandeep's back turned, Adina had an impulse to look inside the purse lying on the table. Despite the allure of thinking it held answers, she knew it did not. Her answers were within the minds of people. Kirandeep was a conduit to her father.

The way she talked to the staff and fiddled with her pockets told Adina she was harmless. At the funeral she had been wearing a dress, while today, she was wearing a woolen sweater that did nothing for her figure.

"Here you go." Kirandeep placed a cup in front of Adina, and she tried to look past the fact that she was drinking out of a porcelain cat's head. The woman took a seat opposite her, brought her cup close, and wrapped both hands around it as if needing the heat. "This is weird, right? Really weird."

"Yeah," Adina muttered. "It's just...yeah. I don't know what to say."

"Me either." Kirandeep half-laughed. "How about I introduce myself properly and start from the beginning?"

"That sounds like a great place to jump off," Adina replied, blowing lightly on her coffee.

"My full name is Kirandeep Narwaz. I grew up in Hopefill City, and I consider myself a successful business-woman. I run a series of cafés across the city, one of which you're standing in."

"This is your café?" Adina didn't look. A vision of her father's home filled with cat memorabilia almost made her laugh. Maybe he had changed because that was not some-thing Adina would have ever contemplated as a part of his life. "I gotta ask. What's with the cats?"

"It's kitten-intense, isn't it?" She smiled. "I do love the little critters, that's for sure. Not completely my fault, though. When I was looking for something unique for the area, I found this area has more cat owners than not, so it seemed like the perfect fit. Just quaint enough to attract customers. Good enough food to keep them coming back."

"Smart." Adina cleared her throat. "I don't know how much you know about me, but I'm the navigator for a small crew, and I'd consider myself a decent engineer as well. I've always been good at fixing problems by taking machines apart to see how they worked and then putting them back together."

Adina could tell the stranger wanted to say something but was holding her tongue. Instead, she took a sip of her coffee. "Your father has told me a lot about you. He's really proud."

"He has a funny way of showing it," Adina grumbled, frowning and looking at her hands, which were clasped in her lap. She lifted her head and nodded at the ring. "Are you two getting married or…"

"We are." Kirandeep smiled as she stared into the distance. "We haven't set a date yet, but soon, I hope."

"How long have you known my father? How long have you been dating? When did this all happen?"

Kirandeep swallowed heavily and took another sip before she answered. "We've been dating for just over a year, I met him through a dating site online, and yeah, that's it really. We got together quickly and took it from there."

"Why was my father at my uncle's funeral? They didn't get along. Was it for me?"

"Mostly," Kirandeep admitted. "Usman wanted to pay his respects, but he was hoping to see you there. When he received the invitation, he was overwhelmed at the prospect of seeing you again."

"I didn't realize he had gotten an invitation," Adina said, but that might've been a mistake on the care home's part. "Why does he want to reconnect now? He's had twenty years to get in touch."

Kirandeep reached across the table and covered Adina's hand with her own. "Usman's been carrying a lot of shame. He never got in touch because he didn't think you could forgive him. I convinced him to go to the funeral."

"So, he *didn't* want to see me?"

"No. I mean, yes, he did, but he was ashamed." Kirandeep's eyes glistened, but she continued without faltering. "He thinks you wouldn't want to talk to him. He failed you. Nothing can change the past twenty years, but what we do with the next twenty is for you and him to decide today. He regrets what he has done and understands if you won't forgive him. He expects it."

"So you know what happened between us?"

Kirandeep nodded. "At least from his perspective."

Adina leaned back in her chair and pulled her hand out from under the stranger's. "I'm having a hard time. I was a little girl when he abandoned me. He knows he doesn't deserve my forgiveness, but my uncle raised me better than that."

"Usman still loves you, Adina." Kirandeep pursed her lips. She was having as hard a time with this as Adina. "If you give him the chance, he wants to be your father again."

"I don't know what to say to that." Adina wanted to vent and scream and give her father a miniscule taste of what he had put her through. Kirandeep had no idea. Twenty years was a snap of the fingers when someone didn't have to live every minute of it.

"You called him," Kirandeep replied. "If it wasn't me that answered, it would've been him. Somewhere deep down, you must want to at least hear him out. For now, that's all he can ask for. He hasn't earned more of your time."

"I'll meet him," Adina conceded. "I can't promise what'll happen after, but I'll meet him for sure."

"I'm glad to hear that. I'd like you to be there when he

gets home from work today. Would you be able to do that?" Kirandeep leaned forward hopefully.

"I'll do it," Adina said, finality in her voice. "Just tell me where."

"I think it's a place you're very familiar with…"

Frontier Zone, City Station Hopefill, En-D Detention Center, Cell A

Jack still couldn't believe he was sitting across from Theo Young. The guy had never looked worse in his life. He was sad about what Theo had become. Once he had been the life and soul of Force de Guerre, a team that kept the peace in a world at war with itself. The unit had been led by Jack, a master of hand-to-hand combat, a cunning strategist, and above all, a loyal and reliable friend. Now Theo was a junkie living on the streets of Hopefill City. Life had not been kind to the man.

"Jack was your big toe?" Tc'aarlat asked.

"We were all surprised at that," Theo replied with a smile. "We're going back a good few years now, when we were all nice and fresh from Terry Henry Walton's merciless training."

"Thank you, sir! May I have another?" Jack quipped.

"Defeat your enemy with your mind, not your body. Now give me five more miles since you dumbasses won't outwit anyone and are better off being cock-strong," Theo recited in his best Colonel Walton impression.

Jack chuckled before turning serious. "What happened to you, Theo? How did you get here from there?"

"Things weren't the same after you were kicked out of

Force de Guerre, Jack," Theo replied. "The next team leader was yours truly, and I was a pretty poor substitute. The missions I led were barely successful, and when Kayleigh died, well, I couldn't forgive myself for it."

"I heard about Kayleigh. It was a shame what happened to her."

"Well, the rest is history. I wish things had gone better, and I wish I'd made a few different choices. No changing that now, though. Just got to get on with it."

"Theo, I'm sorry."

"Don't apologize," Theo replied. "The bad decisions were all mine, leading to trying that crap that has taken over my life. The death spiral ebbs. Juicing in the Pod-doc would probably clear everything right up and make me resistant to its effects. Even my nanos have abandoned me."

"Nanos? I thought it was just me. Had an op, and they wouldn't fix my broken arm. Took another treatment to fix me up. I'll see what I can do."

Theo nodded with a half-smile. "I can't believe you're here, Jack." Theo clapped him on the shoulder, one friend to another. "Speaking of which, why *are* you guys here?"

"I can answer that." Tc'aarlat raised one long finger. "We're doing some work for the En-D. We need to find where Eternity is coming from. You are going to help us get to the top, to Bloody Darling."

"Bloody Darling?" Theo laughed. "That guy ain't real."

"What do you know about it, man?" Jack asked. "Any info at all could help us. This is an important job for us, and it seems it's important for you, too. If we can resolve this, we can get you some help."

Theo sat on his bunk and raked his fingers through his

hair before speaking. "A bunch of people think there's this one guy at the top, supplying all the drugs to Hopefill City, but I can't see that as true. The drug comes in from other worlds like Talth, because a bunch of suppliers exist out there. For one guy to be running the show on Hopefill City, they'd have to be fending off those other suppliers trying to get a piece, you know? For that, they'd need an army and a shitload of influence among the stars."

"That...makes a lot of sense," Jack said. "Still, we can't rule out a top supplier going by the name Bloody Darling. That's who we've been hired to deal with. There has to be a top to this, and we've got to find it. There seems to be a single pipeline into the city. That's the one we need to cut and in a way that doesn't create ten more in its place."

"That ain't an easy task, Jack," Theo replied. "The top doesn't want to be found, and they've taken some serious precautions to make sure it doesn't happen. I mean, fuck, I could be killed just for talking to you guys, and I'm a client."

"Would you be willing to help us anyway?" Tc'aarlat asked. "I can't promise anything in compensation, but I do have a sizeable collection of grubs in the fridge back on the ship that you're welcome to."

"Is...is he always like this?" Theo asked, pointing at Tc'aarlat. "Or is this just an off day?"

"Yollins have a different sense of humor, one that doesn't blend with human humor. And then there's Tc'aarlat, who is even more different. Count your blessings that you don't live with him.

"If you were Yollins," Tc'aarlat said, "you'd be laughing for a long time, no shit."

Theo shook his head. "I want to help, but I can't. I don't want to end up dead, and I don't want to lose the high. Helping you could really fuck me up."

"I get it, but I don't understand. I'm offering you a way out. High risk, high reward. Just like the old days." Jack got to his feet and moved to the exit. When he knocked on the door, it opened quickly to allow him egress. "I hope things work out better for you, Theo. I really do."

"Don't count on it, Jack."

Frontier Zone, City Station Hopefill, WRU Headquarters, Draven's Desk

Draven's stomach had been performing gymnastics, twisting his gut into a knot, and he doubted it was from lack of food. Something clawed at the corners of his mind; it had been there ever since Mikhail May had forced an interview with Jack and Tc'aarlat. That had seemed off. Draven was coming to the end of his report about what had happened on the last mission, including his first-hand observations.

It had seemed like a normal mission at first. They had transformed and tracked the smell of unregistered werewolves to storage units in the building, but when it came time to close on the targets, Draven had accidentally triggered a tripwire and blown them all to kingdom come. He was trying to make sense of it, figure out how he had fucked up so badly, and more importantly, figure out if they had been set up.

If the answer was no and it was just his mistake, then

his career was over. Not because they'd force him to resign, but because he would lose confidence in himself.

"Working late, boss?" Tinio came up behind him, as pleasant-faced as ever. "We were about to head over to the hospital, see how Rola was coming along."

"I've heard she's going to make a full recovery. Back on the team in no time," Draven said, swiveling and giving Tinio a peek at those pearly whites. "You know that tip we got for the storage units? Where did it come from?"

Tinio replied with a nonchalant shrug, "It was called in by the owner of the storage units. Apparently he heard some strange things happening within and wanted it checked out."

"Strange things? Did he mention what those strange things were?" Draven kicked himself for not asking more questions before accepting the mission.

"Nothing besides howling and whimpering coming from within at least two of the units," Tinio replied. "As soon as howling was mentioned on the En-D report they referred it to us, as per the law, and the rest is history, boss."

"What do you think of it all?" Draven wondered. "It seemed like they knew we were coming, didn't it?"

"Maybe it was a trap just for us. No one can find the owner. En-D wanted him for questioning. They're still looking for him."

"Is that right? What about Mikhail? Did he know about this mission before we went on it?"

"I hope so. He's the one who gave the order," Tinio replied, turning to leave. "Anyway, I'll see you at the hospital when you get finished with your reports. We'll be expecting you. Don't go doing anything stupid, now."

"Yeah, I'll try my best," Draven called after him.

Draven watched him go before turning back to his report. As he dove more into the events of that night, questions flashed like neon lights in front of the strip clubs. Why would the people behind the werewolves plant explosives and set a trap? Why wouldn't they just clear the area? Was it simply to send a message to the WRU?

Draven gritted his teeth and snarled. Something smelled funny. His gut renewed its gymnastics until he decided to do something about it. Grabbing his jacket, he made a beeline for the door.

He needed to return to those storage units. He was sure there was something he had missed the first time around.

9

Federation, Base Station 11, Residential Zone 5, Blakemore Block

Another trip back to Station 11, another eight hours of time. Adina hadn't been there since she had turned thirteen.

Whenever she tried to think back on the good times in her family home, she was blocked by the image of her mother's mangled corpse and the guilt she still carried because of it. Her birthday. A day that would haunt her forever.

Still, Kirandeep had brought her here, back to where it had started. Adina walked through the door, freezing once inside. It carried only a hint of familiarity, and that by itself relieved some of her pain. She was little more than a stranger in a stranger's home. One more step and it all came back to her in a rush, like a heavy wave on an ocean moon slamming into her.

She realized it was the same, all of it. Exactly the way she remembered, right down to the photos that lined the walls, her mother's carefully placed knick-knacks. Even the flooring had survived all this time. The rug was gone, though, the one that had been soaked with blood and gore.

Adina found herself staring at the spot with only one thought: *that was where my mother was killed*. Kirandeep led her in like a guest visiting for the first time and offered her the chair where her uncle used to sit.

"Would you like anything to drink?" the woman asked, moving toward the kitchen. "Any nibbles?"

"No, I'm fine, thanks," Adina replied and kept an eagle eye on Kirandeep's back until it disappeared around the door. When she was alone, she knew there was something she had to do. She forced herself out of her uncle's seat and moved toward the stairs. She had to see it. "I'm just popping to the toilet, Kirandeep. Be right back."

"No problem," the woman called. "Upstairs on your left."

Adina knew where the toilet was; she had lived there far longer than Kirandeep. She struggled upward, her feet fighting her when she should have been springing forward. An invisible weight bore down on her.

On the walls, most of the photos were of her mother and her father together and smiling, with an odd photo of young Adina thrown in for good measure. She couldn't ever remember being that innocent. It felt like another person in another life.

Certainly not her.

She moved past the bathroom to the only place on her mind. She pushed the door, only to find it locked. Adina tried turning the handle, even tried applying force, but it wouldn't open. She looked around quickly to make sure Kirandeep wasn't coming up the stairs. When she thought the coast was clear, she focused on one of her nails, transforming it into a long, slender black claw the perfect size for a keyhole.

She fought her desire to avoid the wolf while feeling the clinical need to use the assets at her command. Her mental discipline training was paying dividends she hadn't expected. Despite the stress, she was in control. Her heart rate increased, but she tamped it down, refusing to let it race out of control.

Just like the wolf.

Adina inserted the claw into the keyhole and twisted it. The lock lacked a superior digital design, which meant it could be bypassed easily. Pressing her claw against the tumblers inside the lock, she forced them into the right position, and a second later, there was a click. The door opened.

She hesitated, her hand on the knob. A moment earlier, she had been sure. She didn't know what she'd see on the other side, but she knew she'd regret it if she didn't look. Adina moved through the open door and flicked on the light.

The room was a puke-inducing shade of pastel pink and stubborn yellow. The walls were lined with flowers. Same with the curtains and the carpet, and scattered throughout with a complete zoo of stuffed animals.

Besides a bed, there were three large desks weighed down with piles of scrap parts: circuit boards, screws, bolts, and a variety of mechanical bits. It was exactly the way she remembered it, right down to the last detail.

She knew at that moment she was the first person to be inside this room in twenty years. She stared, mouth agape.

"I've always wondered what was in this room."

Adina jumped at the voice. Kirandeep stood behind her, taking in the colors and the musty smell.

Adina slapped a hand to her chest. Caught! She turned to the woman and forced herself to slow her breathing. "This was my room," she said simply.

"I'm sorry. I didn't mean to give you a fright, dear."

"No, it's okay." Adina smiled. "I was the one snooping around."

"Was this your room?" she asked, stepping in. "I've never seen it."

"Yeah, I guess it was once," Adina replied, looking at everything and nothing. "It's exactly as I remember it, yet I feel like a stranger."

"You *are* a stranger," Kirandeep replied. "Why don't we go back downstairs, sit, and wait for your father?"

"How long until he gets home?"

"I gave him a call in the kitchen," Kirandeep said. "So, soon."

"You—"

"It's okay. He doesn't know you're here."

"Right," Adina said. Following the woman back downstairs, she knew it didn't matter if her father took a minute or an hour. The wait would seem like forever. The stories she would tell herself would be a rehash of the horrible thoughts she'd had over the past twenty years. It wouldn't get better until her father made it better.

Adina didn't know what she wanted from him. Tears? A

tirade? A complete breakdown? After all this time, what did a pound of flesh look like?

Frontier Zone, City Station Hopefill, En-D Detention Center, Cell A

As Jack kept a watch on the entrance to the detention center through the shades of his recently bought glasses, he couldn't help but wonder if this would've been easier with Adina. After all, Theo knew their faces. Before Jack and Tc'aarlat had even left the center, they had decided to wait for Theo to be released from his cell and follow him as he sought his next high.

"So, you've got a historical colonoscopy with this guy?" Tc'aarlat said, leaning against the wall around the corner. They had been waiting for an hour, and it was starting to grate on the pair of them.

Jack knew what he meant but didn't bother correcting the words.

Tc'aarlat pressed on. "Thanks for making it so damned awkward in there."

"You're welcome," Jack replied. "And yeah, you could say we've got a history. I still can't believe that was Theo Young. He used to be a prime warrior, real top notch, and now... Well, *damn*."

"That's government military private contracting scum for you," Tc'aarlat said. "Eat you up and spit you out without a damn for what happens after."

"You're just stringing random words together, you bug-eyed, big-headed no-load. It's not what you think. We were all valued assets until we didn't follow our orders and didn't explain ahead of time. I screwed up. Theo screwed up. We got people killed. There's no coming back from that. I couldn't do it. Theo couldn't do it. We left, and Theo fell through the cracks while I was given a second chance."

"It's hard not to fall into the butt cracks. So very large and hard to avoid."

"I've got to do something for him," Jack replied. "There has to be something I can do to help."

"Maybe you could buy him a sandwich? He sure looks like he could use one," Tc'aarlat suggested.

Jack scoffed. "Was your entire species born without compassion, or was it just you, Tc'aarlat?"

"I had it removed when I was five. Had to make room for my massive sense of humor."

"Couldn't have had that much compassion to begin with then."

"At least I have..."

"Hold up." Jack silenced him with a gesture and straightened, eyes laser-focused on the entrance. "Theo is out. Put on your stealth cap, and when I move, follow me like my fucking shadow."

Theo's head hung low, but his eyes shifted back and forth under his brows. The scabs under his eyes disappeared into the shadows of his face. Jack nudged Tc'aarlat. *Get ready to move.*

It would be difficult to tail Theo without being noticed, but they didn't have a choice. The Shadows in the shadows. They crept after him.

As they followed Theo around the city, he walked with determination in his stride and a clear destination.

Jack and Tc'aarlat had a good idea of where he was

heading. The vagabond shuffled his way from one district to the next, begging along the way and getting nothing but disgusted faces in return. Eventually, they came to an abandoned dock that would have once been used as a place to house incoming space vehicles.

"If I was going to sell drugs...again," Tc'aarlat said, taking in the dark alleys between derelict and salvaged ships, "this would be where I'd sell them, that's for damn fucking sure. Holy crap, the only thing it's missing is a sign that says *Get your drugs here*. Honestly, how is there not a single fucking En-D officer on patrol here?"

"Would *you* want to be an officer on patrol here?" Jack asked. "That would be enough to make me quit my job."

"Fair point, but maybe they could throw in hazard pay."

Jack could only shake his head while wondering if *he* was getting hazard pay as part of the contract. He could have been in Theo's shoes, but with a couple breaks and the largesse of General Reynolds, he had earned a new and better life, one where he was able to watch over Theo. Maybe he would have done the same if their roles were reversed.

They pressed on, keeping as close to the man as they dared, using the chaos of the docks to blend in.

Theo kept moving on a path that he seemed to know well until he slowed with an unnatural noise.

A rough voice called, "Theo, get your ass over here."

Frontier Zone, City Station Hopefill, Dock 9, Freight Bay A

After the mandatory twenty-four hours were up, there

was only one thing on Theo's mind as he exited the detention center: getting high. Unfortunately, his reluctant imprisonment had put him behind a full day in getting paid, meaning he didn't have enough credits to buy a sandwich, let alone a vial of expensive Eternity. Desperate but hanging tough, he had no choice but to try bargaining on his way to the docks, begging as he went for the extra funds but receiving nothing for his effort.

Entering the shadows of the old docks, he couldn't help but scratch at his eyes beneath the sunglasses. Theo's heart was racing with fear, but it was addiction that drove him forward. It had never been this bad before, and over the years, he'd always managed to get enough and then some for the various drugs that came in through Hopefill City. Eternity was different, though; it was a more expensive taste and a better experience, life changing in some ways, and it was the only high he was interested in right now.

That expense, mixed in with the fact that the citizens of the city were less trusting these days thanks to the werewolf problem, was the reason he had his cap in his hand now. Already his vision was blurring as the drug left his system, and the headache he was carrying would cause some people to faint from the pain.

"Theo." The beggar stopped dead at hearing his name. Again, he felt the presence of others behind him but didn't have the presence of mind to act on it.

Riddle came into the light a little ahead of him, followed by the menacing presence of Bonkers, his gigantic and growling werewolf companion. Riddle cleared his throat. "I take it you wants the usual today, Theo?"

"I was actually hoping you could, uh, give me something on credit," Theo replied, deciding to get right to the point. "I got picked up last night, and I'm a little short."

"You look plenty tall to me!" There was a ripple of laughter through the thugs surrounding him. "You know that ain't how this works. Now get the fuck outta here, you cheap-ass fucker."

"No, wait, please," Theo said, moving closer but backing off when Bonkers set his green eyes upon him. "Just a taste, that's all I want. I'll pay you double next time."

"Do you see any old clothes here?" Riddle asked.

"What?" Theo looked confused. He could feel people moving closer behind him, and Riddle seemed to be backing off too. Theo was running out of options. This deal was going south quickly.

"Answer the question," Riddle replied. "Do you see any old clothes, maybe some second-hand gizmos or collection cups?"

"No?" Theo said.

"That's right, you fucking don't," Riddle said. "Cause I ain't a fucking charity shop. Now run away before you get your legs broke."

"Please, just..." Theo lurched forward, and that was enough for Bonkers. The big werewolf leapt across the intervening space and pinned Theo to the ground, its breath hot on his face. It growled, its teeth bared, and for a moment Theo thought it would attack, but it just loomed with drool dripping from its maw.

"You've gone and done it now, Theo." Riddle came close and knelt to get a better look. "You've pissed off a big fucking werewolf. What do you think is going to happen? Maybe I should let him nibble you a little, have a snack."

"Call him off." Theo closed his eyes to the nightmare, his heart going into overdrive. "Please."

"Why should I do a thing like that?" Riddle laughed.

"Because he asked you nicely, dick-cheese."

The gang turned quickly, but not one of them reached for their weapons. Behind them with weapons drawn were the unlikeliest of heroes: a human and a Yollin holding his gun gangster style, parallel to the ground. They all knew what the situation was, and they held their hands up in surrender, not liking the thought of being shot today.

"Yo, who the fuck are you?" Riddle called. "This is a business meeting."

"We're your worst nightmare." Jack trained his gun on him. "Now, let Theo up before I put another hole in your face you can spew shit from."

Tc'aarlat hummed with an approving nod. "That was good, Jack. One of your finer lines. Your bad-guy banter is really coming along."

"Yeah? I can't lie. I didn't have that prepared. Completely off the top of my head."

"It was impressive," Tc'aarlat replied. "I couldn't have said anything finer."

As the two were patting each other on the back, Riddle saw an opening, and he was going to take it. The drug dealer let out a low whistle, a command to turn the attention of Bonkers from the vagrant to the newcomers. The wolf sprang into action and went for Tc'aarlat with the ferocity his species was known for.

"Why me?" Tc'aarlat dodged and rolled to the side, coming up with his blaster at the ready, but Jack was behind the wolf. No clear shot. Tc'aarlat ran, trying to lure the werewolf into a trap.

Jack stumbled out of the way and drew a bead on the werewolf. Bonkers leapt past them and continued running into the wreckage.

Riddle pulled his weapon and snap-fired a shot that sent Jack behind a ship's bulky stabilizer, half-buried in the metal of the deck. Jack dialed the Jean Dukes to a low setting, only two. He wanted to get their attention without killing them. He fired a couple of wild shots in the general direction of the dealers.

The drug crew members hammered their clubs against any metal surface, creating a cacophony that hid their movements.

Riddle fired again, and Jack shot back in the general direction of the dealer. Jack couldn't get a fix on his location thanks to the war drums, but he knew where the thugs were. With each drumbeat, he zeroed in and dropped the clubber. In a matter of five seconds, the crew was down three.

Tc'aarlat had taken himself out of the combat area, thinking he could capture the werewolf and remove its collar if it had one, but the tables turned with the first corner. The crazed werewolf with the mad pair of green eyes had a different idea. The creature was waiting for him, and Tc'aarlat knew it'd only be a matter of a small mistake or a burst of energy to catch him.

"Let's try this on for size, wolf boy," Tc'aarlat said, leaping on top of a broken-down freighter and diving into one of its many access points. As he expected, Bonkers followed, jumping after him.

The instant the wolf's paws hit the flat surface of the derelict's hull, Tc'aarlat squeezed the trigger and sent the werewolf tumbling head over paws with a glancing blow, enough to leave a nasty scar down the creature's side. Tc'aarlat couldn't kill it. *Have mercy, for he knows not what he does,* Tc'aarlat thought. The werewolf tumbled off the hulk to the ground below.

Tc'aarlat had seen what he had suspected. The wolf was wearing a collar, hidden beneath its fur. In a flash of courage, stupidity, or both, Tc'aarlat jumped from his vantage point on top of the ship onto the wolf's back. The beast threw back its head and howled its indignation.

"Settle down, fucker!" Tc'aarlat punched the creature in the back of its head, right between its ears. He grabbed the collar as if it were the bridle on a horse and pulled back, jerking the wolf to a halt.

The Yollin's fingers tingled, then a shock blasted through his hands—enough to make his arms tingle. He twisted the collar, looking for a hasp, but the shocks running up his arms kept making him lose his grip.

"This collar is mine!" he roared, fighting the discharges until he snapped it free. The werewolf bucked, and Tc'aarlat fell back. The creature ran a few steps away and started to change, hair receding and disappearing to expose the flesh of the man beneath.

Jack held off the attacks from Riddle's dwindling forces. "If ever we could use En-D, now would be a good time to corral the losers."

"If you give up now, we can talk about what you did wrong and how you can change your ways. I promise I'll only stun you."

"Fuck this." Riddle took off running, his whistle low and calling for his werewolf buddy. The others who were still standing, upon seeing their leader bail, did the same, and soon Jack was alone with Theo and half a dozen stunned minions.

"Are they gone?" Theo wondered.

"Yeah," Jack replied after standing up and looking around. "At least, I think so."

"That was close." Theo came out of his hiding spot, and Jack did the same. Jack took a moment to catch his breath, and Theo held out his hand.

"What's that?" Jack nodded at it.

"I think you just saved my life, man," Theo replied, thrusting his hand forward. "Least you could do is shake my hand."

"What are you doing, Theo?" Jack straightened. "You just tried to reason with a group of drug dealers. Are you trying to get yourself killed?"

"I don't want to get killed. I just need a little Eternity to keep me going, keep me awake and eager."

"That crap's going to kill you," Jack said. "It's eating you from the inside out."

"I just…it's harder to get off than you think."

"You're right." Jack pointed his Jean Dukes Special at Theo, an impossible range to miss, and before Theo could even materialize a thought about running, Jack hit him with a heavy stun and sent him sprawling. Jack gave his body an idle kick; it didn't respond. "I'm going to help with that, Theo. I'm going to get you clean."

"Little help?' Jack turned around and gave a loud sigh, really more of an annoyed grunt. Tc'aarlat had reached the end of the short alley between two derelicts, and he was dragging a naked man. The Yollin clicked his mandibles happily at a task well done.

"You're unbelievable," Jack said. "What are we supposed to do with that?"

Tc'aarlat shrugged and held up the collar. "For the tech boys, but ones we trust, not the other guys. What happened to Theo?"

"Looks like the same thing happened to your guy."

"Timothy said he couldn't analyze anything until he had a wolf and a shock collar. I've got both right here. Now we can get the information right from the horse's south."

"South?"

"Yeah, you know, the rear end," Tc'aarlat replied with a shrug of his shoulders. "That's where all the crap is."

Jack chuckled. "Any ideas on how we're going to get both back to the ship?"

Tc'aarlat looked around the docks, hoping an answer would jump out at him. It didn't. He shrugged. "Just have to carry them, I guess."

"You're joking."

"Any better ideas?"

Jack gave another disgruntled sigh, knelt before Theo, lifted him until he could get him over his shoulder, and plodded back toward the more civilized parts of Hopefill City. Tc'aarlat did the same thing with the naked man.

"You've got werewolf junk all over your shoulder."

"Takes one to know one," Tc'aarlat shot back, shaking the collar at him.

Frontier Zone, City Station Hopefill, Commercial Zone 1, Storage Units

Draven moved past the En-D barriers that had been set up toward the half-destroyed building on the horizon. He kept his gun steady at his side while he moved with extreme trepidation. He didn't want to be on the wrong end of an explosion again. Moving carefully through the rubble, Draven entered the building via a collapsed wall and went to where he had been when the blast had caught him.

As he made his way there, he remembered the events that had led up to the explosion. It was difficult to remember since the whole thing had happened so fast. He was having trouble focusing on any single detail.

Still, something nagged at the back of his mind.

Trailing his fingertips over the shuttered and bolted storage units, Draven thought it amazing they had survived. It was amazing that *he* had survived.

As he climbed the stairs, now nothing more than a pile

of rubble, he thought about the second before the explosion had occurred. In his mind, he could feel the tripwire and hear the click, and his body had acted of its own volition, dodging into the unit behind him, securing the heavy door an instant before the explosion.

"Okay," he said to himself, reaching the place he thought he had been before. "Let's see what we've got here."

Reaching down, he took a handful of dust and stones and let it cascade from his fingers. The storage unit directly in front of him, the one where he had smelled a werewolf, was gone, suggesting it was where the bomb had been. Any wall standing beyond the explosion's center was charred from the fireball that had rolled past.

Draven didn't know what he was looking for and suspected the En-D had taken anything that might be of value, but he clawed his way through the wreckage anyway. He was desperate to find a lead to justify his gut instinct.

"If they weren't exploding it to send a message," he thought aloud, "maybe they were exploding it to hide something. Say, a piece of evidence?"

There was nothing there. No bomb components or evidence of another crime.

If a group of werewolves *had* been occupying this storage unit, and he was sure of that because he knew what he'd smelled in his wolf form, there would be something left behind. A personal item, some furniture maybe. A damn bed sheet.

A false lead with wolf scent, which meant it was

targeted specifically at his unit, the only one that would track a smell.

He stepped back to study the area. Although the main unit was nothing more than a crater, most of the others still stood.

Draven remembered that while he was heading for the primary unit, Rola had been attempting to open a different one. As Draven approached, he found that unit was still intact, although it had taken some damage. The door was caved in and badly damaged, and while the ceiling had collapsed, the floor was intact. Draven carefully stepped through.

Clues. Evidence. There had to be something.

Like signs of life. He knelt to pick up a length of rope, seared at one end. Someone had been tied up in this storage unit, perhaps recently. Draven found a bit of shiny plastic peeking out from under a brick.

He picked up a card, an ID card. The picture had worn off, either before or during the explosion. The only bit of image that remained was a blurred logo, and he knew he had seen that logo before. The colors, blue and white, rang a bell, and after a moment more, he thought that it might belong to a facility known as the Ice Blocks where they kept the werewolves that were too dangerous for regular society.

"Now, that's interesting," Draven said. "What would this be doing here of all places?"

Draven searched further but found nothing else. He left the half-destroyed building and returned to the hovercar waiting outside. There was no doubt in his mind about where he was going next.

. . .

Federation, Base Station 11, Residential Zone 5, Blakemore Block

Adina had been waiting patiently with Kirandeep, and she had come to understand that the woman was a shining light in her father's life. Love lost, love found.

Kirandeep seemed dead-set on trying to make the situation between Adina and her father better.

They had been sitting in a moment of silence when the front door opened. A beep sounded, the one that had signaled a person's arrival throughout her childhood. Before she knew it, she was staring up at her father, and he gazed back at her. Neither had any words.

"Welcome home, Usman," Kirandeep said, moving to her fiancé and giving him a quick peck on the cheek. "I hope you don't mind that I arranged this for you."

"Adina? You're here?" Her stunned father stated the obvious.

"I'm going to leave you two to it. I need to get to work," Kirandeep said and strode to the front door. After a beep and a click as the door closed, the two found themselves alone.

Adina looked after her desperately, hoping she'd come back. She hadn't expected her to leave so soon or so quickly.

Usman took the couch opposite, the same spot he always sat, and anxiously tried to make words happen.

"You said you wanted to talk to me, to give you a chance to explain," Adina said slowly.

"I...I wasn't expecting you to turn up, given what happened at the funeral." Usman ran his fingers through his thinning gray hair. "It's good to see you're so well. Are you, uh, doing okay? Are you happy in life?"

"I'm here for you to explain," Adina replied firmly. "I'm not here for small talk. I just want to give you the chance to say it to my face."

Usman grimaced and searched the room with his eyes, peering at every memory, the ones carefully chosen from before his wife died, while trying to avoid looking at Adina. When he had the words, he leaned forward and looked at his daughter. "I was wrong to kick you out like that, Adina, and I was wrong to abandon you. I'm sorry."

Adina stood up, eager to get as far away from this awkward situation as she could. "Is that all you have?" She had never answered her question to herself of what she wanted to hear.

"Sorry?"

"Is that what you wanted to say to me? Have you said your piece?"

"Yes. No. I don't know," Usman replied. "I've had this exact scenario play inside my head a thousand times, but now that I'm here..."

"I just want to know if I can leave."

"I know it wasn't your fault, Adina. By the time I realized that hard truth, it was too late for me to have a relationship with you. But you've got to understand; you murdered the love of my life, involuntary or not. My whole world shattered."

"What? You think my world wasn't destroyed?" Adina's voice was louder. "She was my *mother*! I think about it every day. I see it every time I close my fucking eyes."

"*SO DO I!*" Usman roared, his eyes on fire. "I loved her,

and you took her away from me. Of course, I kicked you out. Every time I saw you, I saw the monster that killed my wife."

"Well, now you've fucking moved on," Adina said. "I'm glad to see you've found a new *beloved* to care about, like you ever gave a shit about Mom."

Usman flopped onto the couch, his brief fervor spent. "It's been twenty years, Adina. How much longer do I have to mourn to receive your approval? What do you need me to do? What do you want that is in my power to grant? Yes, I'm engaged to Kirandeep. She's a lovely woman who helped give me a new lease on life. I owe her. I'm sick of being alone. I'm sick of rotting on the inside. I lost everything on that day. My wife. My daughter. And myself."

"I waited for you to get in touch." Tears streamed down Adina's cheeks. "I was a little girl, and I needed you. How do you think I felt about losing both of my parents?"

"I was wrong. I can't change that now, but I would if I could. Kirandeep was right that I needed to reconnect with my daughter if I ever wanted to be whole again."

"Twenty years too late," Adina said. "Way too late. You've never done anything for me, not a single damn thing."

"That's not true."

"Name it," Adina said. "Name one thing, and I'll sit back down."

"If it wasn't for me, you'd still be in the ice blocks," Usman replied.

Adina looked at him, half disgusted, half confused. "What are you talking about? Uncle got me—"

Usman shook his head. "When they took me in and

they talked to me about putting you on ice, I fought for you, Adina. I told them not to because I knew you didn't have control over it. That it wasn't on purpose. But that didn't mean I could look at you."

"Why should I believe you?"

"I've got no reason to lie. When it came down to it, the whole thing was my decision, and I told them not to."

"You abandoned me at my mother's funeral." Adina took a seat in her uncle's favorite chair. "You kicked me out of my family home."

"I know. I'm not saying I haven't done terrible things," Usman said. "I'm saying that I'm sorry for them. I want you to forgive me but understand if you can't. I want to give you some form of finality through my side of it."

"I've...I've never *not* understood why you kicked me out," Adina admitted. "I get what I did, even if it was out of my control, and I get why you did it. I *was* a monster, and through my weakness, I failed you. Most of all, I failed Mom."

"I didn't want to live with what killed my wife," Usman said, scrubbing his eyes with the back of his hand. "Honestly, I thought my disdain for you would lead me to do something terrible. I didn't know if I could control myself. I loved you, Adina. I still do, but there was something... Surely that's the one thing you understand. Losing that control."

"It is." Adina nodded.

They sat in silence for a few minutes, lost in their own admissions, their souls searched but not cleansed.

"Where do we go from here, Dad?"

"I don't know," Usman replied. "*I don't know.*"

"I think I should leave," Adina said. "I've got to think about what I want out of this."

"Are you going to *leave* leave?" Usman asked. "Or will I—"

"I can't answer that right now." Adina headed toward the door. She had to get out of there. "I don't think it's as simple as that."

Frontier Zone, City Station Hopefill, The Ice Blocks

The station was no different from most places. It had criminals who came in all shapes and sizes, and like other places, it had ways of dealing with them. For regular criminals—drugs dealers, murderers, thieves—there was a place below the station. A prison that could hold many, as if a crime wave had been built into the station, prognosticated and prepared.

Rogue werewolves were an entirely different problem. Some were criminals, mainly killers, but others were just lost and confused. They couldn't be placed with the general prison population for fear they'd go into a rage and rip the other prisoners apart. That's where the Ice Blocks came in.

Draven had been there a few times on official WRU business. The Ice Blocks were a relic that helped the station bury their problems in a way that kept them out of sight of the Federation.

It was a marginal program for the rehabilitation of werewolves who could live up to Federation standards. They were being produced outside of approved channels and in ways that would have drawn the ire of everyone within Bethany Anne's circle, including BA. The Hopefill City authorities had gone to great lengths to avoid that.

The werewolves who could manage were placed back into the city and kept under close observation. Those who couldn't became inmates of the Ice Blocks. With no way to control them, the Hopefill City leadership froze them in their cells, keeping them alive but in stasis until such time as a solution could be found. They were neither alive nor dead.

The guards let Draven in the moment he showed his WRU badge and accompanied him to the front desk for good measure. The receptionist was a stern brunette with sour features. She looked like the kind of person who took her job seriously. Draven thought she was at least a decade older than him. Her name was Minerva Stroll, and he had met her before.

"Draven Maynard." She looked at him like a bitter old woman who had just missed the bus. "I've got nothing on the WRU docket to say you've arranged a visit for today."

"This was a spontaneous venture." Draven leaned against the counter and turned up the charm. "I couldn't stay away from you, Minerva."

"That's sweet." She scowled. "Why are you here?"

Draven placed the ID card on the counter and slid it over to her. "I need to find out who this card belongs to. Can you check on it for me or something?"

"It's probably Briona's," Minerva replied without hesitation.

"What makes you say that?"

"She lost her card a few weeks ago, and we had to get her a replacement," Minerva said, grabbing the ID card and running it on her system. A few seconds later, she had her answer and turned the monitor so he could see. "As expected."

"Is she working now?" Draven asked while taking in the information on the screen, knowing there wouldn't be much time until it was turned away. Briona Arnd was the lead scientist in the Ice Blocks. Her official title was Lead Geneticist and Researcher for Project One. Draven was at a loss about what Project One was. He murmured, "I'd like to have a few words with her if I could."

"What is it concerning?" Minerva replied. "People don't get to see her without an appointment."

"I'm afraid that's WRU business." Draven took out his WRU badge to emphasize his point. "It's urgent I speak to her immediately. Where can I find her?"

"Briona has a research facility at the far end of the Ice Blocks," Minerva said. "I'll have a guard escort you there."

"Thank you." As Minerva turned to get the attention of one of the guards, Draven saw the opportunity to nab the ID card he had just handed over, thinking it might be useful to maintain control of the evidence. He palmed it off the desk before sliding it smoothly into his pocket.

He followed a guard through the many hallways of the Ice Blocks, which was like a living werewolf aquarium. People, some mid-change, some fully transformed, others no different from humans, were inside large blocks of ice and on display.

It made Draven sick to his core since they were the same as him. Sympathy tugged at his heartstrings, yet there was nothing he could do to help them. All he could do was keep moving forward and solve the case.

. . .

Frontier Zone, City Station Hopefill, Dock 9, Freight Bay A

Jack held up his hand at the side of the road and waited for the first hovercab brave enough to stop for a group that was made up of a human, an unconscious vagabond, a naked man, and a Yollin.

Tc'aarlat had first suggested they catch the shuttle to Dock 17, which was a good hour walk away from where they had encountered the drug gang. Jack had countered that suggestion with one of his own; a hovercab would be quicker with much less carrying. The only potential problem was if the two woke up in the middle of the trip.

"Here we go," Jack said, putting on an award-winning smile. The holographic letters that read HOVERCAB above the roof indicated his target. Jack waved him down, jumping forward to put his body in the vehicle's path while waving with both arms.

A man on the older side of life wearing thick glasses and sporting a pencil-thin mustache sat behind the controls. He eased to the side and let the hovercab settle to the ground. Jack opened the door, and Tc'aarlat moved the first body in before the driver could protest.

The cabbie took it in stride. "Where you headin', fellas?"

"Dock 17," Jack replied. "We're in a hurry."

"Oh, that ain't no problem. Seems most of my fares have been in a hurry tonight. Why, I just picked up a couple of girls, fresh from a night out, you know, who wanted me to take them to a fast-food place. Fast food? No one appreciates home cooking anymore—"

As Jack listened to the cabbie ramble, he kept a keen eye on Tc'aarlat, who at that moment was trying to stuff the naked werewolf in his overly large human form inside the relatively small hovercab. Tc'aarlat shrugged. "What are you, a road crew manager? Grab a leg." The Yollin pointed at Theo.

With Jack's help, they moved Theo into the cab with a more personal touch as opposed to the naked man who was twisted up, half on the seat, half on the floor. Tc'aarlat climbed in after them, leaving no room for Jack.

"I can sit up front, right?"

"Against the rules. You could fit in back if your carapaced friend wanted you to."

"No laps!" Tc'aarlat called from the back seat. Jack agreed. He wasn't going to sit on a naked man's lap or on Tc'aarlat's.

"An extra twenty credits if you let me sit up front."

"There's always room for a new driver in training!" The cabbie roared at a statement he'd probably made a hundred times before. Jack climbed in and flashed his credit chip to pay the man's personal fund. The official meter was already running and tallying up the credits.

Tc'aarlat struggled to close the door behind him. "Jack, we seem to have a problem."

Jack hopped out and forced the door shut by slamming it against the protruding body parts. Tc'aarlat grunted. The front passenger door had closed and it was locked.

"No passengers in the front seat," the cabbie repeated.

Tc'aarlat's patience was gone. Despite the confined space, the Yollin's blaster appeared in his hand, and he aimed it at the cabby's head. "Listen here, you fucking scamming shit-piece ball-twisting dick-hole festering pustule. Let him in, and let's get going. Your cab sucks, and you suck too, and if you don't open that door, you'll be able to pour your shit for brains out the hole I'm going to put in your head."

"Easy, cowboy. It was funny, no?"

"Not only no, but hell, no and fuck, no."

The door popped open, and Jack returned to his seat without having to say a word.

"...I dropped them off and then I saw you fellas along the road. Seemed to me that you were looking for a hovercab."

"Fascinating." Jack stabbed a finger ahead so the cabbie would do less talking and more driving.

"Been good weather for a change, don't you think?" the cabbie continued as the engines whined to lift the vehicle into the air with the heavy load it carried. The hovercab finally started to move.

"Good weather for what?" Tc'aarlat asked. "What the hell are you talking about?"

Jack waved his hand. "Ignore him. He's a little angry if you haven't noticed. Inside the station, the weather is always the same unless they make it rain. Do they do that here?"

The cabbie laughed and ignored the question. "Where you guys coming from, a night out?" The cabbie took the next corner, cutting off several lanes of waiting cars.

"Just a couple of drinks," Jack said. "Old friends meeting up for the first time in ages."

"And then you get naked and jump in my cab. It's not my place to question why. Your credits are good with me."

"They're good with the next guy who doesn't talk so much, too."

The cabbie pulled to the side. "Get out."

"This isn't Dock 17," Jack replied, making no move to open the door. "An extra twenty to shut your suckhole, or I let the Yollin kill you and we take your cab."

"I said…"

"Keep driving," Jack snarled before the cabbie could finish. He tossed his hands into the air and returned to the driving lane. The cab accelerated toward a connector that would take them to the dock. He didn't risk making further small talk or attempt to extort more credits from his passengers.

Scammers, Jack thought. If we were thugs, we'd rob him and take his cab.

When they arrived at Dock 17 and the familiar sight of the ICS *Fortitude*, Jack paid the fare and wished the cabbie a good evening. Jack took Theo and dropped him over his shoulder. Tc'aarlat lifted the big man, but he got twisted up before getting through the door.

"For fuck's sake!" Tc'aarlat bellowed before turning to Jack. "He's stuck. The big bastard is stuck."

"*This night*," Jack moaned. The more they tried to work him out, the less his body cooperated.

"I've got an idea," Tc'aarlat said. "Just give it a second."

"You fellas need some help?" The cabbie exited the hovercab and approached them, taking in the sight of the man. "Woo, he's a big boy, ain't he?"

Tc'aarlat cracked his knuckles. "Jack, I'm going to lose it in a second."

Jack took the cabbie to the side. "Listen, man, maybe you should—"

The naked man's eyes popped open to find he was wedged inside the cab. The change came at a fantastic speed. Hair grew while his face changed from human to the snout of a great beast. Tc'aarlat twirled the collar that no longer controlled the werewolf. It unscrewed itself from the door and lunged upward, ripping through the roof of the cab. It howled in righteous fury and peeled the roof back.

It burst free with a single leap. Tc'aarlat fired, JDS set to three, the strongest stun setting. The werewolf crumpled to the ground but didn't change back.

"What the hell?" Tc'aarlat complained.

Jack clapped him on the shoulder. "Nice plan, buddy. You carry the hairy one. At least he's not naked with his junk all over your shoulder anymore." Jack laughed. He looked at the cabbie. "Yeah, sorry about that, and before you ask, no, we're not going to pay for it, but this guy will." He contorted himself to keep Theo from falling while he produced Timothy's card.

The driver stood slack-jawed.

"Come here, asshole," Tc'aarlat grumbled at the werewolf. He grunted with the effort to get the great hairy beast onto his shoulder before standing slowly like a powerlifter rising from a record-setting squat. He staggered after Jack. "Slow down, wiper of asses."

The pair left the cabbie to sob on the dock as they moved up a short slope and into the familiarity of their spaceship.

Jack threw Theo into a spare room and directed Solo to

keep the doors locked. Tc'aarlat did the same for the werewolf.

The Shadows met in the corridor. Jack glanced over his shoulder at the locked door before shrugging. "I wonder what Adina is up to?" he asked nonchalantly.

"I wonder what Don Gan'barlo is up to. Don't think I've forgotten because we've been busy with excessive amounts of stupid."

"I don't know why, but I feel like we're closing on the Don with each step toward finding this Bloody Darling. Doesn't this whole drug monopoly smell like him?"

Tc'aarlat stared at Jack. "Sometimes you say things that make you sound smarter than you really are."

"Sometimes you open your mouth and words fall out, but they're nothing more than bullshit. No, wait. That would be all the time. Are you hungry, my friend? I could use something to eat and a good nap, too."

Frontier Zone, City Station Hopefill, The Ice Blocks, Briona's Research Laboratory

The research laboratory carried the same theme as the rest of the Ice Blocks. It was a large circular room with a dozen frozen werewolves arrayed around it like sculptures or works of art.

The laboratory held analysis equipment, complete with racks of vials interspersed with screens filled with scrolling data. In the middle of the room stood a commanding figure, a woman of average height with blonde hair and pale skin. She turned toward Draven and the guard, her neutral expression becoming one of annoyance.

"Who's this?" she asked the guard. "What's he doing here?"

"Draven Maynard." Draven didn't give the guard a chance to answer. He waved him away with a flash of his badge. "I'm an agent for the WRU. I was hoping you'd have a spare moment to answer some questions for me."

"I suppose I have a moment for the WRU." Briona nodded at the guard, and he left them to it. "Do you mind if I work while we talk?"

"Of course not," Draven replied. "Can I ask what you're working on?"

"It's called Project One," Briona said. "Otherwise known as the Werewolf Solution Project. That's what I'm doing here. I'm trying to reverse the process of rogue lycanthropy, that which isn't produced through the use of the Pod-docs."

"Can't we just use the Pod-docs to counteract the nanocytes?" Draven asked.

"There's the rub. We don't have Pod-docs on this station because the werewolves are the most public secret ever. Everyone knows, but the politicians have somehow managed to keep the Federation from getting involved. I get closer every day. It's about rewriting a person's DNA to block the ability to transform," Briona said, and she gestured to the wolves around her. "When I figure that out, they'll be free."

"Seems like a noble goal, and by noble, I mean terrifying, but we should press on." Draven took the ID card out of his pocket and handed it to her. "By any chance, did you lose this recently?"

Briona took it and examined it, running a fingernail

across the charred surface. "Yes, I did a little while ago. Where did you find this?"

"In a storage unit in the northern quadrant," Draven replied. He paid close attention to her body language. "Have you ever visited that part of the city?"

"I haven't," Briona said. "I've no idea how it got there. Someone must have taken it."

"Can't rule it out," Draven replied with a shrug. "Do you have any idea when you might've lost it?"

"A couple of weeks ago," Briona said. "I had to get a new one. I'm sure it's all a matter of record."

"Does this place keep a record of when and where these ID cards are used?" Draven said. "I'd be really interested in seeing if there's been any awkward activity recently, something that might suggest someone's been using the card."

"I believe they do. It's all attached to the computer system." Briona nodded slowly. "If you ask at the front desk, I'm sure they can provide you with the logs, but is it—"

Draven continued his questioning. "Have you noticed anything strange lately? Anything missing, not in its right place, unusual characters hanging about?"

"Not at all," Briona replied. "It's been business as usual, as in, no one comes in here."

Draven couldn't tell if she was lying. If Briona was, she was very good at it, but it seemed a little unusual that someone had taken her ID card and nothing had been noticed. Again, he thought back to Tc'aarlat's words when they were being questioned by Mikhail, hinting at a deeper plot. "The werewolves the WRU takes in...they come here, right?"

"Yes."

"Do you have access to them?"

"I have access to all the werewolves in the Ice Blocks," Briona replied. "For research purposes, of course."

"What do you make of their recent behavior?" Draven said. "Unusually feral?"

"We keep them sedated until they can be put into an ice block," Briona said. "Usually they come in with lacerations, a sign of abuse."

"You don't monitor them?"

"It's the policy of the Ice Blocks to put them directly into storage," Briona replied. "It's out of my control, and I don't think their behavior has anything to do with creating a cure anyway."

"All right then. What about the collars they wear when they're brought in?" Draven asked. "What do you make of them? Do you think there's something more to them?"

"They don't come in with any collars," Briona replied, clearly confused. "Should they have collars?"

"Whenever we pick up a werewolf gang member, they have a shock collar on," Draven said. "I assumed that they'd arrive with the new inmates."

"I don't know what to tell you," Briona said with a shrug. "I haven't seen any come through here."

"Unusual," Draven remarked. "Would anyone take them off before they got here?"

"I can't think why," Briona replied. "Are there any other questions?"

"No, I'll take my leave," Draven said, and he shook her hand with a warm smile. "You've been really useful, Briona. Thanks so much for answering my questions."

"It's no problem. Always happy to help the WRU."

"You said I can get the ID logs from the front desk, right?" Draven asked. "From the lovely Minerva."

After she confirmed that, Draven left the room and moved through the corridor with more unease in his stomach than ever. From all accounts, Briona was telling the truth, but he couldn't shake the feeling that there was something more to this. Something sinister. For one thing, Briona didn't seem too upset at the thought of her card being used by someone else. And what was it doing in the storage units? Draven went to the front desk eagerly and picked up the logs. He was going to get to the bottom of this if it killed him.

11

Frontier Zone, City Station Hopefill, Dock 23, Freight Bay F, ICS *Fortitude*

The howling from the room next door awakened Theo. He went from dream to blurry reality to the shakes of withdrawal. He had expected to see the cold, gray walls of a detention cell, but the bed was softer, and it was a real room. Reminded him of a spaceship, but his brain was muddled. Too long without the drug. Too tired, and no amount of sleep would grant him respite from his fatigue. He threw his legs off the bed and stumbled to the bathroom to relieve himself, followed by splashing water on his face.

A private shower. He didn't usually have such luxuries. He stepped in, still wearing his clothes since they never had the opportunity to get washed either. He let the water run over him until he managed to strip down, then washed his clothes using the available shampoo. The mundane task helped him focus. One small task at a time. He washed himself twice, then twisted the water out of his clothes. He hung them around the small bathroom and wrapped the towel around himself.

Barefoot but clean, he tried to open the door to his room, but it was secured from the outside. He knocked gently, then started to bang on it. *I've been kidnapped*, he thought through the fog, but he had no idea who or why. He tried to access the ship's computer through the screen on the wall, but it wouldn't respond to his iris or hand-print. Of course it wouldn't.

He returned to the door and started banging on it again. "Let me out of here!"

A gentle tap on the other side reminded Theo of prisoners trying to communicate through the walls of their cells, but it was followed by a familiar voice. "Calm down, Theo. Can't have you beating up my ship. You're not in any danger. You are in a spare bunk on my ship, *Fortitude*."

"I feel like shit," Theo replied. "Let me out of here so I can take care of myself."

The door slid open, but Captain Jack Marber blocked the way. "I'm glad you cleaned up. You look a lot better."

"You got any extra clothes?"

"You're not going anywhere except to a Pod-doc, where we're going to get you cleaned up."

"For a second there I thought the dealers had me. Let me out."

Jack pushed him back and moved into the room. He had a breakfast tray in his hands—nothing fancy, just some toast and eggs. The door closed behind him, and Theo couldn't mistake the loud click for anything other than it being locked into place.

"You hungry?" Jack pushed the tray toward him. "Thought you might want some breakfast."

Theo dragged a hand through his hair before taking the tray. He sampled the food and ate slowly, but his stomach heaved. He needed Eternity before he could do anything else. He nibbled for Jack's sake, but the food was revolting. It took an inhuman effort for him to keep it down.

"I want to help you, Theo. I want you to get you back on your feet."

"Don't do this, Jack," Theo warned. "I don't *want* to get back on my feet. I want to get my fix and be done with it."

"Be done with it. Why didn't you fight the dealers until they killed you? That's about all your life's worth," Jack replied.

"I know you feel guilty for leaving. This isn't the way to make up for it. Just let me go."

"No can do, boo." Jack tried to be flippant, but he was torn. Was he helping or not? "I have no idea how long it'll take you to get clean if we can't get you into a Pod-doc. No matter what, I'm not leaving you in the same state I found you. I owe you too much."

"Why can't you just respect what I want? It should be my choice, don't you think?" Theo asked.

"Not this time, Theo. I'll drag you kicking and screaming back to the real world. Your contributions to society are not at an end. You have a lot more in you. It's not you speaking, so I can't respect those wishes. Once you're clean, you can go your own way."

"Don't do this, Jack." Theo grabbed him by the collar, pleading and moaning with his red-raw eyes. "Please, please just let me go. *Please.*"

Jack brushed him off. "No."

"You're a fucking coward, Jack. It's your fault I'm like this," Theo snarled. "If you'd just given that order, I wouldn't have fucking lost everything important. I wasn't a leader. I never wanted to be a leader."

"That's why I'm doing this, Theo," Jack replied. "I knew about you and Kayleigh, and I'm sorry you had to face her death alone."

"I don't need to do anything." Theo scratched at the corners of his eyes. "Let me out of here."

"When the time is right." Jack strode to the door and let himself out. Theo tried to rush him, but Jack fought him off. The towel slipped off and fell to the floor. "There you are. Naked before the world, your ass hanging out. Today starts anew. Welcome to the first day of the rest of your life."

"NO!" Theo screamed as the door slid shut. He pounded on it until he couldn't lift his arms, then slid to the floor, exhausted.

Frontier Zone, City Station Hopefill, Dock 23, Freight Bay F, ICS *Fortitude*, Bridge

On one side of the screen, he had live footage of the werewolf in the ship's quarters, and on the other, he had an open comm with Timothy Grand.

The beast had woken in the foulest of moods and set about ripping apart the mattress and anything that wasn't hardened steel or stronger.

Tc'aarlat watched with mild interest while Myst, his

Raal hawk companion, perched on his shoulder, happy to be with the Yollin.

"Well done on catching one, Tc'aarlat," Timothy said, adding a thumbs-up as if it were a prize in a children's game. "I know someone who works for the Ice Blocks and might be able to give a more accurate observation of the creature."

"It's wild." Tc'aarlat stared at it while fiddling with the shock collar it had worn. By now, he thought the thing would've returned to its normal human self, but it was still a werewolf hours later. It was feral, a relentless ball of fur and fury, and Tc'aarlat was beginning to have his doubts that it had been human even though he'd seen it in its human form. "Who is it? Who should we be expecting?"

"Her name is Briona Arnd. She's a geneticist for the Ice Blocks, and I daresay, she knows more about the werewolf problem than anyone else. I'll get in touch with her right now."

"What have I missed?" Jack came in as soon as Grand signed off.

"Not much," Tc'aarlat replied. "Tim Grand is sending an expert over, and it looks like we're going to need *new* guest quarters."

Jack gestured at the collar in his hand. "Find anything new about that?"

"Well, it's a shock collar for sure," Tc'aarlat replied, throwing it to Jack. "You can tell from those little metal spikes hooked up to a power supply in the collar. I can't see anything else to it, like a transmitter. Then again, I'm not the best with crap like that."

"Have you tried asking Adina?"

"Asking me what?" Adina had picked her moment well, wandering into the bridge with a cup of hot coffee in one hand and her tablet in the other. She looked like hell, with a bad case of pillow face and sleep hair.

Myst squawked a greeting. Tc'aarlat absentmindedly stroked the bird. "When did you get back?"

"Last night." Adina yawned and moved toward her terminal, where she took a seat. "I had a conversation with my father, and it went about as well as you could expect."

"Do you need me to beat his ass?" Tc'aarlat asked. "I will, for you. And for me too because I like it."

Adina took a sip of her coffee and stared at her Yollin crewmate. "What do you want my help with?"

"This." Tc'aarlat threw the collar toward her. She didn't have a free hand. She didn't try to catch it and watched it sail past her head to land on the deck behind her. Tc'aarlat threw his hands up. "You could have caught it."

Adina shook her head, put down her tablet, and retrieved the collar. "What is it?"

"A shock collar that the werewolves are wearing," Tc'aarlat said.

Moving it beneath a light, Adina closely inspected the elements that made up the insides of the collar: the spikes, the small battery, and a metal plate that had a screen embedded inside it that looked similar to a heart monitor. Adina gave a few *umms* and *aaahs* before turning back to the others. "You're right about it being a shock collar, that's for sure, but there's something else. See this plate here? It's a brainwave-scanner and not a very good one. I'd say it's been programmed to give a shock whenever it detects certain thoughts. I'd have to tear it apart and test it to be sure."

"What does that mean?" Jack asked.

"Okay, let's say you put this on a dog," Adina said. "Their brainwaves are low, instinctual, so it wouldn't shock them. I think this thing roots out intelligible thoughts, the kind of ideas that control the decision-making process, and stops them in their tracks."

"That's why that thing is so stupid and feral." Tc'aarlat pointed at the screen, where the werewolf was throwing a tantrum. "No idea if it'll turn back until it calms down and can do it without thinking about it."

"What the hell are you doing with a werewolf?" Adina glared at Tc'aarlat.

"We caught it last night," Jack said. "Do you think the collar and it being feral are connected?"

"It can't be feral as all werewolves start with a sentient form like a human. Could it lose its humanity? That's the right question, and I don't know the answer," Adina replied.

"Suppose we'd better wait for the expert then," Jack interjected.

Frontier Zone, City Station Hopefill, WRU Head-quarters

Draven sat at his desk, running the conversation with Briona over and over in his mind. The Ice Block had given him the logs for badge usage, showing him who was where and for how long since they had to badge both in and out.

He didn't see anything untoward up to the moment the

badge had been stolen. It had been business as usual, with a nothing-burger as main course and zip on the side. That was the baseline from which the deviation was obvious. He found that Briona had gone from a regular routine to a sporadic schedule. In the past two weeks, she had come and gone at all hours. Sometimes she'd stay for a whole day. Other times it was less than an hour.

"What are you up to, Briona?" Draven asked.

"Boss?" Draven was no longer alone in the office. Tinio Attes stood there with a confused expression, holding his regular steaming cup of morning joe in his hand.

"Tinio?" Draven questioned. "What are you doing here so early?"

"I'm always in at this time." Tinio marched up to the desk. "I could ask you the same question."

"I'm following up a lead," Draven replied, showing his subordinate the list he had recovered. "I went back to the storage units and found an ID card in the rubble. It belonged to a lead researcher working at the Ice Blocks, who had reported it lost a couple weeks earlier. Take a look at this listing. You notice anything unusual?"

Tinio examined it closely. "Up until two weeks ago, Briona had a pretty regular schedule. Now it's all over the place."

Draven moved to get up. "I need to bring her in for questioning. This erratic schedule leads up to the explosion."

"Right now?" Tinio asked. "Do you have an address?"

"No, but she'll come into work eventually," Draven replied. "I'll just wait there."

"Do you want some help?"

"I doubt I'll need it. Why don't you brief Mikhail when he gets in?" Draven eyed Tinio suspiciously.

"I could be useful," Tinio pressed. "You're dealing with an employee that handles werewolves every day, and I hate to put you down, but you happen to be one of those werewolves. Chances are, she will be prepared for you. Even if they are unconscious, it's still a place that's been trained to handle werewolves."

Draven had just met with her. She was no threat. Was Tinio on the wrong team? Was he the leak? Best to keep one's enemies close. "Sounds like a winner. Come on, let's have a sit-down with the good doctor."

They walked toward the exit. Once in the corridor, Tinio tapped Draven on the shoulder. A second later, Draven couldn't miss the barrel of a blaster pressing into his back. *You couldn't wait until we were out of the building?* Draven thought, cursing himself for allowing Tinio to walk behind. He'd made his move far earlier than Draven anticipated.

Tinio leaned close and whispered, "This is nothing personal, Draven. You're going around asking all the wrong questions."

Electricity surged through Draven's body, lighting every nerve on fire for an instant until his world turned black.

The blond hunk collapsed into Tinio's arms, and he dragged him outside the building and toward the hovervan they had used to raid the storage units only a few nights earlier.

Double-checking that no one was watching, Tinio dropped the dead weight inside the back and shut the door. In his head, he arranged a quick checklist to make sure his tracks were covered.

First, he had to go back into the building and erase any and all footage of the past hour to make sure no one suspected him. After that, he would have to take Draven to the boss, following the orders she had given him. Tinio wasn't sure what fate had in store for Draven, but he had a good idea where he would be at the end of the day.

Frontier Zone, City Station Hopefill, Dock 23, Freight Bay F, ICS *Fortitude*, Bridge

Briona adjusted her glasses to better focus on the monitor on the bridge. The feed of the werewolf in the guest quarters was different from what it had been a few hours ago. The rampaging monster had curled up and fallen asleep on the tattered remnants of the bed. It looked peaceful, sweet almost, breathing slowly and deeply.

Jack and Tc'aarlat glanced nervously at each other like two patients in a doctor's office waiting for bad news.

"What do you make of it?" Tc'aarlat asked. "Ass-blastingly redonkulous? I thought wolf guys were supposed to change back once they've calmed down."

"That's right, Tc'aarlat," Briona replied. "It is weird that this one has not reverted back."

"There's also this," Jack said, handing her the collar. "It was latched around the thing's throat. Our engineer believes it gives a shock to the wearer whenever it has an intelligible thought."

"How interesting." Briona took the device and scanned it indifferently before turning back to the video feed. "I'd like to perform further tests on it. I'll get the werewolf transferred to the Ice Blocks immediately."

Jack sighed. "Well, if you think that's for—"

"Hold up," Tc'aarlat interjected, thrusting his hand out to keep anyone from moving. "I want to have a word with this guy. Don't you have one of those injector things that can return him to normal?"

"I can do that at the Ice Blocks," Briona replied, not trying to hide her distaste at Tc'aarlat's interruption.

"What's the problem with doing it here?" Tc'aarlat asked.

"Nothing, but I won't be able to administer it here. The only ones allowed to have injectors outside of the Ice Blocks are the WRU."

"We've got a contact in the WRU," Jack said. "I'm sure he'd be happy to help."

"These werewolves are dangerous, not like any you've encountered before. Please, let me take it back to the Ice Blocks," Briona said. "You're violating the law that gives us jurisdiction over any and all captured werewolves."

"You have to know that we work for the Federation, and it seems to me that the entirety of Hopefill City is violating the law. Werewolves are considered equals, not treated like wild dogs running free to be collared. Maybe we should make them aware of what's going on here so they can bring the full weight of Federation law down on your shoulders," Jack countered.

He was tired of playing pattycake with these people. He wondered how it had gotten this far and why the Federation didn't understand the extent of the problem.

Adina stepped onto the bridge, eyeing the woman with Jack and Tc'aarlat. She moved toward her terminal with Isaaca sitting on her shoulder. "I'm not interrupting anything, am I?"

"Hello, *Adina*," Briona said, giving her a smile and offering her hand. "We haven't been formally introduced. I'm Doctor Briona Arnd. Lead researcher and geneticist for the Ice Blocks."

"How do you know my name?" Adina asked suspiciously, shaking the offered hand.

"I've been following your career with interest. I have a list of unusual werewolves, and you're at the top."

"How in the hell is that common knowledge?" Adina glared, but the doctor only shrugged. Adina gestured at the screen. "Why is that one not changing back?"

"I was just telling Jack and Tc'aarlat that I could do a proper observation on the wolf back in the Ice Blocks."

"We probably shouldn't let you have it," Adina said with her fists jammed against her hips. Jack smiled and nodded over Briona's shoulder. "Shock training? Did you have anything to do with that?"

Briona crossed her arms and twisted her mouth. "It's uncertain whether the collar could have that kind of effect. I'm sure you'd agree."

"I doubt it until there's empirical evidence to the contrary. I'll work off my hypothesis at present," Adina replied.

"First things first," Jack said. "Solo, can you put me in touch with Draven Maynard, please?"

"I'll do it now, Jack," was the reply from the ship's AI, and a second later, they were listening to the distinctive beeps of a call being connected. They waited, but no one picked up. "I'm sorry, Jack. I cannot connect this call."

"Perhaps he's busy?" Briona suggested.

"It isn't like him not to answer," Jack said.

"Even if he is a dickhead," added Tc'aarlat.

"Solo, can—"

"I have some sway over at the WRU," Briona interrupted. "If you'd like, I could arrange for some agents to come by with an injector? That way, you can get the answers you're looking for."

"We'd appreciate that, Briona," Jack replied. "Here, let me show you the way out."

"Thank you, Captain."

Adina and Tc'aarlat glared at the back of her head as Jack led her toward the airlock and ramp to the ground, but they didn't speak until she left the bridge.

"There's something about her that doesn't sit right with me," Adina said. "I have the strangest feeling I've met her before."

"If you opened up the dictionary and looked up 'bitch lollipop,' there'd be a picture of her all dressed in glitter," Tc'aarlat replied. "I'll tell you one thing. She does not like us not handing the werewolf over to these Ice Blocks things."

"Do you really think that wolf will have any answers for you when it reverts back?" Adina asked.

"I don't know, but I'm starting to feel sorry for it. And

don't you tell anyone. I don't want my hardass image tainted by feelings like you weak humans show," Tc'aarlat said.

"I got a message from Kirandeep." Tc'aarlat raised a confused eyebrow at her. "That's my father's new girlfriend. She wants to meet up with me later today after she's done a few errands, so that's what I'm going to be doing."

"Still got some daddy issue stuff going on, even though we have a mission that could use you. Not that family doesn't come first, but it doesn't."

Adina looked down her nose at the taller Yollin.

"Well." Tc'aarlat breathed out the word. "Good luck with it. If you need my help with anything, like beating up your old man, I'm only a call away."

"Thanks for the offer, Tc'aarlat." Adina gave him a smile and a quick nudge on the arm. "I'll keep that in mind."

12

Frontier Zone, City Station Hopefill, Dock 9, ICS *Hopeful*

The ICS *Hopeful* was likely the oldest ship on the docks. It had been there since the Hopefill City upgrades almost two decades earlier when the new docks had been built, and it was an uncomfortable eyesore. It hadn't flown in all that time.

It was battle-damaged, with sections missing, craters, charred, scorched, dented. It was little more than scrap metal held together by rust, which was bizarre since metals on space stations tended not to rust.

In a previous life, *Hopeful* had been a battleship, a courageous defender of the Federation and its assets. These days it was something else. It was a base for the Silver Diamonds drug gang.

The ship had been chosen for a number of reasons. It was hidden in plain sight, for one thing. It was large enough to house the operations of the Silver Diamonds and their gang members, and thanks to its previous life, it was defensible when it came to protecting the gang's resources. With so many other gangs creating problems by perpetual efforts to expand their territories, the ICS *Hopeful* had a unique advantage.

Riddle had been avoiding the *Hopeful* like a person would avoid meeting their in-laws for the first time. After what had happened with Theo the other night and the disappearance of his right-hand wolf Bonkers, he knew that at some point, there was going to be a serious conversation. He also knew it wasn't going to end well, so in a bid to protect himself, Riddle had scurried across the city and made a poor attempt at smuggling himself out. He was discovered a few moments later, shocked with a bistok prod, and tossed off the freighter.

Riddle was a tall guy, always had been, and good in a fight. The gang members who had come to retrieve him had twitchy fingers and powerful blasters. They wouldn't deal drugs like he did.

They were the ones who made sure everyone played nice. They were the messengers of pain.

The three of them didn't bother to break out their blasters since he knew he had no choice. He came without causing any trouble, and now here he was, back at the *Hopeful*, or as he was thinking of it, the *Hopeless*. If he ran, they'd just shoot him. If he didn't, he would probably die, but his surrender was complete. He'd wait for his punishment and take it like a man. When someone was a werewolf handler like Riddle was, losing a werewolf had consequences. The creatures might have appeared to be an infestation, but they weren't, and they didn't grow on trees.

A familiar face appeared, one he had seen a thousand times. It stood out in a crowd. It was burnt on one side, with the other side heavily tattooed with crow icons, leading to the nickname "Crow." There was one tattoo that didn't match the others on the side of his neck: a silver diamond, a sign of status in the hierarchy. There was no one higher than Crow, or that's what Riddle thought. He was the top dog of the *Hopeful* and the leader of the Silver Diamonds' drug operations in the city.

Riddle was forced into the room and to his knees. He resisted, finally finding a bit of spine, but it was too little, too late. A baton to the back of his knees convinced him to get down.

Crow glared. Riddle tried to avoid looking at the man. Seeing someone with his authority and power that angry made him quake in fear despite his surrender to his fate. Crow took a seat and let silence fill the empty space in the room. Riddle's breath quickened with each passing moment.

Crow got out of his seat and approached Riddle, leaning down to be on the thug's level and forcing his eyes toward him with one meaty hand.

"What's the rule, Riddle?" he asked calmly. "The one rule."

"Crow, please, I'm sorry. It wasn't me; it was the other—"

"The rule, Riddle. I want to hear you say it. Now."

"We don't let the werewolves get captured," Riddle replied. "Crow, listen, it was—"

"Did you break that rule?"

Crow let go of Riddle's chin. The thug's eyes fell, and he spoke barely above a whisper. "Yes."

Crow stood back up, and for a moment, Riddle thought

he was going to be shot. He closed his eyes in preparation. When nothing happened, he opened them again and saw Crow looking down at him.

"There are consequences for this, Riddle," Crow said. "Not just for you, but for the Silver Diamonds. *She* wants a word with you."

"She?" Riddle looked up, confused. He had never heard of this *she* before, and the mention of a person to whom Crow deferred created a boulder in the pit of his stomach.

Crow grabbed his collar and yanked him to his feet, then pushed him on a slow and reluctant march through the ship. Riddle had no choice. They kept the blasters trained on him, but he was keenly aware that they were taking him to the underbelly of *Hopeful*. To a section of the ship he had never seen before.

Frontier Zone, City Station Hopefill, Dock 9, ICS *Hopeful*, The Recuperating Room

The water was perfect, as she had prepared it to be. It was not a pool in a high-class hotel, more of a large glass container in the center of what had once been the *Hopeful's* engine room. Still, it would do.

Naka-Lee came here whenever she had the chance. It was the perfect place to rest and restore her scaly skin, as well as to think about things that needed to be done. In the past few days, her challenges had tripled in their complexity. She smiled. They were being handled and moving at a pace she deemed sufficient for her plans.

Naka-Lee had made an arrangement with the Silver Diamonds, not that they'd had a choice. In return for her obedient and willing werewolves, just enough to keep them ahead of the competition, they would give her a place to lay low when she was there on business. They would also fulfill her favors whenever she requested.

She was satisfied that the deal was enough to keep her safe in the company of the gang, but she was no fool. She kept her own personal werewolf, her pet and bodyguard Biscuit, close at hand in case of trouble.

The kind of trouble she was expecting in the next few moments.

Naka-Lee's private room was secured by a large steel door, not unlike those on submarines, with a wheel lock.

A vigorous knock came before the wheel spun. A few seconds later, a group of Silver Diamonds came into the room, leading one of their thugs—the one she had been expecting to see this morning—with guns pointed at his back.

They didn't say a word. None of them dared, and that was how she liked it. Naka-Lee always spoke first when it came to matters of discipline, which she called "teachable moments."

Those who couldn't respect that had only milliseconds to contemplate the error of their ways before crossing over to the next life. Swimming to the top of the ad hoc pool as elegantly as any dancer, she pulled herself free of the water's embrace and moved toward the newcomers. Along the way, she shifted the water off her skin and changed into something more human. She mostly looked the same, but she knew the form would put the others at ease rather than being a fish monster.

Naka-Lee stopped three meters from her guests, where

she could see them all without turning her head. She adopted a wide but casual stance, dominating and, above all, unyielding. She pointed at the one called Riddle, who was very close to tears. "I'm going to assume this is the wayward soul we were talking about earlier, Crow?"

"That it is," Crow said and quickly added, "ma'am."

Naka-Lee turned her full attention to the accused. "Do you know who I am, Riddle?"

"N-no," he stammered, "ma'am."

"I'm a collector of sorts," the female replied. "What I collect is perceptions, different points of view from people in a variety of situations, and that's what has brought you here to me today. You see, Crow has told me one side of the story, told to him by gang members who might not be reliable. What I really need, though, is your side of the story. I need details. Are you following me so far?"

Riddle nodded enthusiastically.

"Good," Naka-Lee said. "This werewolf that you fondly called Bonkers was in your charge and in your service the night you lost it. Now, I'm not looking to find out where the creature is. I already know it is with the Shadows. Neither am I asking you to retrieve it. I have far more capable people who can assist me with that side of things. No, what I'm asking you is for the events and why you felt the need to abandon a creature who represents a sizeable investment for your gang. Begin."

Riddle swallowed, not that it did much for his dry throat, and tried to put his thoughts together. "It was a regular drug trade at the beginnin' with a guy we already knew. His name's Theo, right, and he buys a lot o' stuff from us. This time though, he had come lookin' with empty hands, and I was wantin' to give him a scare, teach him a lesson."

"Was this the first time he had come without the means to pay?"

"Yeah, he's usually good for it."

"Interesting," Naka-Lee said thoughtfully. "Please, go on."

"Well, after that, I told Bonkers to leap on him, jump right up, and the wolf did it," Riddle said. "Then, uh, things just kicked off. These two guys came outta nowhere with guns and stuck us up. I thought they were robbin' the merchandise, so I turns Bonkers attention on them instead."

"'These two guys.' A Yollin and a human right?" Naka-Lee asked.

Riddle nodded with wide eyes. "We get in a big fight. Bonkers goes after the bug-lookin' guy while we fight off the other one. Turns out he was too good for us with his crazy weapon that blasted people around corners. The rest of the guys only got blunt weapons. It was too hot, so we took off. I whistled for Bonkers, but he never came. That's the story, ma'am."

"That's because he was captured," Naka-Lee said. "Captured by the Yollin you set him on."

"Yeah, that's—" Riddle never got a chance to finish that sentence. Naka-Lee grew a tentacle at the speed of thought and rammed it into his open mouth. It continued down his throat until it grasped and jerked his larynx out through his mouth.

Riddle gagged and coughed, unable to breathe while blood ran over his lips and onto the deck. He fell to his knees, hands around his throat as if that could soothe the pain roaring within. His eyes rolled back in his head and he fell over, then twitched a few times before he went limp.

"Crow." Naka-Lee only had to say it once. He shot his attention to her in an instant. "I hope this sends a decent message, yes? I'm not known as a forgiving person, and this shitstain has really fucked me over. Because of him, the Shadows have access to one of *my* werewolves. Now I've got to call in a bunch of favors to correct it."

"Message received."

"Good, because if it fucking happens again, it'll be your throat on the floor and those of your whole gang. I am very upset about this, Crow. It's really unprofessional."

Naka-Lee tossed the larynx on Riddle and wiped her hands on Crow's jacket. Hands that moments earlier had been tentacles. "You can leave now, all of you. I've got an important appointment I'd like to keep that I'm already running late for."

Frontier Zone, City Station Hopefill, Dock 23, Freight Bay F, ICS *Fortitude*

Jack and Tc'aarlat left the ship to find three familiar faces from the WRU waiting patiently outside a black car. Tc'aarlat was about to move down the walkway to meet them, but Jack stopped him with a firm gesture. He had an itch that gave him pause. It started with the noticeable absence of Draven Maynard and ended with the determined faces of Tinio, Rola, and Reward.

"We were called in about your werewolf problem," Tinio shouted up to them. "Briona sent us personally."

"Thanks for coming so quickly," Jack shouted back. "Where's Draven?"

"I couldn't tell you." Tinio gave a half-assed shrug. "Draven didn't show up for work this morning, and no one has seen him in a while."

"Is that right?" Tc'aarlat asked. "Where's your injector gun thingy? How are you supposed to change this guy back without it?"

"It's in the car," Rola said. "That's where it's going to stay."

"I ain't feeling good about this. This smells like three rear ends of crap, and never mind the fucking flies. I don't think we should let these guys anywhere near that wolf, not until we hear from Draven."

"I don't think they're giving us a choice," Jack whispered back.

Tinio waved and started walking. "According to the laws of Hopefill City, the WRU is well within its rights to retrieve werewolves that have been proven as threats, are part of criminal organizations, or have a possibility of being a danger to themselves and others. The werewolf you have in there fits all three categories, so move aside."

"What happens when we don't?" Tc'aarlat called. "You're off your head if you think you're going to get past me!"

"That's what we'll do," Tinio said. "We have the full support of the city behind us."

Just behind the trio, a hovercar pulled up. The car was well-designed, posh and expensive looking, but it had security like heavy metal doors and bulletproof windows. The backdoor opened and out came Timothy, still looking like hell but smiling all the same. "The En-D have it within their power to hold a citizen in a holding cell of their choosing for twenty-four hours."

"Timothy Grand?" Tinio stood back to let him pass. Timothy continued toward *Fortitude's* ramp. "What are you doing here?"

"I heard the WRU were moving to take the werewolf, and I thought I'd make sure the exchange was clean," Timothy called over his shoulder as he strode toward Jack and Tc'aarlat.

"Thanks for the assist," Jack said with a nod.

"That werewolf is part of an ongoing investigation," said Tinio. "We're well within the law to—"

"Yeah, I know the law," Grand replied. "Here's a lesson for you. When it comes to cases outside of werewolf inter-ference, the priority lands with the En-D. This wolf has a connection with a known drug-trafficking gang and is still in the interview process. According to the law, we can hold him here for twenty-four hours, after which we will hand him over."

"So beat it, you hairy-butt bunch." Tc'aarlat held up two fingers and waved them. "Before we have you arrested for trespassing on our ship, or near it anyway."

Tinio glared but had no choice. "Twenty-four hours. We'll be back at this time tomorrow to take the wolf."

"Bring Draven. We're more than happy to work with him rather than lackeys," Jack said. The car lifted into the air and slowly maneuvered away from *Fortitude*. Jack clapped Timothy on the back with a short laugh. "You got here just in time. We were gearing up for a fight."

"That wouldn't have been a smart decision, Jack,"

Timothy replied. "If you fight them, they'd be within their rights to arrest you. All I've done is bought you some time."

They went inside the ship, making sure to secure the hatch behind them.

"What now?" Tc'aarlat said. "Without that injector thing, we can't turn that guy back. He has answers to our questions. I know it."

"There's an obvious solution you're not seeing. We've got to get our hands on one." Jack raised his eyebrows.

"You aren't suggesting what I think you're suggesting?" Timothy inquired. "Because if you are, as head of the En-D, I've got to close my ears to it."

"If they won't hand us one, we're going to steal it instead," Jack said.

"Draven would be really useful here," Tc'aarlat said. "He could get us inside, no problem. It's a shame he's never around when you need him."

"Wait, that's it." Jack snapped his fingers and turned to Timothy. "When Draven was in the En-D, did you run him through any imaging software for facial recognition?"

"Yeah, why?"

Tc'aarlat laughed. "Of course. We have a machine that can create realistic masks! We stole it from that doctor guy we encountered a few months ago."

"I think we've got our way in," Jack said. "And we'd better act on it quick. We have twenty-four hours."

13

Federation Hopefill City, Commercial Zone 1, Gray Sun Café

Adina had gone to the familiar café and grabbed the booth she had come to think of as familiar and comfortable. For perhaps the hundredth time, she checked the time on her communicator, then looked at the clock on the wall and checked that, too. Kirandeep was late by about an hour, and it seemed uncharacteristic for her. Adina worried that something was wrong.

Adina thought about what could be keeping her and went back to the other night with her father when she had rushed off so quickly. Kirandeep had told her that she ran several cafés across Hopefill City, which made her a successful businesswoman, and wouldn't they have been open when she was meeting her father for the first time? Or would they? For a scientist, she had not done her research when it came to her own family.

"I'm sorry I am so late," Kirandeep said when she finally

arrived. "A café across the city was having a supply issue, and of course, they couldn't solve it without my help."

"No, that's okay," Adina replied. "I was just thinking about the other night with my father."

"Yes, I'm dying to know how it went." The woman held up her hand to one of the cashiers and made a gesture to get some drinks for the table. "I'm all ears."

"I think it went poorly." Adina frowned. "I'm not sure I'm interested in renewing a relationship with him. I believe him when he says he's sorry, but I don't think I can forgive him."

"That makes me tremendously sad, dear," Kirandeep said, reaching for her hands. "I wanted you and your father to reconnect."

"Why would you want me to come into your life?"

"I've seen the pain it causes him. I've seen him cry in his sleep for you and grow depressed whenever he sees your photo. He lost everything once, and he seeks a better level of normal. He is extremely proud of all you've accomplished."

"He could've done that any time," Adina shook her head. She couldn't get past the idea that her father wouldn't have anything to do with her until he was sure she had the werewolf under control. Maybe he had been too afraid to do anything before now.

"Because he didn't have me before," Kirandeep said, and she looked down at the floor, avoiding Adina's gaze. "I know what it's like to lose the people you love with your mistakes."

Adina sighed. "No, I can't do—"

"Just one more time," Kirandeep urged. "You've both

gotten over the initial discomfort of seeing each other after such a long time. Maybe the connection is only one conversation away."

Adina thought she might be right. She understood where he was coming from. She *had* killed her mother, and when she put herself in his shoes, she couldn't imagine doing anything different.

"I'll meet him one more time, but not *there*. I'll meet him for coffee. I won't ever go back to my former home."

"Yes, somewhere public," Kirandeep agreed easily. "You could meet at one of my cafés, like the one I was looking after today? You'll love it. It's this little place with a seating area outside that overlooks one of the city's parks. Really beautiful. I love sitting there and admiring the flowers."

"Yeah, sure," Adina said, not thinking it mattered. "Just tell me when and where."

"How about later today? An hour before the shops close?" Kirandeep stood up, threw her purse over one shoulder, and gave Adina a warm smile. "Would that work for you?"

Adina nodded through her apprehension while looking up at Kirandeep. The light caught her in a way that she was surrounded by an aura like an angel. Adina couldn't remember meeting a more pleasant person. "Which café is it?"

"The Sweet Surron."

"I'll be there." Adina smiled. She couldn't put her finger on why, but she liked this woman. She could see what her father saw in her. She was sweet and caring, and above all, she reminded her a lot of her mother. The way Kirandeep was always smiling, her jokey personality and humble nature. Those had been her mother's traits, too. Quietly she decided that she would do something nice for Kirandeep, for all the effort she was putting in to reconnect Adina and her father. She would surprise her at the café with it.

Frontier Zone, City Station Hopefill, WRU Headquarters

The mask had such an uncanny resemblance that Tc'aarlat jumped back and shouted, "Dickhead!" when Jack came out of his room wearing it.

They boarded a transport and headed to WRU Headquarters. Thanks mostly to Nathan and his crystal-clear images of Draven, they had a plan, and Jack was ready to play the part.

They surveilled the building for an hour, trying to determine the best course of action to acquire the injector. They had no plans for the building or a clue as to which room was what. Jack knew he had to avoid everyone. The mask changed his voice but not his mannerisms.

"Project confidence while being completely ignorant and looking for something that isn't going to be in the open. Got it. This is a fucking Shadow plan at its finest: make it up once we get there. What could go wrong?"

Tc'aarlat leaned close and studied Jack's new face. "We abandoned planning because nothing ever went right. It's better not to constrain yourself. It's also important to note that I'm glad it's not me in there. Go get 'em, fuck-boy."

"No plan? We have a *damn* fine plan. Should we go over it again?" Jack needled his friend.

"If you want," Tc'aarlat groaned.

"I just want us both to be on the same page," Jack replied. "No offense, Tc'aarlat, but sometimes your mind wanders."

"What?" Tc'aarlat asked. He had let his mind wander. "Sorry, I faded out there for a second."

"Listen up." Jack leaned into him, laying out the plan with overexaggerated hand gestures to keep the Yollin's attention. "I, disguised as Draven, am going to go into the building and search for one of those injectors while doing my best not to draw attention."

Tc'aarlat nodded. "It's simple and easy to remember, one of our better plans."

"You, Tc'aarlat, are going to create a diversion if I call for help so I can escape. Got it?"

"Jack, come on. It's not pocket science."

"I'm already regretting this." Jack took a deep breath and rubbed his fingers against a growing headache. "Warn me if there's any danger, like mobs of officers heading my way, okay?"

"You got it. While you're in there, do you mind if I go and grab some lunch?"

Jack stared at him. "Yes. I mind."

After a few more deep breaths and much trepidation, Jack, his Draven mask firmly in place, headed toward the headquarters. He strode briskly. People who walk fast tend to look like they know what they're doing, like they're on a mission. Tc'aarlat used an outside ladder to get to the roof of the building across the road.

Jack slowed to let another employee go ahead of him.

"Sorry." Jack smiled as he pushed in beside her before the door closed, hoping his mask hadn't slipped.

The woman rolled her eyes. "That's okay, Draven. Stop forgetting your ID card."

Jack shook his head and threw his hands up in response.

He was in, and seeing no other way to navigate, he decided to follow the stranger in front of him. The woman led him through the headquarters, doing an admirable job of ignoring him. People gave him strange looks, which suggested Jack had gone where Draven was not a frequent visitor.

Eventually, they reached a large room with a series of work cubicles. Jack shuddered at the setup. The woman headed to a desk he assumed was hers. That left Jack to adopt a different course of action. He strode confidently to a small area where coffee had been set out. He took half a cup to carry around because with the mask, there was no way he was going to attempt to drink it.

He held his cup in two hands and meandered through the cubicle wasteland, searching for Maynard's desk. Jack saw a saucy calendar that depicted a Malatian woman getting raunchy with a water hose. He strolled there to find the terminal labeled Draven Maynard. The desk was covered with small model spaceships, a commemorative glass from the Picky Pouncer, and most egregiously, a framed holophoto of Draven in a club, cool as a cucumber, with his arms around four scantily clad women.

Jack saluted the cube dwellers with his coffee cup before sitting down.

A neighbor leaned in behind Jack, making it clear why

there was a small mirror attached to the top of the monitor. "Since when did you start drinking coffee?"

"Fuck off," Jack grumbled.

"Same old, Draven, a sparkling personality in the morning. Maybe it's good you've taken up a relationship with sad bean-water."

"Busy." Jack waved dismissively over his shoulder. When the coast behind him was clear, he started his search through the drawers and then the file drawers.

It's not here! Jack thought after his search, although he helped himself to an ID card in the top drawer, probably one of the last things tossed in. Jack thought it was a little unusual. It was charred and scratched to hell, so much so that he couldn't make out any of the details. The card was lying on top of a log of access entries. Jack put both in his pocket in case they were useful, and as he was thinking about his next move, a blinding light flashed in his eyes.

"DRAVEN!" Jack turned in his chair to find Mikhail May marching toward him. A number of heads popped over their cubicle walls to see what was going on. Jack couldn't shake the feeling that he was about to become a spectacle. "Where the hell have you been?"

"Uh, I...busy," Jack stammered before thanking the engineers that the mask came with a voice modulator. "I'm sorry, sir?"

"Get in my office, now." Mikhail pointed the way. "We're going to have a serious conversation about your conduct."

. . .

Frontier Zone, City Station Hopefill, Rooftops near WRU Headquarters

Tc'aarlat could see the cubicle farm through the upper windows and had been watching when Mikhail May appeared behind Jack. They walked together toward Mikhail's office, which was in a part of the building where there were no windows. Tc'aarlat decided he would have to wait. It wasn't time to create a diversion.

For a few moments there was nothing, then from the corner of his eye, he spotted a hovervan. *The* hovervan. The one he and Jack had ridden in with the other WRU werewolf agents.

The van settled to the ground at the front entrance. There were three people inside, people he recognized: Tinio, Rola, and the big guy, Reward. They were talking to one another animatedly. Acting on instinct, Tc'aarlat rushed across the rooftop toward them, trying to maneuver himself into a position where he might be able to hear what they were saying. The Yollin leaned close, but the windows were up, and the muffled sound from within was unintelligible.

Tc'aarlat could feel that something was up. He raced to the ladder and climbed down, jumping the last three meters, and he maneuvered close to the van until he could lean against it.

"Why is it our responsibility to take her in?" Rola was saying. "Why are we doing her dirty work? The WRU isn't her private army?"

"Well, for one thing, we want to stay off the menu," Tinio replied. "Not to mention the big payday."

"Sorry, but I've got to agree with Tinio," Reward added.

"She may not be the friendliest of people, but she *is* paying us to put up with her crap."

"Anyway, can we get inside now before someone sees us?" Tinio asked. "You never know who could be listening."

"Fine!" The doors popped open. Tc'aarlat ran for it before they were outside. He rounded the corner and stopped, pressing himself against the building. He leaned close to the corner but not around it.

He heard the footsteps as the group headed for the entrance. Rola continued talking. "I was just saying that it's going to look unusual when the three of us show up out of nowhere. Won't anyone ask questions?"

"They won't care," Tinio replied. "Not as long as we're taking in rogue werewolves."

"We have to capture her quickly," Tinio said. "If we don't, she could escape, and we'll really be up shit creek."

"It seems like the risk isn't worth it," Rola replied. "What if Mikhail asks?"

"We'll say we were in the area," Reward said. "Sorry, didn't mean to interrupt."

"No, you're dead-on," Tinio said. "In fact, we'll mention to him now that we're going to the café, and when it happens, we'll be—"

Tc'aarlat didn't catch the last word. The three WRU agents flashed badges at the access pad and entered the building.

He had no idea what they were talking about, but their conversation had given him useful insight. Those three were in someone else's pocket. He was sure of that now, but the question was whose?

"Maybe it'll be worth following them?" Tc'aarlat said to

himself, going back to the roof. "If Rubber Gut gets a damned move on and gets that injector."

Frontier Zone, City Station Hopefill, WRU Headquarters, Mikhail's Office

Jack marched past the many eyes of intrigued employees. He chose the lowest profile option, which meant he clasped his hands above his head and shook them as if crossing the finish line first and celebrating his victory. He pointed at people and gave the thumbs-up until the office workers ducked their heads to keep the big boss from seeing them laugh.

Jack-as-Draven and Mikhail entered an office that seemed more like a hunter's lodge than an executive's office. The décor included portraits of noble men with pistols and hunting rifles. Shadow-boxed weapons hung between the portraits. Mikhail kicked the chair opposite his desk and gestured with his chin for Jack to sit. Mikhail took the seat at his desk, right behind a miniature guillotine that was impossible to miss.

"Draven, you've got some nerve." Mikhail stared at Jack, daring him not to blink. "You haven't been showing up for work, and when you do, you fail your missions. When I first headhunted you from the En-D, I asked you if you were willing to put in the work and you said you were. What's happened?"

"I, uh, don't know sir," Jack croaked. "I guess I'm just—"

"Is this about Nathan Lowell and his *Shadows*?"

Jack eyed him, curious. He no longer wanted to play

defense; he wanted to know what was going on. "What do you mean, *sir?*"

"Don't deny that you haven't been a bit distracted with Nathan's golden boys. The En-D are having such trouble that they're bringing in outsiders to solve their problems, which highlights everything going on. Do you think Lowell is going to be happy when he finds out we have werewolves? Bah! You're falling into it."

"The Shadows have a good record," Jack said. "But they're candy asses. Ignore those lame fucks, just like I'm doing. I'm working on the exploding building case, and here you are giving me a ration of shit. You pull me in here to do, what, give me a bunch of shit for not doing what you are keeping me from doing? Fuck off! I got shit to do." Jack stood up.

Mikhail stood and thrust his chest out. "Sit the fuck down, dick."

"Fine. Say your piece, and let's get it over with." Jack crossed his arms and tried to make his mask face look angry.

"The Shadows aren't the issue. It's what they can tell Nathan Lowell that is. The werewolf menace threatens the city and it's only getting worse. We've all got to chip in. It's only a matter of time before something serious happens." He leaned back and kicked one foot onto his desk. "Did I ever tell you how I lost these arms?"

"I don't believe so," Jack replied, all ears since he had been wondering that ever since they had met in the interview room.

"My son was a werewolf," he replied. "Good boy. Strong. One day he starts snarling for no reason, and a second later, I'm being eaten as a midnight snack. He ripped off both of my arms when I tried to stop him, and it was only through pure luck that I survived the encounter by cauterizing the wounds on the stove. It was touch and go after my maids found me unconscious and the stove still on. They got me to a doctor."

Jack was on the edge of his seat. "What happened?"

"My family used to be hunters back on our homeworld, and this is going back to primal times when we weren't all zipping off to space. The hunting gene is in me and strong."

"Why didn't you replace your arms with bionics?" Jack asked. "Surely that would be easier than this?"

"I don't trust that technology trash. It can be hacked too easily." Mikhail curled his lip.

"Did you ever see him again? Your son, that is?"

Mikhail nodded. "Yeah, when he was taken to the Ice Blocks. He's still in there, waiting for a cure because being a werewolf is a disease. Do you know what the point of that story was, Draven?"

Jack shook his head. Mikhail was talking, so no reason to interrupt.

"Werewolves are dangerous, even if they don't mean it, even if they simply can't control it," Mikhail said. "I don't want to see them killed, I want to see them cured, but until that happens, we can't have them on the streets posing a danger to the innocent. Just because they kill by accident doesn't mean we should allow it. We're here to protect people."

"What if there isn't a cure?" Jack asked. He knew werewolves were the product of nanocytes acting on Kurtherian-manipulated DNA. But he still didn't know how there could be such a thing as feral werewolves or any that wouldn't be under the control of the Federation. Then again, Adina had been a surprise. She wasn't the only one, and here was a whole city of werewolves who couldn't control their actions, unlike the rest of them throughout the Federation. Jack's face twitched under the mask as he wrestled with the dichotomy of what he knew versus what he was seeing.

"Then I hope they like the cold. Someone is capturing these wild werewolves, training them, and selling them to the drug gangs that plague the city. It's always been your team's responsibility to find out who. It's all very well and good bringing in werewolf after werewolf, but if we can't find a source it's pointless."

"I'm on it. I am confident there was a lead at the storage units where they tried to kill me, no one else. That tells me that I'm getting close. Give me a little more time."

"One last chance, Draven," Mikhail said. "Only one. You can leave now."

It took Jack a couple of moments to remember that he wasn't actually Draven.

With Mikhail away from the others, Jack had the opportunity to explore the building since he had been escorted into an area he would not have otherwise been allowed in.

Where would you keep the injectors with the special turning serum? Jack asked himself.

Frontier Zone, City Station Hopefill, Rooftops near WRU Headquarters

Tc'aarlat had lost track of Jack. Mikhail's office was out of his sight, and from there, it was impossible to tell where Jack had gone. The Yollin cursed the situation until he found a new subject to watch. Tinio was in the room full of cubicles and was talking to a few people.

"I wish I could read lips," Tc'aarlat said, paying close attention to their body language rather than their words. A riot of emotions was playing over Tinio's face as he discussed something with another agent in the room. Tc'aarlat recognized confusion even on that ugly mug, but it went from that to disdain and finally to rage. Tinio grabbed Rola and Reward, pulled them to the side, and gave them a series of angry commands punctuated by wild gestures. They split up and headed beyond the windows where Tc'aarlat couldn't see.

There was only one explanation for why they'd suddenly go on the offensive; they knew that there was an intruder in the building, and Tc'aarlat had no doubt they knew who it was. He didn't know how.

He just knew.

Tc'aarlat rubbed his temples, his mandibles clicking as he tried to decide what kind of distraction he could make to help Jack get out of the building.

He made his decision and jumped off the roof, parkouring his way to the bottom by bouncing from ledge to ledge. He hit the ground with a roll, came up fast, and ran toward the WRU building.

Frontier Zone, City Station Hopefill, WRU Headquarters

The room had been easier to find than Jack had expected. The only problem he had was getting into it since it was secured by a vault-like door that was only accessible from an ID pad. He knew he had the right place, though. That was obvious from the sign on the front which read ARMORY. There would be no beating his way inside for this one. Neither could he trick the computer system itself into thinking he was Draven. Jack would have to find another way.

He rested his back against the door, deep in thought, and almost missed the figure watching him from the end of the hall.

Tinio. The ragged-faced brute marched toward him, and Jack couldn't help noticing that his hands were curled into fists. At first, he thought that they were going to fight, but when Tinio saw that Jack wasn't reacting, he calmed down considerably.

"Draven," he said with a wide smile. "I wasn't expecting to see you in today."

Jack pushed off from the door. "Why is that?"

Tinio grinned, the kind of smile that told Jack he was hiding something. "I thought you were ill. You said you wouldn't be in all week."

"Funny, that," Jack replied. "I don't really get ill."

Tinio gestured to him with a half-laugh. "I guess you're right. Here you are, at work and all kinds of perky. Did you have any success with your latest lead?"

Jack knew this guy was testing him. That meant that if he didn't answer this right, he could expect a world of trouble to fall on him. Jack thought back to what he had seen in the office, particularly what he had seen in

Draven's desk drawer. "Do you mean the ID card I found?"

Tinio's grin dropped. Jack had him. As the guy got closer, Jack took the opportunity to look him up and down. There was an ID card hanging off his belt, the kind that might be able to get him inside the room.

He thought about a quick throwdown and taking the badge, but he wasn't sure he could take Tinio in a straight-up fight.

"Did you find out who that ID card belonged to?" Tinio stepped closer.

"I'm sorry?"

Tinio was as close as he could get, close enough that Jack could see his pupils dilating. "Did you find out who that ID card belonged to?"

"Not yet."

Jack tensed. Tinio reached out to grab him. A klaxon sounded, and with a woosh, fire retardant foam sprayed from the ceiling. Jack made a fist and reared back to deliver a knockout punch, but shouts and many pounding feet approached. Jack backed away, keeping his hands up in case Tinio came at him.

The entire floor's worth of employees waded through the foam toward them, past them, and down the corridor. Jack pressed against the wall but Tinio got caught up in the stampede. Jack snatched his badge as he moved down the hallway, finally surrendering and disappearing out the door.

Jack held Tinio's keycard to the access pad. The door popped and soundlessly moved toward him. Jack found himself in a vault filled with weapons and other items the WRU wished to keep secure.

The walls were lined with shelves holding everything from guns to gadgets and devices built to perform specific tasks. It was immaculate, unlike the rest of the WRU building, which was like an old-school law enforcement office.

Jack reached for a suitcase emblazoned with a medical emblem and pried it open. He was rewarded with an injector and a tube of liquid fitted to the top of it. The label said Humanize. Jack slipped the injector and vial into his coat and ran out the door and after the crowd.

Frontier Zone, City Station Hopefill, Rooftops near WRU Headquarters

Tc'aarlat hurried away from the window through which he had fired into the smoke detection system and set it off. He'd thought there'd be less foam and more water, but despite this place having the appearance of a planetary town, it was a space station, so foam was easier to come by than water.

He tried to get across the street and out of sight before the WRU employees and agents streamed out of the building.

The first ones rushed out to the street in a panic, administration types who weren't looking for a ne'er-do-well Yollin scampering into the shadows. Tc'aarlat raced up the ladder to the roof and resumed his position, scanning the crowd for Jack in his Draven mask.

Nothing.

Tinio! "You bastard!" Tc'aarlat whispered. The agent

was covered in foam. He found his compatriots Reward and Rola. They put their heads together before pushing their way through the crowd, hopping into their van, and speeding away, sending evacuees scrambling for cover.

A hand on Tc'aarlat's shoulder nearly sent him over the edge. He rolled to the side and lashed out with a leg in an attempt to drive the stranger away. "Draven!"

"Dumbass," Jack said in the modulated voice.

"Fuck, Jack! Give a guy a warning next time, will you? You almost got yourself killed."

"Almost. I could feel the warmth from your exploding heart and eyeballs, suggesting you were ready to pass out. You couldn't hear me walk across the roof?"

"Stealthy knuckle-dragging, ass-wiping dickface. Yes. That's you. Next time, maybe I *will* kill you, just to confirm that you shouldn't fuck with me."

Jack peeled the mask free. "That would put a damper on our relationship." He removed the injector from his jacket. "Got it. Let's go before someone finds out."

They hurried toward the ladder. "Did you pull the alarm?"

"Yeah. I saw those guys we met the other night, and I thought they might be after you," Tc'aarlat replied with an enthusiastic nod, spreading his arms nonchalantly to express his pride. "Pretty smart, right? You can say it. I know, I'm not playing with a full load of bocci balls."

"I agree," Jack said. "You *aren't* playing with a full load."

"Speaking of that trio, though, I managed to get an ear on a conversation they were having when they arrived," Tc'aarlat said. "They were talking about taking a girl, but not only that, they mentioned they were working for someone and they didn't want no-arm Mikhail to know. For a *she*."

"I made some discoveries of my own." Jack took out the ID card and handed it to Tc'aarlat to inspect. "That was in Draven's desk, I think it has something to do with what he was investigating, and get this—people haven't seen him for a while. Draven's disappeared."

"You think he fell into something?" Tc'aarlat asked. "Like, a deep hole. *Hopefully*."

"More like he became a real investigator, seeking the truth and not just using his position to rough people up." Jack snatched the card back. "I think he's in danger, and I guarantee Tinio had something to do with it."

"The three-headed wanksplats left in a hovervan, so we can't follow them, but we can look for them."

"They might know we're on to them," Jack suggested. "Tinio confronted me. He could tell I wasn't Draven. I don't think he knew who I was though."

"They said they were going to take that girl near a café," Tc'aarlat said. "No idea which one. I imagine there's a good few hundred cafés on the station."

"They might've already gone then." Jack let out a sigh and shook his head with a reluctant grimace. "We've got what we came here for, and we should follow the lead we have. Afterward, we can come back and keep an eye out for them."

Frontier Zone, City Station Hopefill, Dock 9, ICS *Hopeful*, the Recuperating Room

Naka-Lee stretched off her most recent form with a

yawn and moved past her tank with a yearning to get inside and recuperate from the tiring nature of dealing with humans and their ilk. She couldn't, not with her hectic schedule. She had much to do. Naka-Lee stepped from the comfort that this room provided and to the next room with the thrust of a lever on the door.

In its previous life, she had no doubt that the room was a storage unit of some kind, perhaps for the many tools and resources the engineers of the *Hopeful* had needed to ensure the engines continued service. In more recent weeks, it had been transformed into her own personal space, a little laboratory. Nothing impressive, but enough to serve her immediate needs.

Two individuals were there, one in a makeshift cell and the other strapped into a chair by metal bands. He had a face many people would notice moving down the street. Draven Maynard, the beautiful man-agent for the Wechselbalg Response Unit.

The one in the cell stood and watched with his hands behind his back as if he were a professor contemplating a class of miscreants. Naka-Lee glanced toward him, enough to let the man know that she knew he was still there.

"Lovely lady. Your methods continue to be barbaric. How I wouldn't enjoy demonstrating on you far more effective techniques for extracting information."

"Don Gan'Barlo. You are more than a small and insignificant soul." She changed form and became the one in the cell. "You see, you no longer matter at all."

"Then why am I still here? You must need me."

"I don't really, but in case I need to make a statement, I can execute you in public and toss your body before my enemies. I save you for that sole purpose. I trust you are eating well?"

"I think you should go fuck yourself."

"You say that as if you want to do me while I look like you. In essence, banging yourself. That's messed up, Don. Too bad you can't get professional help for your homo-erotic fantasies."

"When I get out of here, I'm going to kill you. The last thing you'll see is my gloating face. You'll regret keeping me alive." He kept his hands behind his back and watched her.

She flicked her hand as if chasing away a pesky fly. "No. I won't. You are a piece on the chessboard, nothing more than a pawn to be sacrificed at the right time." She continued her march toward the second captive. Don Gan'Barlo glared at her, helpless for the moment.

Draven Maynard flexed and pulled but he couldn't create enough space to work a hand free or even stretch his tortured muscles. Draven's good looks had lost their luster. His hair was matted with sweat and blood.

He looked like a man one step from death. He had lost weight, which was made obvious by his lack of a shirt, and his face wore the defeated look of a man that had suffered for too long. There was still resilience though, resistance to what was happening, probably borne by the nanocytes coursing through his blood.

Naka-Lee would have to break his defiance before he could serve her needs. Not that she minded. She had become very good at breaking dogs.

"How are we feeling today, Rex?" She moved close, casually running her fingers over the old-school medical instruments she had left on the nearby table to tease him. A surgeon's ransom in chrome and steel.

"My name's Draven, you fish-faced cow," Draven spat at her, but his mouth was dry and the words came out as a croak and a rasp.

Naka-Lee ignored the jibe and took one item from the table. Draven closed his eyes and fought an epic battle between the anticipation of more pain and the need to engage with a calm body.

She had used that item on him before. It was a pair of goggles that had what appeared to be blackened lenses, but on the inside, there were two screens designed for hypnotic suggestion. Departing his body and watching from the outside as his thoughts were reshaped made him want to scream.

"We can talk about this."

"Talking is not for wolves." Naka-Lee moved up to him and despite his resistance and jerking his head to foil her efforts, she placed the goggles over his eyes and flicked them on. His eyes popped open of their own accord. He was already losing control.

His body went from squirming and struggling to eerily still, as if the goggles had taken away his desire to fight back. "Unfortunately, I don't have the facilities to get any real work done, but for now, these goggles should do."

There was a knock on the door, and before Naka-Lee could turn around, Crow stepped across the threshold. She stopped him with a scowl. "What do you want, Crow?"

"There's rumblings through the city that the Red Scythes are planning on moving in on our territory," Crow said. "Some of the boys, me included, were thinking that they might have more firepower than us, and we're a werewolf down right now."

"Maybe if someone brought me more werewolves before the WRU got to them?" Naka-Lee said. "Maybe then I'd be a little more productive."

"They're constantly a step ahead, and we—"

"Don't worry, you still outnumber the other gangs," Naka-Lee waved dismissively. "I know. I sold them their wolves."

"I'd still prefer our chances with another—"

"You'll get another wolf when the time is right," Naka-Lee snapped. She pointed at Draven, frozen in place on the chair he was bound to. "Is that all you wanted?"

"No, there's something else. I'm taking a few of the boys to make a first strike on the Red Scythes, teach them not to mess with the gang. I'm leaving a few here for defense, so don't be surprised when you see fewer around."

"That doesn't matter to me anyway," Naka-Lee replied. "I won't be here to find out. I have another appointment I need to keep in a couple of hours."

"Appointment?"

Don Gan'barlo watched the exchange intently. Crow gave him the finger.

"It doesn't concern you."

Frontier Zone, City Station Hopefill, Dock 23, Freight Bay F, ICS *Fortitude,* **Jack's Room**

The moment Jack's foot crossed the threshold of the ship, Solo appeared on a nearby screen with troubling news. Theo had escaped. Jack set his gun to stun and rushed around the ship despite Solo's assurance that Theo was not on board. He returned to the room where Theo had been held to stare at the emptiness.

Tc'aarlat readied the injector to address the werewolf. Tc'aarlat accepted Theo's escape for what it was and prepared for yet another chase, if need be. In the interim, they had a werewolf to break free from its anthropomorphic state.

The only thing of Theo's that remained was his amazing odor, the kind of aroma that could only be obtained from years of living on the streets. Jack plonked himself down on the bed.

"Fuck." The word was simple but effective, an accurate representation of the way Jack was feeling right now.

Solo appeared on screen and for the first time in a while, Jack experienced the motherly nature of the face on that screen. He was staring into the face of an AI who used his mother's image, which was surreal. "Is everything all right, Jack?"

"We were a great unit." Jack looked at her, needing to get it out and not caring who it was to. "I know it's easy to look back on the mistakes and focus on those, but it was only *one mistake*. A big mistake, sure, but still only one. Together we toppled terrorism and rooted out Dark Tomorrow wherever we could find them, and the missions were successful. We worked together for years and in that time, the whole unit became more than friends; we were family. I know a lot of people say that about old groups, but it doesn't make it any less true."

"I can imagine it's hard seeing someone you care about go through a hardship like Theo's."

"Theo is my brother," Jack said. "I love that guy. Theo was funny, witty, and man, could he throw a punch. I remember the first time I ever met him, right after he'd completed training. I was thinking to myself that this guy was going to go much farther than me. Theo was gonna go beyond, be better than the rest of us knuckle-draggers."

"Now he is addicted to Eternity," Solo said. "There are facilities on Hopefill City for drug rehabilitation. In fact, there are—"

"He'll never do it. He's already at the bottom of that rabbit hole. If it has a bottom, that is." Jack waved her off. "I can't blame him, either. I know what's happened to him. That doesn't mean I should stand by and do nothing; that guy hasn't had anyone to care about him for a long time.

But now he has me. I've got to find him. I've got to. I have to help him because if I don't, no one else will."

"He was very clear that he didn't want your help. He will fight you."

"I know. He can't help it. But I have to win that fight. I have to get him the help he needs."

Jack stood up and left the room, resolute in his stride. When he was gone, a hand reached out from under the bed, Theo crawled out of his hiding place and stood up. The vagabond had heard everything Jack had said, and although he had been touched by his words, Eternity's call was far stronger.

"I'm sorry, Jack," Theo whispered as he snuck through the open door. "I think you're a bit too late to help me."

"Please be safe," Solo said. Theo looked at her.

"What?" he enquired to the air. "Why are you letting me go?"

"I have been studying you for these past few days Theo," Solo replied. "Correlating your actions to the various studies I have found on drug behavior. I believe you can be made clean with one trip to the Pod-doc, and I believe you can stay clean."

"Then why not tell Jack that?" Theo waited at the door, ready to bolt.

"This last step is something you must do on your own, according to the research. You do not need those drugs; you can turn it all around."

Theo wanted to laugh, but he didn't. He frowned instead before turning away. "You're wrong."

. . .

Frontier Zone, City Station Hopefill, Dock 23, Freight Bay F, ICS *Fortitude*, Tc'aarlat's Room

Myst squawked up a storm on Tc'aarlat's shoulder as he waited for Jack to arrive. The Yollin had prepared the injector and was ready to get into it, while his Raal hawk was eager to get back to her perch in a room where Tc'aarlat had not been spending much time lately. He gave her a loving stroke while whispering in her ear, "Calm down, we'll be back in our room soon."

"Sorry about that." Jack walked up, shaking his head in frustration. "My reluctant guest has done a disappearing act on me."

"That does not surprise me," Tc'aarlat replied. "That guy did not want to be here."

"Yeah, well, I'll find him again," Jack said. "Speaking of disappearing acts, have you seen Adina?"

"No, but I know she's meeting up with her swept-mother," Tc'aarlat replied. "She'll probably be gone all day."

"*Step*-mother," Jack corrected. "Not swept. Where are you getting swept from?"

"Like she swept in and took her mother's place?" Tc'aarlat primed the injector. "We doing this? Or are we going to argue about what words are correct and incorrect again?"

"No, let's get this over with," Jack said, eager to move forward. "Before the WRU arrives."

They took their places at the door, ready to rush in. "Solo, a quick look inside, please."

The screen showed the werewolf crouched in the middle of the room, ready to launch itself at the door.

"New plan," Jack said. He pulled his Jean Dukes Special

and set it to the lowest stun setting, one. He aimed at the doorway, checked the wolf again, and nodded to Tc'aarlat. He waved his hand in front of the pad. Jack fired the instant the door popped, catching the wolf mid-leap.

Tc'aarlat lunged forward to drive the injector into the beast's side, but the creature twisted in mid-air.

Jack fired again. Tc'aarlat fell back as the werewolf hit the deck and jumped on top of him. Jack hit it once more and the wolf teetered and fell over. Tc'aarlat pushed himself out from under the massive beast, picked up the injector, pleased that it hadn't activated, and plunged it into the heavy leg muscles. The spring sent the dose through the needle and into the creature. Tc'aarlat stepped back, eyes wide.

Nothing happened.

"That was disappointing," Jack said. "No, wait…"

They watched as the transformation started, increasing in speed.

The head started to shrink and the muzzle retracted into a rounding face. Out came a tuft of auburn hair and a beard to match. A human, with tattoos in place of fur.

When all was said and done, they were looking at the man they had seen earlier, before he changed back. His eyes were wild and frightened. Burn marks reached across his skin like a giant's fingers. There was no denying this stranger had been tortured. He had a hard time getting off the floor from the combination of getting stunned and a forced transition.

"Wh-where am I?" the stranger questioned. "Wh-who are you?"

"It's okay, friend," Jack said, lowering his gun and

moving closer. "I'm Jack, this is Tc'aarlat. We're not going to hurt you."

"Then what are you going to do with me?"

"We want to ask you a few questions." Tc'aarlat stepped forward. "That's all. After that, you're free to go."

"Free to go?" He rolled the word *free* around in his mouth. "I can't. She'll come for me."

"What's your name?" Jack asked. "Where are you from?"

"I'm Chalky," the stranger replied. "I'm from Hopefill City. Oh, God, this *is* Hopefill City, isn't it?"

"It is. You're home," Jack assured him, then took a step back. "Tc'aarlat, can you get our guest some clothes, please?"

"He won't fit in mine," the Yollin replied, nodding at Jack.

"You hungry?" Jack asked. Chalky shot his gaze straight past Jack at Tc'aarlat, his eyes filled with all the hunger in the world. "I'll take that as a big fat yes. Tc'aarlat, get him something to eat while I get a jumpsuit from my quarters."

Chalky didn't seem to care that he was naked. He didn't seem to care about much except that some woman would come for him if he stepped outside *Fortitude*.

Frontier Zone, City Station Hopefill, Commercial Zone 12, Shopping District

For all the troubles in the station, it had great prospects for tourists. The downtown area had hundreds, if not thousands, of stores. Hopefill was a crossroads of trade, even though it was at the edge of Federation space.

It was a maze of shopping; one you could easily get lost

amidst the flashing signs and iridescent windows with neon mascots to entice potential customers inside.

Turned out it was exactly what Adina had needed. Since she had joined the Shadows, she had earned a decent wage, but one big problem was finding a place to spend her credits. There was the occasional visit to a world that carried decent goods like Talth, but they had been working, and it felt out of place to go shopping. Now Adina had a chance and she was taking it, going on a major-league shopping tour, leaving other thoughts behind as she refreshed her wardrobe along with other items both necessary and frivolous to spruce up her quarters and the whole ship.

Searching high and low in every shop she thought might have something worthwhile, Adina eventually came upon a cute sweater with a kitten logo on it. The knitwear had a button on the nose that when pressed, brought the kitten to life in a hologram, something that could be played with. If she knew Kirandeep's tastes, and hopefully the kitten café was a good indication of that, her stepmother would love this.

In high spirits about her purchases, Adina elected to take a hovercab to the café and made great time because of it. She was an hour early, but just in time to show her appreciation to Kirandeep for all the effort she had put in to reunite them. Adina paid the fare, grabbed her bag, and moved toward the café.

It was hard to ignore the surroundings as she strode toward the door. Kirandeep had picked a good spot. Across the way was a public park with the flowers her future stepmother had mentioned. They covered its breadth, between the trees and across the grass, in skillfully tended flowerbeds. Beyond, people were bustling by, kids played on the trees, and dogs acted as could be expected. This café was directly opposite on a quiet road, with a seating area outside where people could watch.

Adina shook herself out of her reverie and pushed open the door to head inside. It was old-fashioned and picturesque. It made her feel like she was stepping into a darling saloon run by someone's grandmother. Oak was the theme of the day, from the furniture to the walls, and it was hard to miss the beams that ran across the ceiling. Adina hadn't thought they made buildings like this anymore.

Despite the appearance, she moved past tables upon tables of patrons enjoying coffee or tea to the counter. There she was greeted by a friendly face, a man she thought might be a decade younger than herself. His nametag said Anthony and she made a note of it, along with an engorged mole that was like a fat leech on his neck.

"Hello there. How can I make you smile?" he asked politely.

"I'd really like a coffee," Adina replied. He turned to a coffee machine, twirling a cup. "Is Kirandeep around?"

"Sorry?" He turned and pricked up his ears.

"I said, is Kirandeep around?" Adina repeated louder. "I know she owns the café, and I'm supposed to be meeting her here."

"I haven't seen her for a couple of weeks," said Anthony, pouring the hot liquid in her mug. "We thought she'd gone on vacation or something."

"What do you mean?" Adina asked. "I thought she was the owner?"

"She is," he replied, handing her a cup of hot java. "It's just she hasn't been around lately. Kirandeep has kind of left us to get on with it. Usually she comes in every day, but lately…"

"Is it unusual not to see her?" Adina enquired. "When was the last time?"

"About two weeks ago," Anthony said. "Nothing since."

"She said she was checking on this place today after she stopped by yesterday?"

"That's news to me." Anthony shrugged. "If you see her, tell her April needs to talk to her about the books. She's been going mad trying to sort out the expenses."

Adina took the mug thoughtfully, and as a result, half-assed her response. "Yeah, no worries."

Once again, her thoughts returned to the night she had met her father for the first time in years, Kirandeep had disappeared to go to work. Adina didn't know many cafés that were open at that time, but she assumed it had been administrative: doing the books, getting payroll done, that kind of thing. Now she wondered if there wasn't something more to that.

Frontier Zone, City Station Hopefill, Dock 23, Freight Bay F, ICS *Fortitude*, Galley

They sat around the small table in the galley, with Chalky across from Jack and Tc'aarlat. Jack couldn't remember the last time he had seen someone so hungry, and he waited politely but eagerly for Chalky to finish. Finally, the scrawny gentleman swallowed the last of his second sandwich and leaned back in his seat.

"I can't tell you how much I needed that," Chalky said. "It's exhausting being forced to be a werewolf all the time."

"I can only imagine," Jack replied. "You up for a few questions?"

"You guys saved my life," Chalky said. "If it weren't for you, I'd still be at the wrong end of a bistok prod."

"Always nice when we don't have to torture someone for information," Tc'aarlat said. "My first question is, what the hell? The werewolves are considered to be feral, but here you are, not a caveman at all. You sound educated."

Jack eyed the Yollin. He wasn't wrong, but it sounded odd coming from Tc'aarlat.

"I can't remember much, but I can tell you it's been a while." Chalky sat up and drew his chair forward. "I was a druggie. Am a druggie, I don't know. I think I might be clean now because the urge is gone. Anyway, I got approached by the Silver Diamonds. They'd found out I was a werewolf and offered me a whole lot of Eternity in return for a favor. It was better than selling body parts, or that's what I thought at the time."

Jack stared intently at the man wearing one of his jumpsuits. "What kind of favor?"

"They wanted me to kill someone for them since I was a werewolf and all. I agreed to do it and they took me toward the back."

"It was a trick." Tc'aarlat pounded a fist on the table. "I'm calling it."

"Don't interrupt the man." Jack nudged his friend with an elbow, but it bounced off Tc'aarlat's carapace.

"No, he's right," Chalky replied. "They took me through to that huge but derelict ship they use as a base for their operations, and in the back there was this woman. Except she wasn't a woman, she was a fish. Like, a fish woman."

Tc'aarlat leaned forward and took a deep breath. "Did they give you drugs before they took you back to their base?"

"No, I saw her," he replied. "Next thing I know, I'm being strapped to a chair and hypnotized or something. It was that woman; she brainwashed me. I remember going wolf, turning and changing, but then everything becomes fuzzy. I can remember trying to change back, but every time I did, I got a shock from a collar around my neck. Eventually I wasn't thinking at all, I was just...feral, like you said."

"*MIND CONTROL!*" Tc'aarlat shouted, making everyone around the table jump. "Knew it! Fucking *knew* it!"

Jack rolled his eyes and tried to stay on track. "Is that all you can remember? Nothing else?"

"It's all really fuzzy. Sorry, guys."

"Don't be sorry. You've given us good information. Do you think you could take us to that base you mentioned? You remember where it is? And were there any others there? Like, how many people will we find?" Jack leaned back, not expecting to get anything else worth hearing, but he had to ask.

Chalky shook his head. "I'm not going back there. It's easy to find. It's the biggest ship on Dock 9. Derelict, but the access is open but guarded. I'd say there were at least a dozen gangbangers there, probably a lot more. I didn't see very much of the ship before they strapped me down. Oh, there was some dude in a cell to the side in the big room where they worked on me. Some dude named Don."

Tc'aarlat's bolted upright. "Don Gan'barlo?"

"Yeah, that's it. She seemed to take great pleasure in taunting him, making him watch what she was doing."

"Why does she have the Don as a captive? He's not a werewolf."

Chalky shook his head and shrugged.

"Solo." Jack turned to the screen in the galley and it came on with a flourish, with Solo awaiting his commands. "What do you have on fish people? Any potential races this woman could be?"

"There are hundreds of races that fit that descriptor in the galaxy, Jack. You'll need to be more specific."

Tc'aarlat turned to Chalky. "Anything else? Come on, think."

"Uh, she was golden," Chalky said, thinking fast. "Like a big goldfish."

"Mutanaraian." Solo said the word easily. "There are many fish-like races in the galaxy, but only one that resembles the Earth goldfish in appearance when they are in their natural state."

"This Mutanaraian is enslaving werewolves," Jack said. "I think we've just found where these rogue wolves are coming from. They're being trained like dogs to kill for gang warfare. Mikhail was right; it *is* someone in the city. What else can you tell us about Mutanaraians, Solo? Any weaknesses?"

"Mutanaraians have a remarkable ability to change their form," Solo said. "They can appear as any person as long as their target shares similar aspects. Same height, width, and skin tone. They're mostly known for being shape-changers. As for weaknesses, they have a preference for being in water."

"Well, fuck," Jack exclaimed. "That means this person could be anyone. Hell, we might've already met her."

"I bet if we could capture her, she'd know who Bloody Darling is. I think we know what we need to do. It's clear to me." Tc'aarlat crossed his arms.

"Then make it clear to the rest of us," Jack requested.

"The woman is Bloody Darling and by using the Don's assets, she has built her own empire, a monopoly. I bet she is the sole importer of Eternity. She is the one we've been looking for. Take her down and we accomplish our mission. Take her down, and we can face Don Gan'barlo. I can't wait to give him a knuckle lasagna."

"I didn't hear a plan. Are we going to walk into a gang's fortress and hope for the best?" Jack asked.

"First day with the Shadows?" Tc'aarlat asked. Jack closed his eyes. The Don. Bloody Darling. A gang and a fortress. They needed an army and a better plan.

1 5

Federation Hopefill City, Commercial Zone 8, The Sweet Surron Café

Adina had been sitting in the outside space, watching people in the park and thinking about her father, trying to recall the good times they had as a family. The clock was quickly running past the time they had arranged to meet, and she could see no sign of either Kirandeep or her father.

Adina started to feel sick from the anticipation. Had she been abandoned again? Deep down, she thought she might have made a mistake; that maybe she already had everything she needed when it came to her father. She doubted they could have a real relationship. Maybe this would be a final goodbye instead.

When Kirandeep came around the corner, her hair was wild, the same as her smile. She hurried to the café, where she took the seat opposite Adina. She tried to apologize, but her words were lost in a flurry of nonsense.

Adina had crossed her arms and leaned back to take in the woman who ran a series of restaurants, yet couldn't string two words together when she was late. What was the woman who was to be her stepmother hiding?

"Sorry I'm late again," Kirandeep finally managed to say with a strained chuckle. "I swear, these cafés are giving me the runaround."

"Where have you been?" Adina asked. "Aren't you the owner of these places? So if anyone is giving you the runaround…"

"I was checking in here, but I got called away to one of the others," Kirandeep replied. "It's like they can't run without me. I'm sorry you came here and couldn't find me. This café is off the beaten path and the manager keeps it on track. I only need to check in on occasion to give him a pat on the back."

"Aren't you the manager?"

"No, I'm the owner," Kirandeep replied and half-laughed. "What, did you think I ran *all* of these cafes by myself? I wish I had the time."

"The other night when you said you had to go to work," Adina questioned. "Wasn't it a bit late to—"

Kirandeep interjected with a short chortle. "I wasn't going to work, dear. It was just an excuse to leave you and your father alone. I thought you two might need that to get started."

"Yeah, I suppose that makes sense." She pushed the bag across the table and Kirandeep took it eagerly. "Here, I got you this. It's just a little thank you for all the effort you've gone to."

Silently, Adina agreed that *was* a good explanation for why she had gone missing, but she still had a feeling, a suspicious feeling, that something was wrong. She tried to drive the thought from her mind, but it refused to go. Perhaps her time with the Shadows was making her mistrust every stranger she met. She took another sip of her now-cooling coffee.

Kirandeep opened the bag and pulled out the sweater. She squealed in such a high tone of voice that Adina had to put a finger to her ear. The woman hugged it to her chest, apparently over the moon. "Oh, my goodness, this is so lovely. Oh, thank you, Adina. This is such a thoughtful gift!"

"It's no problem," Adina replied casually. "Just wanted to show my appreciation. You seem to be trying to make things right. Speaking of which, where's my father? Is he going to be here soon?"

"I'm sure he'll be here shortly. For now, though, I'm happy talking with you."

Adina nodded. She was there, Kirandeep was there. Might as well make the best of it.

The conversation was light between the two of them. Occasionally they would laugh at a joke, and the banter came with plenty of questions. Kirandeep asked about the Shadows, and Adina related some of her adventures, then Kirandeep acted amazed. Adina had to admit she was having a good time with her future stepmother, but she couldn't help feeling the absence of her father, and eventually it became too much.

"Where is he?" Adina checked the clock on the wall. "It's been over an hour."

"I'm afraid I told you a fib." Kirandeep blushed. "He isn't going to be here today. In fact, he doesn't even know we're meeting."

"What?" Adina was furious.

"I know a teensy little secret about you, Adina. Something I don't think you even know yourself, and well, I didn't think it was prudent to bring your father in on it."

Adina looked around, confused. "I'm sorry?"

"It's this." Kirandeep rummaged through her purse and pulled out a small device, one Adina recognized as a data disk, before throwing it toward her. Adina picked it up carefully and studied it. "There's information on there that you don't want to be made public. The fact that you are a werewolf."

Adina exhaled with a low growl. "The people who care about me already know, and those who don't, don't matter. If you don't mind, I'll be on my way, you fucking bitch."

"You're not going anywhere." Kirandeep pointed to Adina's seat. The happy-go-lucky café owner was gone, replaced by a cold and calculating harpy. "An individual named Benjamin recorded a video suggesting that you turned into a werewolf and slaughtered fifty people on a planet called Renasta."

"No, that wasn't me." Adina knew what she was talking about. Back on Renasta, they had found fifty villagers ripped apart. She had thought it was her fault, that she had done the killing because her werewolf side was unstable. Jack and Solo had assured her it had been another race of technological beings called the Onbir and her hands were clean. It all made sense now. "Jack said it was—"

"He was lying," Kirandeep said dismissively.

"Who are you? What's your role in all of this?"

"I'm an agent for the WRU," Kirandeep said. "I couldn't

just stand back and let you get away with it. Not this time, Adina."

"In one instant, you've destroyed any chance of a normal relationship," Adina snarled. "Damn you to hell. Do what you want with your little video. I'm out of here. I'll send a message to my father since I'm sure you won't tell him the truth, and I will reiterate my earlier point. You are a fucking bitch."

"I had to, Adina," Kirandeep replied. "By any means necessary."

Wendy's words came to her, that the En-D had taken in her uncle. That the day before he had been as healthy as he had ever been, then the next day he was dead. *By any means necessary.* She swallowed past the rising tension and asked the question she was most afraid to ask. "What do you mean, by any means necessary?"

"I feel like you already know," Kirandeep replied calmly. "We had to manufacture a way to bring you here, Adina. One that meant you would stay for a while. Something urgent you wouldn't say no to."

"*You...you...*" Adina's breath was frenetic as the fury rose within. All her meditation and self-control were shoved aside in an instant. There would be no stopping her. Kirandeep had killed her Uncle Youssuf, and for that, she deserved to die. Adina had the means to make it happen.

Frontier Zone, City Station Hopefill, Dock 9, ICS *Hopeful*

Theo didn't know what he was doing. He did it all the same.

What he had refused to tell Jack or Tc'aarlat was that he

knew where the Silver Diamonds kept their drug supplies, it was in a large ship known as the *Hopeful* that had been out of service for years. If the Silver Diamonds weren't interested in bartering for some Eternity, he would steal it and hope he didn't get caught.

The ship was easy to find. It stood out from the other derelicts, looking like nothing more than scrap until one got close enough. Inside was a maze of corridors and rooms that were nearly impossible to navigate. Luckily, Theo had been watching the ship for a long time, studying the comings and goings of the Silver Diamonds, and above all, he'd been listening. Being a homeless person didn't offer much, but it did allow a man to go unnoticed while others talked.

Theo could infer a lot about the *Hopeful* from the ramblings of the men he bought drugs from. One thing he knew was that there was a secured room filled with supplies, all their supplies.

The ship was guarded, that was true, and he had always preferred to pay for his Eternity rather than to steal it in fear of getting caught, but now he was looking to avoid both problems. Theo had that itch, that damned insatiable itch, and it was getting worse the longer he went without, even though the initial detox should have passed during the days he'd spent aboard *Fortitude*. Theo had gotten over the shakes a day ago. Gotten over the headaches too, but the urge that remained. The addict's demon. That voice that spurred him to make bad decisions.

Theo tactically moved to the top of a scrap pile nearby. He hadn't forgotten everything he'd been taught in the Force de Guerre and the Bad Company. He stayed low and out of sight, moved without shifting what was beneath his feet. From his perch, he had a better angle on the *Hopeful*, and he watched to confirm a secondary entrance to the ship. A secret entrance only used by a privileged few. A hole blasted through the outer hull during a space battle long ago.

Quietly he stole down from his perch and toward the access point. He maneuvered slowly through the junk in the yard because quick movements drew the eyes of the inevitable watchers wherever they were. Slow movements avoided unwanted attention. He moved half a step at a time, waited, moved again while exposed to imminent death should someone see him.

He breathed a sigh of relief when he was finally able to lean against the outer hull of the hulk. Inside the hole, a door had been installed. To its side was an access keypad. He used to be good at getting through technical obstacles. He hoped his refreshed mind would serve him in resolving the challenge.

Theo expected this wouldn't be the only puzzle he would have to solve. He was happy to work on it without someone shooting at him, unlike the old days with Jack. They had always been under fire, but they had laughed it off and shot back with bigger and better weapons.

He tore the cover off the pad and with a small piece of metal, cross-wired the elements while shorting the locking mechanism. The door popped.

When he stepped inside, Theo didn't know what to expect, but thought there would be no resistance since the access only opened for those who belonged there. He thought there might be people milling around, though.

The Silver Diamonds were the largest gang on Hopefill City. They controlled over half of the drugs going out to people like him, not to mention they controlled an equal number of werewolves. As he moved into the old ship, he realized there weren't many people inside. It took big numbers to be on the streets and rousting the locals.

Perhaps he had gotten lucky and arrived at an opportune time? He snorted quietly at the thought. He wasn't the sort who got lucky. He checked the overhead, expecting a guillotine blade to fall on him. That was the kind of fortune that fell his way.

With the absence of people came another problem: finding his way around. The *Hopeful* had been built to house thousands of passengers and crew. It was a massive beast with a labyrinth of corridors and multiple confusing decks. Theo meandered, searching for a clue that would take him closer to the supply room.

Finally, he heard footsteps. Theo moved silently into the shadows and waited. The single set of heavy steps suggested a gang member.

Theo decided on a course of action. When the steps came even with him, he launched from his hiding spot and pounded a fist into the person's solar plexis, driving the air from him. The man doubled over Theo's rising knee, snapping his head backward. The gang member fell. Theo relieved him of his pistol.

On the floor was a man, as big and furry as the rest of them with arms covered in urban-style tattoos, moaning from the violence done to his body. Theo stood up straight and looked down at him. "What stupid name have you got?"

"Derrick," the man grumbled, nursing his head with one hand. "Who the hell are you?"

Theo leaned close. "Where is the supply room where you store the Eternity? It would suck to die because you didn't tell me."

"I can't do that. Crow would—"

"I'd be more concerned with what I'm going to do to you if you don't tell me where it is. Way I see it, Crow isn't here. It's just you and me, and I've got your gun."

Derrick gasped something. As Theo leaned closer to hear, the man tried to grab him. Theo rotated his torso and delivered an elbow to Derrick's mouth.

"I'm not going to ask you again."

He nodded and pointed. "I have to show you."

"That's bullshit, but I don't think you want to die, and if you dick me, you'll die first and you'll die ugly, watching as I kill your buddies one by one."

With Derrick leading the way, the going was no longer haphazard. They turned back and forth through passageways, going up and down to get around areas that had been blocked by damage. They passed others based on the sounds Theo heard, but anytime they got close, he would pull Derrick back and throw his hand across his mouth to stop him from sounding the alarm. It was a slow process that only agitated him further, but eventually, after many turns and long corridors, they made it to the room he had heard so much about. Theo was standing in front of a large steel door with a wheel lock. He threw Derrick into it.

"Open the door."

"Listen, I can't," Derrick pleaded. "If Crow finds out, I'm

a dead man. He'll cut my head off. I've seen him do it to other guys."

"I can cut your head off right now if you want," Theo said. He didn't like playing this kind of role. His temper was usually much calmer, but he was being driven to the edge by his addiction and he could feel time running out, forcing him to resort to intimidation. "It's your choice."

The thug shook his head and stared at his feet. Theo chanced a look at the door. No lock, only the wheel.

"You know what, D-man? I don't want to go in there either. Why don't you show me the way out of here?"

Derrick smiled in relief. He took one step and pointed in a different direction from the one they'd come. Theo swung before he could change his mind, cracking his pistol across the man's skull. The sickening sound of a watermelon getting thunked preceded the body hitting the deck.

"Sorry," Theo told him before turning the wheel to unsecure the door. He pulled the door open slowly to look over the barrel of his weapon checking the space beyond.

Inside was Theo's paradise, number one on his list of dream getaways. The room was filled to the brim with tubes of Eternity, thousands of them. They lined a hundred shelves like little soldiers standing at attention. Theo threw himself into the room and started stuffing vials into his pockets, abandoning all reason as he did. Theo only stopped when he heard the door slam closed behind him. The wheel spun. On this side, there was nothing to spin. The interior wheel had been cut off.

Theo collapsed to the floor. "Fuck." He had no idea who'd closed the door, and it didn't matter. He'd been caught like a rat in a cage. Nowhere to go. At least there was light, pale like that of a full moon, but it was better than nothing.

"I-is someone there?" A female voice brought focus to his chaotic mind. Theo looked beyond the nearest shelves to where the voice had come from.

"Hello?" Theo called. There they were, right at the end of the aisle, two women. One had pale skin and blonde hair and the other was lying in a heap, unconscious and barely breathing.

Something awful had happened to the two of them, ending with them getting tied up. From their state of distress, Theo guessed they had been in here for a while. Theo hurried over to undo their bonds. The smell was horrible. They'd not been allowed anything and were soiled from head to toe.

"What's happened to you? Why are the Silver Diamonds keeping you prisoner?"

"It's not the Silver Diamonds," she said in reply. "It was a woman, a woman who looked just like me."

Theo untied her bindings and set her free, not that it would do much good for the whole minute she'd get to stretch her legs. "It's okay," he soothed. "We'll figure something out. I'm Theo, Theo Young. Who are you?"

"My name is Briona," the woman replied. "Briona Arnd."

"And her?" Theo nodded at the other woman, the one who did not look like she was in good shape.

"Her name is Kirandeep," Briona replied. "She needs help."

·　·　·

Federation Hopefill City, Commercial Zone 8, The Sweet Surron Café

Adina couldn't control the urge; it was too much. She breathed in and out slowly like she had been taught, but whenever she tried to clear her mind, she saw her conversation with Jack, her father's betrayal, and the fact that this woman had killed the last family member she had given a damn about.

Adina let go. Her nose and mouth became a snout while her forehead became more pronounced. The hair erupted from her skin as she went to all fours. The second her paws were on the ground, she launched at Kirandeep.

She roared her fury. Kirandeep dodged easily, as if she had superhuman speed and was well-trained in the martial arts. She ducked the next attack and sidestepped the one after that. Adina paused, her fury almost spent.

Kirandeep wasn't what she pretended to be. The woman was like a stream of water, ever graceful and never stopping, moving out of the way of each blow like she was born to it.

"Oh, Adina, what have you gotten yourself into?" Kirandeep asked. "Why did you kill all those people?"

Adina pushed harder. She *hadn't* killed those people. The Onbir had, and then they'd tried to kill the rest. She knew that.

"Everyone run!" Kirandeep shouted for all to hear, sending the people into a frenzy. "There's a werewolf on the loose! Run for your lives!"

She then ran across the road toward the park, and in her rage, Adina gave chase. The woman was fast, but Adina guessed she wasn't invincible. Kirandeep jumped for a nearby tree and grabbed a low-hanging branch. She swung around like a gymnast and threw herself upward to land on the next branch, standing upright and looking down at Adina, taunting her with her smile.

Adina didn't need such grace. She just needed to jump using her powerful legs. Soon she was among the branches, unsteady on her four paws but managing to stay upright. The mystery woman in the turtleneck sweater was gone.

Adina howled in frustration.

Kirandeep came out of nowhere, and Adina had no time to react as the woman had launched herself with the speed and agility of a master ninja. She kicked wolf-Adina in the ribcage. Adina, stumbled back, lost her footing, and fell out of the tree to hit the ground hard. The wolf was strong, but the pain was great. She regained her breath quickly, but it was too late.

She was surrounded.

Three WRU agents closed on her. Adina felt a prick in her hip, and a few seconds later, she was back to her old self, if a little dazed by the fight. The ugliest of the three forced her on her face and jerked her arms behind her back to snap heavy steel handcuffs on her wrists. He pulled Adina upright and plopped her on her feet.

Adina didn't have to wonder how they had gotten here so quickly.

A crowd of civilians appeared, and they were ugly too, hurling invective at the beast. Their fear found a target in Adina, and their relief heaped praise on the three WRU agents.

Adina looked over her shoulder to find Kirandeep smiling.

The woman marched up to her with a face like a cat that had caught a mouse, and Adina sneered at her.

"Adina, this is for your own good. For what it's worth, I'm sorry."

"What have you done with my father?" The van doors opened and rough hands tossed her inside like a common criminal. "Was any of this real?"

"Of course it was. I needed your father to carry out my plan," Kirandeep said. "He played the perfect part in keeping you distracted while I did what I had to do to keep the universe safe from the likes of you."

"Who are you?" Adina asked. "Really, I mean?"

"For now, let's just say I'm someone who has a lot to gain from you. You're going to be my prized possession."

"Just answer me one question, please," Adina said and Kirandeep leaned in to listen, loving the use of her word please. "Was my father in on any of this? Did he know what was going to happen?"

"Of course, dear. He knew everything," Kirandeep lied. Adina knew she was lying because of how she tried to sell it.

The doors shut, preventing any more conversation. Kirandeep rapped her knuckles on the door to let the agents know it was time to go. The hovervan pulled away. Adina didn't have to wonder where she was going. There was only one place on City Station Hopefill where rogue werewolves were taken: the Ice Blocks.

Frontier Zone, City Station Hopefill, Dock 9, ICS *Hopeful*, **Supply Room**

Theo didn't know how much time he had left, but he suspected there was precious little of it. After he finished untying Briona, he set to work on Kirandeep, and soon they were free to roam about the supply room. That was when the urge hit him, and he remembered where he was. With the distraction gone and Briona attending to the other woman, Theo returned to the shelves of drugs and began filling his pockets once more. The urge was strong; he needed to get high.

"What are you doing!" Briona barked. "We need to get out of here."

"There's no way out," Theo assured her. "We have a few minutes, maybe not even that, but there is plenty of time to get a few of these down and ride the torture through a grand delusion."

"Please, you have to help us," Briona pleaded with their savior.

Theo's eye started to twitch. He had the tubes in his hand; in a moment he could be high, his hunger sated, every desire granted. Theo couldn't remember the last time he'd had a responsibility like this. He also couldn't remember the last time he had been this lucid.

"I can't save you." Theo looked at Briona. "I can't do—"

THUD. THUD. THUD. The gang had arrived. He heard the wheel spin and the locks retract. Briona braced herself against the door as if that would keep them out.

Theo weighed the balance of each course of action: try to save the women, or lose himself in an Eternity stupor. Either way, he was going to die. One way would be painful, while the other would be painless. Except for the mortal cry from his very soul. It called to him now.

"Talk to me, Theo," Briona said, her back against the door. "Can you help us, or should we just give up like you? Do you know what they do to female captives?"

"I lost everything," Theo muttered. "I lost everything that I was, starting with Kayleigh. She was the love of my life. I can't. I can't go on being sober. I'm sorry."

Theo popped a vial and tipped his head back.

Briona started gasping for air, losing the fight to keep the thugs out. The door slowly moved inward. She screamed.

"Forgive yourself for fuck's sake and get over here!" Briona managed.

Theo dropped the vial and ran. He braced against the door and it stopped moving. Even through the thick metal, they could hear the cries of rage from those on the other side. Shouted orders were followed by a renewed effort. Theo leaned into the door and held tightly. Briona demonstrated a renewed surge of energy.

Theo saw with exceptional clarity. He could hear the voices beyond. He let go and stepped back. "Let them open the door," he said in a low and dangerous voice.

"Are you sure?" Briona asked. "We should look for—"

He aimed his pistol where the faces would look through. "Let it go. Now is the time to fight. Five men on the other side of this door, and I have eight bullets."

"Doesn't sound like good odds to me."

"You're right. They're going to need four more before things get interesting. Let it go."

Briona lifted her hands away and stepped back.

16

Frontier Zone, City Station Hopefill, Dock 9, ICS *Hopeful*

The thug faltered, tripping over his own feet and falling into the wall. A second thump of a weapon fired to stun sounded. The man slammed into the wall a second time and slid down it, slumping to the deck. Tc'aarlat brought the tip of the barrel to his mandibles and pretended to blow the excess smoke away like the cowboys he had seen in Jack's movies. JDS didn't produce smoke, but the result was the same.

Thanks to Chalky, they had found the *Hopeful* and the ramp leading inside, along with three guards protecting the entrance.

Jack and Tc'aarlat had made easy work of disabling them, removing them from the equation. Now they were faced with the enormous task of finding their way through the colossal ship.

"You sure you can lead us through?" Tc'aarlat asked their new best friend. "It's pretty big. Ha-ha! That's what *she* said."

Chalky grimaced but nodded. "I've been through here before, and it isn't something you forget."

"I just hope this isn't a wild Bruce chase," Tc'aarlat said.

"Wild *Bruce* chase?" Chalky questioned.

Jack grabbed his shoulder and gave him a slight shake of the head. "Don't get into it. You'll regret it."

"I know it isn't too far from here. I just need to get my bearings," Chalky told them.

As they moved through the derelict, the trio came to the conclusion that it was unusually empty. Every now and then they encountered an individual who they quickly dispatched through a double blast of two Jean Duke Specials on the number two setting.

Chalky led them through a series of twisting corridors and around obstructions, and eventually they worked their way toward the aft end of the *Hopeful.*

Chalky came to a sudden stop and pointed at a door that would be at home on a submersible vehicle. "It was right through there. That's what I remember."

"Are you coming?" Jack asked, already knowing the answer since Chalky's feet seemed to have welded themselves to the deck.

"No," Chalky replied.

Tc'aarlat dialed his weapon to six and Jack did the same. Chalky watched the pair go. They approached the door, spun the wheel lock, opened it, and disappeared through it.

A moment later, he was on his own in the dimly lit corridor. Chalky shook with a fierce chill from a non-existent wind, as if there was something there.

Chalky could feel eyes on him, and it was making the hairs on the back of his neck stand on end. He searched frantically, but he couldn't see a thing. He listened intently, but the only thing he could hear was his own breathing.

In front of him was the door Jack and Tc'aarlat had disappeared through, and behind him was the long stretch of corridor they had just come through. Dark and intimidating.

"Hello?" he called into the dark, but only silence answered him. Chalky wanted nothing more than to get out of there. He turned to run. In the space of a heartbeat, his fears materialized in the form of a massive beast blocking his way. His breath caught in his throat, and he froze.

He stood eye to eye with the monster. Its blond hair was knotted. Drool dripped from its exposed fangs. Chalky could feel its voracious hunger. Worst of all, it was wearing a pair of goggles modified to fit around its head. Chalky had seen those goggles before. They were the ones he had been forced to wear. Beyond the werewolf's skull, a collar wrapped around its hairy neck—a shock collar that assessed the beast's thoughts and delivered pain should the mind stray from the desired path of obedience and violence.

Chalky couldn't transform into a werewolf to fight the beast, not with the serum flowing through his veins, so he took the only option available to him; he ran. He made it two steps before the great beast slammed into him.

Frontier Zone, City Station Hopefill, Dock 9, ICS *Hopeful*, the Recuperating Room

Jack and Tc'aarlat found themselves in a large room

with a thousand or so pipes leading from massive turbines that had powered the ship once upon a time. In the center was a large circular tank filled with water. Stairs led to a platform from which a person could easily get into or out of the pool. The pair fanned out to search the room.

"So, it's just a really big fish tank?" Tc'aarlat pressed his hand against the tank and felt the cool of the water behind it. It was large, perhaps twice as large as him, and filled with crystal-clear blue water that he found engrossing. "Does this mean we've found the right place?"

"I'm more concerned about this." Jack held a long and powerful chain attached to the wall with thick bolts. The kind of thing you expected to see used for a wild and dangerous animal, except this was much larger and the other end had broken off, as if whatever it had been attached to had snapped it in an impressive show of strength. "We don't know what kind of guards she might have here."

"Uh, yeah, we do Jack," Tc'aarlat replied. "Werewolves." The Yollin threw one hand up while waving his pistol with the other.

"I should've gotten more of that injector stuff. Why did I only grab one?"

Tc'aarlat didn't look at Jack as he answered, "Because coming here was not on the horizon, over the horizon, or even on the planet." Tc'aarlat scanned the room, not finding anything of importance except another door leading out of the room. He could hear an intense buzz coming from just beyond, like the static from an old television.

Tc'aarlat pulled a lever near the door, and it opened with a creak. "Hey, Jack, check this out."

Jack went first while Tc'aarlat aimed his pistol over the captain's head. Inside they found rusting metal, an examination table splattered with blood, a chair with straps, and chains attached to the bulkheads. Everything that made a torture chamber the center of the worst horror stories.

It also contained a cell with a single individual. The man stood, and his frown deepened. The bags beneath his eyes and sagging skin suggested he'd been there for a while.

"Would you look at that?" Jack said once he was sure they were alone. "Don-fucking-Gan'barlo. How's it going, cockwad?"

Tc'aarlat pushed past Jack and rushed across the small chamber. "I ought to kill you right fucking now, as much bullshit as you piled on my head. Fuck you! Can you hear that? *FUCK YOU!*"

"Hey, buddy," Jack warned. "Everybody can hear that, and they really shouldn't. Kill him and let's get out of here."

Don held his arms out, resigned to his fate. "Please, kill me. You'll be doing me a favor. That woman assumed my identity a long time ago. I have no idea what anyone has done to you, but I'm sorry for it. Help me get out of here and I'll do right by you, starting with Fish-Head. She needs to die in a big way, a big ugly way."

Tc'aarlat dialed his JDS to ten and aimed at the Don's head.

"Whoa, buddy," Jack cautioned once again. "That might give us away as well as bring the entirety of this wreck down on our heads. How about four as a setting? It's not like he's going to fight back."

"I hate this guy. Killing him will be the epitome of my life's work." Tc'aarlat's hand shook with anger.

"When you use words like 'epitome,' it suggests your mind is not in the right state. Maybe you can fuck-bomb the Don to death. That would be something."

Jack eased toward the Yollin in the hope of reducing the tension.

"Fuck-bomb?" Tc'aarlat sighed and looked at the Don through new eyes, seeing his sorry state. "You deserve this."

"I don't," he replied simply. "No one deserves this. I might have done some questionable things in my life, but nothing like what she's doing. What she makes me watch. Kill me. You'll be doing me a favor."

Tc'aarlat lowered his weapon. "I won't do you any favors. You're fucking Don-fucking-Gan-fucking-Barlo. You are the biggest asshole in the universe."

"Not anymore," he replied before lowering himself to sit on the edge of his bed.

Jack put his hand on Tc'aarlat's shoulder. "She's turning the werewolves to her purposes, isn't she?"

"Torture, the glasses for mind control, and the shock collars to keep them from turning back. I'm not sure she needs the torture, but she likes it. That's why she does it."

"You don't look like you've been tortured," Tc'aarlat noted.

"Not physically, not lately anyway. She's all about the mindfuck."

"You're not a new man," Tc'aarlat countered, his hand twitching as he fought his desire to kill the Don.

"Not at all. I only want to get back to running my empire and having hot and cold running women at my beck and call. My people doing my bidding. But I don't think she's left me with much. I think she has her own people in place of those I trusted. Maybe it's time to retire, I don't know. Not as long as I'm in here. Tc'aarlat, I know people need what I have to offer. Money, drugs, political influence. I'll cancel your debt and throw you an extra hundred thousand credits if you get me out of here, assuming I still have a hundred thousand credits."

Tc'aarlat turned away, refusing to look at the man. Mind games weren't beneath him. He wasn't as happy as he'd thought he'd be, seeing the Don as he was.

"Goggles?" Jack asked.

"They're what's making the noise." Tc'aarlat held up a pair and pressed them to his ear holes. "This is where the buzzing is coming from. Damn, I thought I was going crazy for a second there."

Jack took the goggles and gave them a listen. "It's just static. I'm not sure how these would get into their heads."

"Visual and aural stimulation to make the wearer susceptible to suggestion," the Don offered.

"What's this?" Jack pulled a data disk from a pile on a table and held it in his palm. He looked at it sideways because it looked familiar. "Wait, I know what this is!"

"We might need to take a pain check on that." Tc'aarlat tapped Jack on the shoulder. "We've got bigger problems."

"It's not a pain check, Tc'aarlat, it's a—" Jack turned around. It wasn't what he expected. A blonde werewolf bared its fangs. Once it had the attention of the torture chamber's occupants, it growled and started to move forward. The werewolf wore strange goggles, held in place by a strap around the ears with a secondary strap under its chin, like it was wearing a muzzle.

"Where did you come from, you ugly bastard?" Tc'aarlat raised his pistol.

"Not ten," Jack reminded his partner, knowing who the werewolf was. "Hey, Draven. How's it hanging?"

"I knew he was a dickhead, Jack," Tc'aarlat said. "I've said it a bunch of times."

"But he's being controlled. Set it on three." He dialed his JDS to the heaviest stun setting and took aim. Draven the werewolf moved laterally, sizing up its prey, knowing they were dangerous. It looked for an opening.

"Oh, yeah," Tc'aarlat replied. "Well, he's still a dickhead."

Frontier Zone, City Station Hopefill, Dock 9, ICS Hopeful, Supply Room

Years of training came back to Theo in a flash. Clarity of thought coupled with body control established through repetition, sparring, and individual practice.

He took aim as the door opened. Theo fired at point-blank range into the first face, exploding the head behind it. He took one step into the newly cleared opening and fired at the next target. He ducked and aimed, firing a third time and removing a third target.

The fourth and fifth scrambled for cover, but Theo was faster. In less than three seconds, he fired five times with four kills. The final individual had dodged the worst of it and was on the deck, trying to crawl away.

Theo hurried forward, looking for a new target as the

sound of the pistol reverberated through the corridors. Theo reasoned it would draw gang members from near and far. There was no way they'd tolerate an intruder within.

Theo reached the injured man, relieved him of his club, and used it to bash him in the head. He didn't care if the man survived. He only cared that he wouldn't interfere with their exodus from the *Hopeful*.

Briona moved into the outer area, careful not to step in the blood and gore from Theo's assault upon those who would have done them harm. She returned to the supply room and tried to carry Kirandeep, but she was too weak. "Help me," she pleaded.

Theo blinked away the blood lust and listened for a short while longer before backing toward the vault door. He kicked the body of the first man across the threshold to make sure no one closed the door on them. "Put her over my shoulder."

He continued to face the doorway, sure others would be coming. He helped guide the unconscious woman over his left shoulder, where she felt like she weighed barely more than a backpack. He kept his pistol aimed outward. They recrossed the threshold to put themselves one step closer to freedom.

"Check these men for guns. If they have any, take them." Theo hadn't seen a firearm during the hyperaware state pure warriors attained during the heat of combat, but just in case, he wanted a backup. He only had three rounds remaining and suspected there would be more than three obstacles attempting to keep him from escaping.

Briona searched but only found clubs. She took one

that fit her hand and swung it to get the feel. The look on her face suggested she wanted to use it. Payback was coming.

"Do you know the way out?" Theo asked.

Briona shook her head.

Theo clenched his jaw and contemplated the woman before him. "You make me want to quit Eternity."

"Then do it," she replied. "As soon as we're out of here."

He looked down at the pockets of his jacket, filled with vials. Briona made a decision. She pulled them out and hurled them into the supply room. Theo had been jonesing hard for a fix, an escape, but he did nothing to stop her.

Once his pockets were empty, she removed a vest from a dead thug, one that had a lighter she'd discovered during her earlier search. She lit it and chucked it into the supply room. The Eternity on the floor caught fire and burned hot. It exploded nearby vials that burst into flame, spreading and cascading through the supply room. She left the door cracked to provide air to fuel the conflagration.

"Just in case," she told him before stretching up to kiss him on the cheek. He wasn't sure if she meant to allay his temptation or save others from being subverted. "How about we get the fuck out of here?"

"I love it when hot chicks swear."

"Hot chicks? Have you smelled me?"

He smiled. "Besides that. But I'm with you. How about this way?" He pointed.

She shrugged. Theo took off, walking quickly. He glanced back only once to make sure Briona followed. She walked in his shadow. He felt different than he'd felt in a long time. He was thinking clearly.

There was no Eternity in his future.

If only they could get off that ship intact.

It didn't take long for Theo to realize they were lost. They stopped after a sharp turn where wreckage blocked the corridor. "I didn't come this way."

Briona thought about that. "We need to go back then. Try to retrace our—"

A long howl made the hairs on his neck stand up. "Werewolf," he whispered. "How far to the last corridor?"

"A hundred meters, maybe?" she tried.

A second howl told him they would never make it.

"Can you fight it off?" Briona asked. "Like you did those others?"

"Not really," replied Theo. "Werewolves are different. There's an innocent underneath that fur. He doesn't know what he's doing, and I don't think I can kill him."

"You are a strange man, Theo Young."

"Listen, I'll fight the werewolf, and you run for your life." He put Kirandeep down.

"I can't leave her. I can't leave you," she argued.

"You have no choice. You can't carry her, and none of us will get away if we try to go together. You have to save yourself and bring back help. Bring the whole WRU, En-D, local cops, anyone who will follow you in here. Do you hear me?" Another howl added to his urgency. He stretched his arms and flexed.

She nodded tightly.

"When I run, you run. I'll take on the wolf, and you find your way out. No matter what you hear behind you, keep running."

"Theo..."

The heavy thump of the beast's paws echoed in the corridor. "Follow me." Theo clenched his jaw and bolted around the corner. The werewolf ran with its snout to the ground. It brought its head up at the sound of Theo's footsteps and opened its jaws. Theo jumped off the side wall to drive the werewolf away from the center, creating space for Briona to get past.

Frontier Zone, City Station Hopefill, Dock 9, ICS *Hopeful*, the Recuperating Room

The Draven werewolf snapped at Jack to drive him backward and twisted sideways toward Tc'aarlat. The move was so fast that Jack's shot found empty space. Tc'aarlat tried to backpedal and in that instant, the wolf was on him, bowling him over.

Energy sparked through the collar, and the werewolf spasmed and convulsed. When the energy stopped coursing through the beast's body. It bolted like a shot out of the room. The footfalls rapidly disappeared into the distance.

Tc'aarlat stood and brushed himself off. "What it is with these werewolf assholes trying to bite me?"

"Maybe you taste good?" Jack suggested. "I always imagined you'd be good fried up and served with barbecue sauce."

"Have you been thinking about eating me?" Tc'aarlat swatted Jack upside the head. "You can eat me, Jack, but not like that."

"We should go after him." Jack moved to the door. "Make sure he doesn't hurt himself."

"Go after him?" Tc'aarlat repeated. "He's a dangerous psychopath, and that was *before* he turned into a werewolf."

"Are you two always like this?" the Don asked.

"Fuck you, Don." Tc'aarlat gave him the finger as an exclamation point.

"We have to take him with us," Jack nodded at the cage.

"You have got to be shitting me. *Shitting. Me.*" Tc'aarlat waved his pistol at the cage. "I still want him dead."

"Then you're no better than him."

"That's what goofy fuckers always say when they are too weak to take care of business."

"I'm pretty sure it's not. We'll take him with us. Then we'll come to an agreement. Wouldn't it be good not to have a contract on your head? If we turn him in to the Federation, we'll still have a price on our heads. If we kill him now, nothing changes, which means a price on our heads. Have you forgotten that people are trying to kill us?"

Tc'aarlat clicked his mandibles rapidly in agitation and thought aloud, "I don't know. I think it would have its benefits. Not having to think for myself might be a nice break from my daily life. Train two birds to kill a rock. Come on, Don. Don't get yourself killed trying to get away, and don't double-cross us. You want to live? We're your best chance."

Jack blasted the lock on the cell and kicked the door open. The Don walked forward hesitantly. Once outside, he closed his eyes, let his head fall back, and breathed deeply. "It's been such a long time."

"How about you get those legs working, fuckstick?" Tc'aarlat snapped.

The Don tossed his hand up at the Yollin but nodded.

Jack walked quickly from the torture chamber and started running once he hit the fish-tank room. At the far end, he stopped and listened. "I think I hear him." Jack took off running.

Tc'aarlat swiped a device off the table and shoved it into his pocket because he thought it looked important. He pushed the Don in front of him. "Keep up, dick. There's no way I'm letting you get behind me."

"I'm free, and I stay free if I keep up. I need no other motivation, dick."

"Fine, dick."

"Dick," the Don shot back, smiling and shaking his head. He hurried after Jack, but he was soon huffing and puffing, although he didn't falter. He wasn't taking his freedom lightly.

"I don't think Draven can see properly," Jack said. "I think those goggles are obscuring his vision. That's why he came into the room sniffing for us. He couldn't actually see us so maybe he was attracted by our voices."

"I was beginning to ponderate why we hadn't seen any other werewolves with goggles on," Tc'aarlat said. "Maybe they're like training wheels?"

Jack replied over his shoulder, "Agree. I think they're a short-term solution to keep the wolves under control while this fish woman rewires their brain. That's good news, though. If we're correct, we can just take the goggles off and Draven should go back to normal."

"It is nice to know what Draven's been up to," Tc'aarlat said. "What do you think he's even doing down here?"

"I bet he was on this fish woman's case, so she grabbed him."

"Probably using those guys in the WRU as well," Tc'aarlat replied.

"Bloody Darling is the fish woman and she has her fingers in the WRU. No wonder the werewolf problem in Hopefill City isn't being resolved," Jack replied.

The sound of scratching claws caught Jack's ear. He waved Tc'aarlat to silence and slowed to a stop. He peeked around a corner to find Draven scratching the walls of a dead end. The beast snapped out of it at the gentle scrape behind it. It turned around and faced them.

Jack clicked his JDS to the one setting and fired. The werewolf jerked with the impact but didn't go down. He roared at the ceiling. Jack pulled the trigger twice more, not knowing if three shots at the number one setting were the same as one shot at number three.

He learned the answer was no when the werewolf charged him. The impact knocked the pistol from his hand.

The Don backpedaled while Tc'aarlat charged. He shoved the Don away and dove, ripping the goggles off while he wrestled with the beast's head.

"Come out of it, fucker!" Tc'aarlat growled into the beast's ear.

Jack pushed and turned, trying to get the weight off him, but with Tc'aarlat on top of the werewolf, he was trapped. The werewolf drooled on Jack's face, but its violent attempts to free itself lessened. Soon, it collapsed.

With a firm hand, Tc'aarlat slapped it upside its head, and the werewolf recoiled with a high-pitched whine. "That's for the Pegasus, you jerk!"

"*TC'AARLAT!*" Jack shouted.

The slap renewed the werewolf's energy. It drove itself upward, coming to all fours and bucking Tc'aarlat off its back.

Jack lashed out with a foot and kicked the beast's front legs out from under it. Draven planted face-first into the deck. The beast huffed once and collapsed. It started to change; the blond hair extended while the snout withdrew. The head changed to human and fur disappeared.

"That was fun," Jack grunted.

"Gentlemen. Congratulations on a battle well-fought," the Don said, leveling Jack's Jean Dukes Special at Tc'aarlat.

"I think you should tell him," Jack said, easing away from Draven as he returned to human form. The beautiful agent was just one more naked guy lying in a rusty corridor.

"I'm having cake and eating it," Tc'aarlat replied. "Or is it eating cake, then having it? I thought confronting Don Gan'barlo would be more gratifying, but he's just another dumbass."

"Give me my gun." Jack stood up and motioned for the Don to hand over the pistol.

"I think not." He dialed the weapon to seven. "I shall be free, and I will owe you nothing. How does that sound for a compromise?"

"Dick!" Tc'aarlat shouted. He turned his head toward the groaning Draven. "And you can shut up." Tc'aarlat stepped toward the Don, raising his hands to rip the weapon away.

The Don pulled the trigger.

And nothing happened.

He jerked it again. Still nothing.

"Dick. Those weapons are keyed to particular people. Don Gan'barlo, dumbass. Whodathunkit?" Tc'aarlat swept his long-fingered hand through the air and grabbed the pistol. He tossed it over his head to Jack. "Hang onto that."

"Did you forget the no double-cross part of our arrangement?" Jack asked.

Draven groaned again while holding his head in both hands. He blinked rapidly to clear his eyes.

Don Gan'barlo's expression suggested no remorse. He shrugged. "You know I had to try. This is me we're talking about."

"I want to kill him," Tc'aarlat said. He pointed at Draven. "We make him carry the body out and take lots of pictures of the naked man hauling the Don's dumb ass to the dock."

"Guys? Oh, my God! Are you okay?" Draven asked.

"Yeah, we're good," Jack replied, trying his hardest to look anywhere but at Draven. "Just doing our jobs. Can you help us get out of here?"

Draven shook his head. "I was brought in with a bag over my head. As a werewolf, I remember colors and shapes because of the goggles, but not passages and corridors."

"What happened to you, Draven?" Jack asked. "How did you get here?"

"It was Tinio. I stumbled onto a lead that was bigger than I expected. He knocked me out, and the next thing I knew, I woke up strapped to a chair."

"What was the lead?" Tc'aarlat asked.

"It was Briona Arnd," Draven said. "I went back to the

storage units, and I found an ID card there. It was all scratched to hell, but I tracked it back to the Ice Blocks. Briona is a researcher there, and her behavior has been erratic these past few weeks. I had the ID logs to prove it."

"You mean this card?" Jack pulled the ID from his pocket, along with the logs. "I took this from your desk when we...went searching for you. Because obviously, we were worried."

"Thanks, guys," Draven replied, missing the jibe.

"You don't think this could be *her*, do you, Jack?" Tc'aarlat asked. "The fish woman?"

Jack nodded. "No doubt. It's her."

"I know the fish woman," Draven said. "She's the one who put the goggles on me!"

"She's a Mutanaraian, a race that can shapeshift," Jack said. "We think she's been disguising herself as someone in the city. Maybe even several people."

Draven stared at the wall. "I thought there was something off about her, the way Briona just shrugged off the fact that she had lost her ID. What does that mean?"

"She's a researcher at the Ice Blocks, right?" Jack asked.

"Yes, and having unlimited access to the werewolves and a lab filled with scientific equipment puts her in the prime spot to subvert everything that's going on," Draven replied. "Sounds like we'd better get the WRU onboard."

"You can't!" Tc'aarlat exclaimed. "We don't know who to trust in there. Any of them could be in caboots."

"Does that mean you trust me, Tc'aarlat?" Draven asked. The Don snorted.

The Yollin scowled at him, regretting his words.

"Tc'aarlat's right," Jack added. "We should only be bringing people in that we can trust completely."

"Then I'm going to Mikhail," Draven said. "This is very much a WRU problem."

"Can we trust him?"

"I had my doubts, but from what I remember, Tinio didn't like him, so maybe he is one of the good guys. We've got to get someone from the Unit involved. We can't do this on our own," Draven pleaded.

Jack looked skeptical. "I don't know. Are you sure?"

Draven nodded. "As sugar."

"Can sugar be sure?" Tc'aarlat wondered.

Draven shrugged and pointed at the Don. "Who's he?"

"Don Gan'barlo, head of a major crime family. He's a dick," Tc'aarlat replied. "I'll probably end up killing him before we're off the ship, and you'll have to carry him. I have confidence that you're up to the task. He used to be much fatter. A jailbird's life has served him well."

The Don didn't change his expression as he looked from Tc'aarlat to Draven and back again.

"Time to go." Jack took one step and stopped, his fingers had felt something in his pocket, something he had forgotten about. He brought it out, a smaller circular device with an integrated holovid. It was the data disk he had found in a pile of other items, the one he had recognized. Draven and Tc'aarlat looked down at it as he began to play with it.

"What is that?" Tc'aarlat asked. "Well, I know it's a data disk, but what's on it?"

"It's a blood report on Adina," Jack said. "With Draven chasing us, I completely forgot about it."

"Wait, what do you mean?" Tc'aarlat said. "Why would that be here?"

"The fish woman is after all werewolves, especially those who are established elsewhere. It's like a sport for her. You don't think..."

"Why else would it be here? Adina has become resistant to the dampening drugs. I think someone using werewolves as weapons would be interested in something like that."

"Didn't Adina say she had a new stepmother?" Tc'aarlat added. "Could it be—"

"We need to get back to *Fortitude*!" exclaimed Jack. "Now!"

17

Frontier Zone, City Station Hopefill, the Ice Blocks

It was the chill, above all else, that woke Adina. A fierce cold, well below any comfort level. Adina shivered uncontrollably.

She opened her eyes to find herself in a cage and on display. A cold fog rolled across the floor, obscuring it and stopping only at the confines of her glass prison. Adina was inside a glass cube, freezing and in the company of others similarly restrained.

She examined the cage as a scientist would, looking at the construction to find stress points and weaknesses. There were none. It was as if the cage had materialized around her. She flung herself at the center of the clear screen, only to bounce off. Running faster and hitting it harder would accomplish nothing more than beating herself up.

Which she thought she deserved, having been drawn in by the evil Kirandeep.

A blonde woman with a devilish smile strolled in. She

wore a light jacket, but otherwise, she seemed to be unaffected by the cold.

"Wh-who are y-you?" Adina managed to say through chattering teeth. Her breath hung in a cloud in the air before her as she hugged herself, trying to maintain the last of her warmth. "Wh-what do y-you want?"

"Oh, Adina, I'm surprised you don't know who I am," the woman replied. As Adina watched, her form shifted. Her skin darkened, her eyes grew exotic, her facial structure shifted. "Do you recognize me now?"

"K-kirandeep?" Adina questioned. "Wh-why?"

"I'm not Kirandeep. She's safe and sound elsewhere. Well, maybe not safe and probably not sound either, but she could very well be alive. I can't be sure. I've been enjoying her life, especially the saucy bits with your father." She waited to see if that got a rise from Adina, but the young woman was too cold. "My name is Naka-Lee Patnee and I'm here to expand my business, but not into cafes."

"Wh-what do you want w-with me?" Adina watched her carefully while having a hard time focusing through the cold.

"I suppose you deserve an explanation," Naka-Lee replied. "I'm a weapons dealer, and a successful one. What I sell isn't just weapons and explosives, though. I've recently gotten into selling werewolves."

"Y-you're going to s-sell me?"

"Yes, but that's not why I was after you," Naka-Lee continued. "About a month ago, I was approached by Benjamin. I'm sure you remember him. He came to sell me the plans to that terraformer I know you delivered to Renasta, but not just that. Benjamin had details on you, a werewolf who had become resistant to the DNA-damp-ening drugs.

"See, that's the one thing holding my werewolves back. The WRU injectors can easily change them back into the simpering fools they were before. If I can figure out what makes you resistant, I can put it in all my wolves. They'll be unstoppable, and that will make them worth a small fortune each. I could sell them to more than just gangs. They could be assassins and thieves. They could change the current landscape of war."

"W-what are you talking about?" Adina said. "Were-wolves have b-been fighting f-for the Federation for generations."

"I'm not talking about the Federation." Naka-Lee smiled. "I'm talking about everyone else."

"W-why not just t-take me, then?" Adina asked. "Why d-did you have to go through my f-father?"

"There are rules in this city. Laws, especially when it comes to werewolves," Naka-Lee said. "If I just took you, people would come after me, especially those misguided friends of yours. If, however, you broke the law on your own by turning into a werewolf on the streets somewhere I knew there would be a bunch of witnesses, you could be arrested. Then everything would be nice and legal. It works out perfectly because there's no better place in the galaxy to study a werewolf than right here in the Ice Blocks. To do that, I needed to build up your emotions, get you to change, then capture you."

Adina started shivering again. The heat left her body as quickly as it had come. "S-so, you lured me here by kkilling my uncle j-just to study me? Y-you better hope I-I don't g-get out of here."

"You're going to make me a fortune, Adina. You're my prized possession. It doesn't end with studying you, either. I'm going to turn you into one of my loyal bodyguards as well."

"Y-you're crazy. You're g-going to pay for m-messing with my family. I promise." Adina felt the heat rising within, but it wasn't enough to change form. Only enough to stop the shivering.

Naka-Lee turned herself from Kirandeep into Adina and pretended to wipe away tears by holding her hands against her eyes to mock her. "Oh, wah, wah, wah. You should be grateful. I've locked up a dangerous werewolf— you. Now you'll only hurt the people I tell you to hurt."

"Never," Adina growled.

Naka-Lee turned to leave, and Adina had the surreal experience of watching herself walk away. "I've got work to do, Adina. Enjoy freezing your ass off. Don't bother trying to transform either. You see those bars at the top of your cell? They're called scramblers; they jumble your thoughts and send down cascading waves of energy specially designed to prevent you from transforming into a wolf. Enjoy not being able to concentrate on anything but being cold."

Adina tried weakly to transform but she couldn't concentrate or couldn't raise her ire. She would have to sit and wait for someone to come to her rescue.

Frontier Zone, City Station Hopefill, Dock 9, ICS *Hopeful*

Crow stepped into the base with a sense of pride and a team of werewolves at his back, werewolves who were covered from head to toe in blood from their most recent business.

The Red Scythes had decided that today was the perfect opportunity to move in on their territory with what they claimed was a more powerful hit of Eternity. This had led to an all-out war that had ended with Crow teaching a few people significant life lessons. The Silver Diamonds had cemented themselves once again as the most powerful gang, but walking into the *Hopeful*, he didn't feel that.

One member, a guy he recognized as Derrick, approached, his head a bloody mess. Crow looked him up and down and asked quickly, "What the fuck happened to you?"

"We were attacked. A homeless guy managed to get into our supply room. He killed some of our people and whacked me a good one. He had the bitches with him."

"Was it the Red Scythes?" Crow asked, fearing the gang had outwitted him by creating a distraction so they could steal his stuff. "Did you see what they looked like?"

"By the time we got to the engine room, they were gone," he said. "And Biscuit, too."

"She's going to be pissed about that," Crow replied. "What about the supplies?"

"Fried. All of it. They fucking torched it all."

"Tell me you're joking. Prisoners are gone. The Eternity is gone. Biscuit is gone," Crow said through gritted teeth. His lip curled into a snarl, caught halfway between white-hot anger and blinding terror. "Did they get away? Tell me they're still in the ship somewhere."

Derrick pointed to his head. "Maybe. I just came to. I have no idea how long I was out."

"You stupid fucker!" Crow blurted. He waved at the werewolves. "Search the ship and find them. Find anyone who's not supposed to be here and kill them. Kill them all!" Crow mashed a button on his remote and the werewolves twisted in pain before the shock settled. The creatures bolted down three different corridors with their handlers close behind. The baying of the wolves echoed through the ship.

Frontier Zone, City Station Hopefill, Dock 9, ICS *Hopeful*, Unknown Corridor

"Take this," Jack said as he handed Draven a dirty towel. "I'm tired of knowing that your dangling dino o' doom is flopping around back there."

Draven wrapped the towel around his waist and tied the corners together. "While your head is twisted backward in regards to my modesty, maybe you can find me something to wear on my feet, too. These aren't like my paws. This metal is a little cold."

Draven held up a foot to show the sole was blackened. "I'm going to need a mani-pedi after this."

"If we survive," Tc'aarlat offered, followed by pushing the Don with the barrel of his gun. "And you better help us, or your plight with fishface will be worse since you helped us."

"I never helped you," Gan'barlo shot back. "You can't force me to help you and then claim I helped you."

"Truth doesn't matter. Only what people believe. Isn't

that something you used to say?" Jack added after peeking around a corner and waving the group forward.

"The Dickens you say!" Tc'aarlat blurted.

"We don't deserve to live," the Don muttered. "At least, not you assholes. The naked guy and me? We do, but not you two idiots."

"Thank you very little," Tc'aarlat shot back.

Jack raised his fist to stop the group. "Stand over there." He waved his pistol at the Don. "And you, watch him." Draven nodded.

Jack leaned close to study Tc'aarlat's face.

"What the fuck is wrong with you, buddy? You're not yourself."

"I have to be me. Who else could I be? To be me or not to be me, that is *not* the question."

"Nope. That's not you." Tc'aarlat's face glistened. Jack used a finger to squeegee a thin layer off. He sniffed the result and his face dropped. To confirm his suspicions, he checked the Don. "Eternity."

"I'm not a doper, Jack!" Tc'aarlat nearly shouted, stamping a foot and punching the bulkhead beside him for emphasis.

"I know you're not. None of us are. Look at the lights. See the rainbow around it and the discoloration? That shit is in the air." He pulled his shirt up. "Cover your faces."

Jack recoiled when Draven pulled his towel off and wrapped it around his head like one of the sand people adorning the centerfold of *Hunky Men Horn Dogs*.

"This keeps getting better and better. The Don. A fish-woman who can look like anyone. Werewolves. Adina probably captured, and now dope on a rope," Jack muttered. He looked around the corner once more before waving the others forward.

"We forgot about Chalky," Tc'aarlat said from the back of the group.

Jack rubbed his temples. "He'll have to make it out on his own since we're lost and can't do jack shit for anyone, not even ourselves. Next person we run across, we're going to capture them and make them show us the way out."

Tc'aarlat thrust a thumb in the air. "Fucking A! I'll rip out as many fingernails as it takes to get them to talk."

Jack looked at the Don, who shrugged and shook his head. He frowned. Jack frowned. Draven looked around as if seeing the world for the first time, a world of rainbows and crystalline waterfalls.

"Come on," Jack growled and quickened his pace. He looked for any traces on the deck that someone had passed recently, zigzagging across the deck from port to starboard and back to the port side before climbing one deck higher and repeating the pattern.

He stopped abruptly and held up his fist. The others ran into him. They muttered until a werewolf howl froze them in place. Jack dialed his JDS to three and ran.

Frontier Zone, City Station Hopefill, Dock 9, ICS *Hopeful*

Theo dodged the head and wrapped his arms around the neck of the hairy beast, climbing onto its back to stay away from the jaws. If he fell to the deck, the werewolf would use its powerful jaws to make short work of him.

Briona brushed past as Theo hung on. The head swiveled and snapped at her, then the wolf howled and bucked, trying to drive the human off its back. Theo refused to give up, and the werewolf wouldn't succumb.

Theo braced a leg against the wall to keep the werewolf under him, but his grip started to slip. He grunted with the effort, holding on for his life. Sparks started flashing before his eyes since his body wasn't up for the effort. It had been years since he'd demanded this kind of physical performance.

Sad years.

Purposeless.

At least he'd die doing something that mattered. It was his time. He pushed off the wall to wrap himself better around the creature's throat. A scream came from behind him, followed by the thud of a club hitting a body. The wolf howled before flopping to the deck. Theo rolled underneath it, breaking his grip.

Briona stood there with a club, brandishing it while the werewolf twisted away and rolled free. It came to its feet. Theo scrambled forward, throwing himself between Briona and the beast—one last act of defiance before they lost the fight.

He closed his eyes and said, "Run," but he knew she was done running. He hadn't managed to save anyone or anything except his dignity.

In the end.

The air compressed, and Theo's ears popped just before the great beast landed on him.

Frontier Zone, City Station Hopefill, Dock 9, ICS *Hopeful*, Down Quarters

Crow ran through gang berthing and kicked the remaining few from their racks. The fight with the Red Scythes had depleted their ranks. Others were out selling product. Dismal numbers. The greatest gang of Hopefill looked anemic. They couldn't even protect their stash from a homeless guy.

"Get up, you lazy bastards. Grab your shit. It's war!"

He led ten disheveled men out of the space. Derrick looked at them but didn't say a word. He had the feeling this battle would determine the primacy not just of the Silver Diamonds but the entirety of Hopefill City.

Werewolves howled from all quarters as they picked up the scent of their prey. Some raced up stairs, others went down, while the last few shot aft down the long main corridor.

"What the hell is up with them? One homeless guy can't be in three places." He stared at Derrick as if he'd have the answer. All Derrick knew was that his head hurt and none of it made sense.

Crow expected an answer. Derrick found his tongue. "He's running for his life and may have sent the women captives on different routes as a distraction. Will the wolves kill them, too? *She* will be pissed."

"She's going to be pissed no matter what. Our entire stock of Eternity is gone. Two of her captives are gone. Is anything else missing? What haven't you told me, you weaselly piece of shit?"

"I don't know. We should probably check her private space."

"Good thing she's not here," Crow grumbled. "This way, you stupid fucks."

He led the way down the nearest set of stairs to the bowels of the ship and aft to the engine room. The howls of hunting werewolves filled the corridors.

"They're onto something," Crow said, glaring at Derrick. They reached the space with the crystal-clear blue-water tank to find it undisturbed. "That's a good sign." The door to her private room stood open. "But that's not."

He started to run, slowing before he moved through the doorway. Inside, he found his worst nightmare. Not the torture room, but that he had failed Naka-Lee. It was empty, and the master controller for the shock collars was gone.

"You've killed us all!" Crow shouted. He grabbed Derrick by the throat, and with a roar, lifted him into the air. The few men who followed him suggested he needed every pair of hands he could get, so he put Derrick down. "When the time comes, you better fight like a wolf possessed or I'll kill you myself."

Derrick gasped for breath but nodded. Message received, but it wasn't as Crow had delivered it. Derrick heard that when the shooting started, he needed to kill Crow.

18

Frontier Zone, City Station Hopefill, the Ice Blocks, Briona's Research Laboratory

Adina had been prodded, poked, and pinched by every device the Ice Blocks had to offer to extract every vital bit of medical data to build a complete genetic profile. Naka-Lee had operated with smooth efficiency despite the extreme temperature that made Adina sluggish, limiting her ability to fight back. Had she tried, the result would have been the same. The shapeshifter had her DNA, and Adina was too tired to lift her head.

Knock. Knock. Adina lifted her head at the tapping on the glass of her prison cell to find the image of her future stepmother, Kirandeep. She couldn't help but be disgusted. Naka-Lee grinned at the response. "Don't go to sleep just yet, Adina."

"Wh-what do you want now? Y-You've got everything."

"You're right, I do. There's the little matter of what I'm going to do with you."

"H-how about a big bowl of fuck you?" Adina conjured her best Captain Jack Marber to come to her aid.

"No, thank you. I'm going to bring you to my personal playhouse, where I can wipe your mind and turn you into one of my pets. You're going to be the first prototype of a new series of werewolf weapons."

"S-suck my ass." Adina's head fell back in defeat. She couldn't fight back. Jack and Tc'aarlat were elsewhere trying to complete the mission. She was alone.

Completely alone and unable to protect herself.

"Before we go, though..." Naka-Lee walked over to a terminal, and Adina looked after her desperately. The shapeshifter pushed a button, and shortly thereafter came a ringing, followed by the voice of a man she didn't recognize. It was a low tone, threatening, and Adina couldn't see the face from her cell.

"Tell Crow I have a task for him," Naka-Lee said. "I want him to kill Kirandeep and send her body to the address I just transmitted."

"No!" Adina tried to shout, but she was too weak.

Naka-Lee ended the first call and called someone else. Adina heard the familiar voice of her father, Usman Choudhury, and could only listen as the conversation played out for her edification.

"Hi, dear," she said. "How are you?"

"Kirandeep," Usman replied. "I thought you were working."

"I am, but there's a business opportunity that will pull me off the station for a while. I have to go immediately before someone else moves in. This could expand the cafés beyond my wildest dreams, but I am going to be gone for a while."

Adina tried to summon the strength to shout, but she had nothing left. She croaked a warning to her father, but it didn't make it to his ears.

"That sounds like a great opportunity. Seize the day, as you always say. How long will you be gone and where are you going?"

"Station 11 for maybe two weeks," Naka-Lee replied. "I love you, honey, so much. I'm so happy to have met you."

"I love you too," Usman replied. "Just be safe and have a good trip. I'll see you soon."

Naka-Lee tapped the screen before smiling at Adina.

"Y-you're a monster. My f-friends are coming, and th-they'll stop you. I'll s-stop you."

"By the time they get anywhere near us, we'll be gone. Shame."

The temperature in Adina's cell started dropping with such intensity, it sucked the breath from Adina's lungs. She struggled to draw in air, but her diaphragm wouldn't cooperate. Her limbs refused to move. She forced her eyes closed before everything went dark.

Frontier Zone, City Station Hopefill, Dock 9, ICS *Hopeful*

Jack pulled the stunned werewolf off the person beneath it. Theo coughed and rolled to his knees. "Jack Marber. Your timing could not have been more impeccable. I can't believe you came to save me."

"We didn't," Tc'aarlat replied.

"We did. Of course, we did. That's why we're here, if it

makes you feel any better. We need help finding our way out of here." Jack helped Theo to his feet.

"Why do you guys have your faces covered, and by the gods of Olympus, why is that man naked?"

"I don't mind," Briona said with a weak smile, leaning heavily against Theo.

"I'm Don Gan'barlo." He offered his hand, but Briona didn't take it.

"He's our prisoner," Tc'aarlat added.

The Don gave the Yollin a hearty side-eye. "That device you took will remove the collar on this hairy bastard." Don held out his hand.

Tc'aarlat pulled the device out of his pocket and aimed his JDS at the middle of the Don's chest before handing over the controller unit. Don studied it for a moment before tapping two buttons. The collar on the werewolf at their feet popped off, and he crushed it into the deck under his heel, then ground the parts into the steel.

"Without that, she won't be able to regain control. Maybe it'll change back into a man and resume a normal life. Until then, without the collar, it shouldn't be violent toward us. These things are much smarter than the locals give them credit for. They are as smart as their hosts."

"Tell us something we don't know, dick." Tc'aarlat motioned to get the controller back.

"Kirandeep!" Theo said. "She's around the corner. We have to carry her out. I'm sorry, we got lost too, looking for the way."

"Well, now we're twice the number and still don't have a clue. Pretty soon, we'll be able to hold hands and fill all the corridors until we find the way off the ship."

"We could blast a hole in the side," Tc'aarlat suggested, waving his pistol in the air.

"The longer I'm on board this ship, the more I like that idea." He gestured toward the shirt pulled up over his nose and mouth. "Cover your faces. Eternity has gotten into the air ducts, and it's messing with anyone who breathes it in or gets it in their eyes."

Draven returned from around the corner with the unconscious woman over his shoulder. "I'm not a med tech, but even I can tell she needs help."

A wolf howled a long way off. Theo pointed. "Coming from that way."

Jack checked his pistol. "From where the wolves come, the heart of darkness beats. We will drop them one by one, leaving their unconscious bodies in our wake without collars, uncontrolled but alive. They aren't our enemy. She is. The gang is. And I've had enough. The only one who gets to remain upright is the motherfucker who will show us the way out because we have people counting on us getting them to freedom."

"Or we blast a hole in the hull," Tc'aarlat reminded.

"Whichever comes first. Follow me." Jack strode briskly down the corridor with his pistol held before him. Theo and Briona walked hand in hand. Draven carried Kirandeep. The Don fell back until he felt Tc'aarlat's pistol in his back.

Within two minutes, the werewolf appeared and ran toward them. Jack hit it head-on with the max stunner blast. Tc'aarlat tapped the Don on the shoulder and gave him the collar control device.

The Don released it and took the collar with him as

they continued. Tc'aarlat ripped it out of his hand and twirled it like a rope until it had enough speed that when it slammed into the metal corridor walls, it shattered, scattering shards over the group.

"Watch it, dick," the Don snarled.

"Leave the dick alone!" Briona snapped.

The Don snorted and started to laugh. Jack glanced over his shoulder to see the surprise on Tc'aarlat's face. The Yollin settled for giving Don Gan'barlo the finger.

Another howl. Jack turned in that direction and found the creature bounding up the stairs toward him. He blasted it with the stun setting and headed downward. The Don disconnected the collar, and Tc'aarlat destroyed it. They kept moving through the ship like a well-oiled machine.

A commotion ahead caused Jack to finally stop. A man yelling.

Jack didn't recognize the voice, but Theo's eyes grew big.

"It's Crow. He's the leader of the gang but rarely goes out in public."

Jack dialed the JDS to nine and flexed his arm muscles. He wasn't strong enough to fire it on ten and suspected nine might break his wrist, but now wasn't the time to risk anything less.

Jack stepped around the corner and blocked Crow's way. "Hey, boys, what's up?"

Crow glared, took a step, and froze. The pistol caught him off-guard. He studied it through narrowed eyes. He waved his boys forward, but they didn't like the look of the weapon aimed at them either.

"Looks like we're at an impasse. I want to get out this

cesspool you call a home, and you seem to be keeping me from doing that. Here's what's going to happen. You'll try something stupid. You'll die. The next one will think they are less stupid than you. They'll die. Then the rest of these clowns will run for their lives, and they'll die if they stick their ugly heads out where I can see them."

Crow stood tall. "You have me at a disadvantage, sir. May I know your name? For the annals of history, of course, because that's what you'll be. You're not walking off this ship."

"Kill him," Theo urged in hushed tones.

Jack had enough combat experience to know that without Crow, the others would disperse. Crow wasn't going to negotiate or surrender. He was going to do everything he could to see Jack dead.

The decision was simple. He squeezed the trigger. The JDS sent a microscopic dart at hypervelocity into Crow's chest, exploding his body and those of the five men closest to him. Their bodies acted as projectiles to flush the corridor clean.

Theo stepped into the corridor. "Eleven with one shot. Nice thunderstick, Jack. If we'd had those when I was in, we could have done some damage."

"Genius killed our tour guide. Couldn't leave one alive?" the Don complained. "You are such a dumbass. I'm embarrassed to have been captured by you."

"Shoot him, Jack!" Tc'aarlat called.

"Shoot him yourself," Jack snapped and started walking. "This way."

He tiptoed through the gore to get to the far end of the corridor.

"I think this is the one I brained with my pistol. I thought he was dead," Theo noted.

"He is now," Briona said with sincere indifference.

Jack moved with purpose.

Another werewolf, another unconscious creature, another destroyed collar. He started to run. "Hey, you!" The man accelerated away from them. Jack dialed his weapon to one and fired at the deck. The stun skipped off and tripped the runner.

Jack ran him down. "Show us the way off this ship," he growled into the shocked eyes. "Chalky?" The young man raised one shaking arm and pointed at an open hatch filled with the dome's artificial light. "That's more like it! By the way, Crow is gone, the others are gone, and that frees you." He stepped over the man and headed outside.

"What about *her*?"

"She's next," Jack called over his shoulder.

Once in the fresh air, he pulled his shirt down to take a deep breath. "Draven, if you would be so kind?"

Draven handed the woman to the Don so he could move his towel back down around his hips. He recovered Kirandeep and the group headed away from the ICS *Hopeful*. For those left aboard, there was no hope at all.

Jack waved down a cab that had braved the docks with a dodgy passenger. He let his rider out and Jack looked in.

"You!" the cabby shouted.

"My friend!" Jack climbed inside before the man could drive away. "I need to use your comm."

The cabby shook his head.

"Are you going to make me shoot you? Just when we were rekindling our relationship."

Tc'aarlat tapped the glass with his pistol. The cabby gave his comm to Jack, who handed it to Draven. "Call Mikhail at the WRU and find out what the hell is going on. Tell him not to trust Tinio or any of those fucks."

Draven made the call. "Mikhail, good to hear your voice. We've cleaned out the Silver Diamonds' lair, the *Hopeful*. All the threats are neutralized, and the good news is that the werewolves are on their way to recovery. We found out what was happening to them."

"Get in here and debrief."

Jack shook his head.

"No can do, boss," Draven replied, then mouthed, "Why?"

Jack gestured at the device. "Jack Marber here. Don't trust Tinio, Reward, or Rola. They are providing information to a shapeshifter who is behind it all, we suspect. We also think she has our shipmate Adina. We could use your help in locating her. She could be masquerading as a woman named Briona or one named Kirandeep."

"Briona Arnd? She's the scientist behind the Ice Blocks. Is this your number? Let me call you right back." Mikhail clicked off.

The cabby wanted his device. "Need it for a little while longer." The others milled around outside. Jack held up his credit chip. "How much for a ride to the nearest full-service hospital?"

"For a normal person, twenty credits, but for you, one hundred."

"Charge one hundred credits," Jack said and waved his chip in front of the device. "As soon as we have our information, take these two women and Theo to the hospital, and we'll be out of your hair."

The man removed his cap to show a bald head. "Want to try that again?"

"Fuck off!" Tc'aarlat yelled through the window.

"Is he always like this?" the cabby asked, trying to keep things light.

"No. Sometimes he's worse."

The device buzzed and Jack answered. "Hey! Why are you answering my buddy's phone? Where's Cletus?"

"He's fine and will call you back in just a few. We're waiting for a call, so how about you wait your turn?"

Jack hung up on him. It buzzed again, but from a different number. Jack accepted the call.

"Jack?"

"Mikhail."

"Briona Arnd just left center with a woman in cryogenic storage. They boarded a van that is at Dock 9 right now."

"We're at Dock 9." Jack looked around.

"Dock 9 is pretty big. Head toward the bow of the *Hopeful* and keep going. She's in that direction."

"On our way." Jack tossed the device to the cabby and hopped out. He waved, and Theo and Briona entered the cab. Draven deposited the woman known as Kirandeep inside and stepped back. "Come on!" Jack sprinted off. Tc'aarlat grabbed the Don and dragged him along, but he was holding them back.

Draven popped the Don in the head and caught the man as he slumped, tossed him over his shoulder, and ran.

"Don't let him out of your sight!" Tc'aarlat said before sprinting after Jack.

Frontier Zone, City Station Hopefill, the Ice Blocks, Briona's Research Laboratory

Briona pushed the frozen body in a cryogenic hover-case. She waved her badge as she passed without slowing down. She made it to a waiting van without getting stopped. Her leaving with specimens didn't cause concern since she had been doing it for months without anyone raising the alarm.

What was another prisoner transfer?

She shoved the case into the storage area and climbed up front with the driver. "Dock 9, a cruiser called the *Escapee*."

"Right away, ma'am," the driver responded politely, pulling out of the loading dock area and accelerating into the main thoroughfare. He lifted to the second level of traffic and raced toward the destination. He didn't bother with small talk since the woman beside him was lost in her own thoughts.

The van made it to the dock in record time. Naka-Lee climbed out without saying a word to the driver. She removed the hovercase herself and pushed it toward the ramp of the *Escapee*, then disappeared inside the ship.

Frontier Zone, City Station Hopefill, Dock 9, *the Escapee*

Jack and Tc'aarlat found the small executive transport easily. Built for speed, it was hidden between a number of larger derelict ships. They stayed to what shadows they could as they ran, but speed was called for. They sprinted across the final open area to get inside the ship before it took off.

"How are we going to get inside?" Jack hissed in a whisper. They had reached a cargo hatch they assumed led into a small hangar, but there was no button, no lever, no way of gaining access. "Do we just knock?"

"I've got an idea," Tc'aarlat replied, moving away from the hangar door and working his way beneath the ship's belly. "These cruisers aren't built like proper spaceships. They're small and sleek, not very good in a fight and only built for short trips."

Tc'aarlat raised his blaster. "Any damage done to this ship is going to set off its emergency systems."

"How does that help us?" Jack asked.

"The cruiser should shut down its primary power to rectify the maintenance issue. Like, two seconds max," Tc'aarlat said. "If we time it right, we can blast our way inside."

"Wait, what?"

"Yeah, we can shoot our way inside." Tc'aarlat grinned. "In those few moments, the shields will be down. One massive blast should tear a hole wide enough for us to get in. This isn't made of stern stuff like my ship *Fortitude*. It's not built for fights. It's like a hovercab."

"Well, it's not like we have many other options," Jack said, raising his pistol to do what needed to be done.

. . .

Frontier Zone, City Station Hopefill, Dock 9, *the Escapee*, Bridge

Naka-Lee had prepared for this moment these past few months. The frozen Adina was locked in another room, and the ship was prepared to take off and never look back on City Station Hopefill.

In the second before she pushed the button to start the ignition sequence, the power went out. It was followed by a concussion that came from the main hangar.

"Maybe I didn't give her friends enough credit," Naka-Lee said to herself.

She whistled for her faithful pet Biscuit, having forgotten he wasn't with her, but the werewolf never came. "Fine, you ungrateful toad. I'll do it myself." She pulled a laser rifle from the armory cupboard at the rear of the bridge and stalked out.

Frontier Zone, City Station Hopefill, Dock 9, *the Escapee*, Storage Room

Unknown to Naka-Lee or Jack or Tc'aarlat, there had been another consequence of reverting the small cruiser to emergency power. The cryogenic systems that were keeping Adina frozen had been taken offline. All of them.

The thawing process was nearly as quick as the freezing. Her eyes shot open and she started coughing, a racking, rasping cough that made her lightheaded. When she finished, she had the strength she had lacked inside the Ice Blocks.

She discovered that the scramblers that had been keeping her down had been knocked offline too.

There was anger in her mind for everything Naka-Lee had done to her family. Playing with her father's feelings, impersonating his fiancée, planning her murder, kidnapping Adina to turn her into a pet, and of course, killing her uncle. Naka-Lee had killed Yousuf just to bring Adina here so she could capture her.

There was no way in hell she was going to let Naka-Lee get away with it, but Adina couldn't force herself into werewolf form. The fear of what she might do made her hold back. Despite assurances from those closest to her, she was not convinced she hadn't hurt those settlers on Renasta.

Breathlessly, she tried to remember the exercises to control that part of herself, but she found that Draven was at her ear then, speaking from her memories. *It's like anger. It builds up and up until one day, it gets released. You need to find an outlet for your anger to stop that from happening.* Adina had never enjoyed transforming, and she didn't enjoy it now.

There was no denying that this thing was part of her. Perhaps on some level, Draven was right; her unwillingness to allow it was keeping her from being a whole person.

At some point she had to let it out, control it, make it bend to her will so she could learn to not fear it. That was why she had been losing control and having those dreams.

Adina forgot about the exercises and took deep breaths, allowing herself to transform into a werewolf.

Not out of fear, not out of necessity or anger, but because the wolf was part of her. She broke through the glass easily in her stronger form, and there was only one place she wanted to go next. It was time for Naka-Lee to pay for her crimes.

Frontier Zone, City Station Hopefill, Dock 9, *the Escapee*, Hangar

No sooner had Jack and Tc'aarlat crawled through the blasted opening than a laser beam cut through the air millimeters from Jack's head. He threw himself to the deck and rolled out of the way. Tc'aarlat fired at the source, but the fish-woman had moved.

Jack snap-fired over a crate, rolled to the side, and fired again.

The laser scorched the wall behind him. Tc'aarlat fired close to a flanking position. She backed out of the cargo bay and shut the door.

"Go after her!" Tc'aarlat shouted. He had the better covering position, so he kept his JDS leveled at the door. Jack ran to it and popped the access button. Nothing happened. He backed away while Tc'aarlat joined him, pried open the panel, and got to work shorting the access.

Frontier Zone, City Station Hopefill, Dock 9, *the Escapee*, Bridge

Naka-Lee returned to the bridge. She heard the steps of a wolf entering the bridge. Biscuit had finally joined her.

She swiveled to coo to her baby, but the wolf standing there wasn't hers. Naka-Lee tried to bring her laser rifle up, but Adina was too fast. She launched herself at the shapeshifter and ripped the weapon away with a toss of her head. She stalked around the captain's seat.

Naka-Lee transformed into Kirandeep and assumed a confident pose. "You wouldn't ruin your father's one chance at happiness, would you, Adina?"

Adina growled.

"I could stop them from killing Kirandeep," Naka-Lee said. "It was your fault Adina. Like it or not, you were the one who killed your mother. Doesn't he deserve some happiness?"

"Adina!"

Adina the werewolf turned and there was her father, Usman Choudhury. She wanted to ask him how he had known where she was. She wondered if he was a second shapeshifter. He held his hands up and approached slowly, but his wide eyes alerted her to his fear.

Naka-Lee fell to her knees. "Thank goodness, Usman dear. She was about to kill me."

"I know that's a lie," Usman said. "I know you're not the real Kirandeep."

Naka-Lee held her breath. "What?"

"I put it together after your call," Usman said. "For the past few weeks, you were too interested in getting me to reconnect with Adina. Then I saw her name come up on the news, and you said you were leaving."

"Very smart."

"Where's my fiancée?" Usman stepped forward, and Adina did the same. They both wanted the answer.

"I die, she dies," Naka-Lee said.

"You're lying." Usman approached her, his eyes narrowing as he mastered his fear, thinking only of his family. "You messed with my fiancée, messed with my daughter, and I'm sure you had something to do with my brother's death. We're going to make sure you get locked up for good."

Adina transformed back into her human form and looked at her father with newfound respect. She had been ready to tear Naka-Lee apart, but her dad was right; it was time to end the killing. "On your face, asshole," Adina snapped. Naka-Lee didn't move.

"I'm sorry about everything, Adina," Usman said.

"I'm sorry, too," Adina said, adding, "Dad."

Frontier Zone, City Station Hopefill, Dock 9, *the Escapee*, Just outside the Bridge

Tc'aarlat peered in and held up his hand. He looked back at Jack. "Looks like they're sorting some things out in there. Should we go in?"

"We'll give them a minute," Jack said, leaning close to look in. He only had eyes for the shapeshifter who currently looked like Kirandeep, a healthy version. The one they found, the real one, had been starved while suffering mightily at the hands of Naka-Lee and the Silver Diamonds.

"Yup," Tc'aarlat replied. "Hey, how do you pronounce 'cress ant?'"

"Do you mean 'croissant?'"

"Yeah."

"It's 'kwa-sont.'" Jack activated the hatch and headed onto the bridge. Adina and her father turned in time to see Jack fire three times at the creature who called herself

Naka-Lee. Three shots at the highest stun setting collapsed the woman. "Hey." Jack tipped his chin toward Adina.

She nodded. "I never doubted you'd come for me. Do you know what she'd look good wearing?"

Tc'aarlat stepped forward. "Hey, I know the answer to this one. Manacles while standing on a gallows?"

Adina chuckled. "The cryogenic case she used on me. Then we don't have to bother waking her up. She would befoul Jhiordaan, so we might as well keep her out of the limelight."

"Touché, Engineer," Jack agreed.

Frontier Zone, City Station Hopefill, WRU Headquarters

Tinio crept into the shadows, making a beeline toward Rola's desk. "Rola." He kept out of sight. "Draven just called Mikhail. I heard it. He's neutralized the Silver Diamonds or some shit. There's about to be trouble."

"I thought you dealt with Draven?"

"He must have escaped. It was probably that Jack," Tinio replied. "I don't think we've got a choice. Can you round up the sympathizers?"

"Do you really think it's come to that?" Rola asked.

"I'll access the ear in Mikhail's room. Just get everyone ready."

Rola stood up from her desk casually and went to move about the room, whispering in every sympathizer's ear, including Reward's. Tinio took her spot and placed an earbud in his ear. The ugly thug navigated her software and brought up a real-time audio feed from the bug he had planted in Mikhail's office. Tinio had to be sure he was in trouble before they acted.

Silence greeted him as he bent his head to listen.

He nearly jumped out of his skin at a bump against his back. He found Mikhail looming over him with two bulky security guards. Tinio shot to his feet, but the guards seized his arms. He looked for help, but Reward and Rola were nowhere to be seen.

"Motherfucker," he whined. A commotion in the hallway suggested they had not gotten away. Gunfire erupted. Most people ducked, but Tinio tried to bolt. He took Mikhail's knee to his groin and collapsed to the floor. The firing stopped.

"All clear. Two down," a voice shouted over the cubicle farm. The guards yanked Tinio to his feet and hauled him toward the building's temporary cells. They passed his two compatriots lying on the floor in pools of their own blood.

"Live to fight another day, Tinio, but there won't be any fighting. You're going to the Ice Blocks. Don't pass Go. Don't collect two hundred credits."

Frontier Zone, City Station Hopefill, Dock 9, *the Escapee*

"Pop the hatch and get that bastard Don Gan'barlo in here." Jack accessed the external cameras in time to see Don bash Draven over the head and start to run. Draven picked up a rock, and with the strength of a werewolf, he hurled it unerringly at the back of the Don's skull. It connected, and the Don went face-first onto the dock's hard deck.

Tc'aarlat was off like a shot. "No, you don't!" he shouted as he raced for the cargo bay.

He jumped out through the hole they'd made and ran for the Don, who hadn't moved since Draven beaned him.

Blood oozed from the wound in a way that told him the Don's skull was fractured and his brain was swelling with the trauma. Tc'aarlat checked the Don's pulse on both sides of his neck. Nothing.

"This is it? You fucker. You never lifted the price on my head." Draven approached, and Tc'aarlat stood up. "Draven, you bastard! I was supposed to kill him!"

"He was going to get away. I did you a flavor."

"Flavor?"

"Mint chocolate chip. Why? What's your favorite?"

Tc'aarlat pointed at the Don. "What about him?"

"I don't know his favorite. He never said, and it doesn't matter now, does it?"

"You take lots of pictures and get it out on the intergalactic wire that Don Gan'barlo is dead after a chase, a firefight, some space battles, and a drug-infused orgy." Tc'aarlat stamped his foot before kicking the Don's body. "You bastard. Fuck you and the whore you rode in on." He searched the Don to find the collar control device and took it.

"Horse," Draven corrected.

"I haven't seen any horses," Tc'aarlat replied.

"I see. You can count on me, Tc'aarlat. I'll make it known that the Don is dead. Really dead."

Tc'aarlat stood there and stared. He wasn't sure what to do now that it was over. An idea popped into his head.

"That means it's *my* ship! Jack stole it from me, and I'm stealing it back." He strutted away.

Jack opened the hatch to the cruiser. Adina and Usman walked out, pushing the hovercase with the frozen creature inside. Jack waved. "Come and take a look at this."

"I need to talk to you," Tc'aarlat replied.

Jack disappeared inside the ship. The Yollin followed Jack to a small medical lab where a rough-looking Pod-doc sat. "This is where she was changing people into werewolves, seeing if it took, and then capturing those who showed the ability." Jack dialed his JDS to five and took aim.

"Don't you think Nathan might want to look at that?"

"This thing is dangerous. It needs to not exist." He pulled the trigger and blasted the unit into a million pieces.

Frontier Zone, City Station Hopefill, Dock 23, Freight Bay F, ICS _Fortitude_, Bridge

Jack and Tc'aarlat had quickly explained the collar situation to Adina, and she worked with Solo to broadcast the signal from the remote across the city. In a few moments, she had disabled every shock collar on the base, and the ensuing howls could be heard from one end to the other. Gang members suddenly found their werewolf servants free of all restraints.

"I think I'm going to remain here for a while," Adina said. "My father needs me, and I'm sure Kirandeep, the real one, will need help recovering. Do you know how she's doing?"

Solo appeared on the screen. "She is still in critical condition. There is no prognosis at the moment."

"I better get my dad and take him to the hospital."

"Make it so, Solo," Jack ordered. The AI called a cab, and Adina hurried off the bridge to get her father. He was in her room, keeping her Raal hawk Isaaca company.

After she was gone, Jack and Tc'aarlat looked at each other. Tc'aarlat opened his mouth, but Jack spoke first. "Not your ship. *Our* ship."

"I'm the captain," Tc'aarlat said.

"No." Jack spun the captain's chair around. "Solo, get me Nathan Lowell.

It took Jack fifteen minutes to complete his report.

"Well-done again, Shadows," Nathan said. "I talked to Timothy, and he was impressed with your work."

Jack shrugged. "Just doing our job."

"Bloody Darling was Naka-Lee, but she wasn't really the Darling. She only maintained that persona for use with the gangs. There was no Bloody Darling."

"It was her who built on the back of Don Gan'barlo's smuggling and drug ring. It gave her an inordinate amount of power, but that's ended. She's in a block of ice in our cargo bay, close to the airlock in case we get a wild hair up our asses. Do you have any more work for us?"

"Maybe." Nathan's image faded to black, leaving Tc'aarlat, Myst, and Jack alone on the bridge.

"Pistachio," Tc'aarlat blurted.

"What the hell is that?"

"My favorite flavor."

Jack was taken aback. "Do you even know what that is?"

"I don't, but that makes it that much more exotic. Like gold flecks in vodka. Who wouldn't want to drink that?"

"'No one' is the correct answer." Jack fired up navigation, followed by the engines. "Solo, get us the fuck out of here."

"Fucking A," the AI replied.

Finis

AUTHOR NOTES - CRAIG MARTELLE

SEPTEMBER 23, 2021

Greetings, Shadows fans! Thank you for picking up your copy of Shadow Vanguard 6 – Family Reunion! You are contributing to the legacy of our departed friend. By buying this book, you are putting money directly onto the table of Tommy's family. They count on the income from these books to simply survive. So thank you, from the bottom of our hearts.

We tried to have this book written by a third party, thinking that we'd be able to tweak it... That was book five and book six was even worse. So Craig wrote book six almost entirely from scratch. That's why it took so long and sorry about that.

This book was about Adina and her back story, plus more about renegades and how a simple desire for a complete monopoly can spiral out of control until the vortex pulls everyone in. Even the authorities were taken in and subverted. The evil mastermind behind it was never obvious so they created a figurehead. And that mystical being was the one behind it all.

How easily people can be swayed. Until outsiders arrive. The Shadows bring a fresh and skeptical viewpoint. They see through the layers and they take action. And that bastard Don Gan'barlo! It was time for his comeuppance. What a sandy little butthole he's been. No more. We brought that thread to a close and the series with this latest book.

Tommy had written three complete books before the decline in his health. He delivered six outlines to us in the final weeks of his life to make sure that these stories carried on. We looked at our budget and decided to have three stories written and then give the funds from the other three directly to Tommy's wife. Money now and money later. The last three stories in the series will probably be shorts that we write at some later time when we have a few moments and as a way to reenergize the series.

Shadow Vanguard. A fun and wild ride with some crazy characters.

That's it – I'm working on Judge, Jury, & Executioner 14 – Jack the Ripper, another book set in the Kurtherian Gambit's Age of Expansion. (You can order that book here)

Break is over, back on my head. Lots of words to gather into a nice, trim package, known as a story.

Peace, fellow humans.
Craig

AUTHOR NOTES - MICHAEL ANDERLE

SEPTEMBER 23, 2021

Thank you for not only reading this series but these author notes here in the back as well.

When I met Tommy a few years ago, the first thing I noticed was his smile and his happiness. And yet, he was already pretty sick.

While we were separated by a large ocean, I did get a chance to see him a few times at an event or two and my memories are still that while he lived, he had joy in his heart.

I am glad that Craig asked me to be a part of extending Tommy's legacy. His stories which Craig brought back and made sure to finish after his passing and our ability to publish his stories to keep his memory alive.

There is no easy way to support another brother from another mother, but I believe Craig has exemplified the trait and through his actions I am proud to call Craig my friend as well.

I hope to see you when reading another book or two in the author notes.

Have a good weekend (or week) and talk to you soon!

Ad Aeternitatem,

Michael Anderle

www.ingramcontent.com/pod-product-compliance
Lightning Source LLC
Chambersburg PA
CBHW020403110726
47899CB00006B/1841